ALSO BY DAVID HOUSEWRIGHT

Featuring Rushmore McKenzie

A Hard Ticket Home

Tin City

Pretty Girl Gone

Featuring Holland Taylor

Penance

Practice to Deceive

Dearly Departed

Dead Boyfriends

Dead Boyfriends

DAVID HOUSEWRIGHT

 ST. MARTIN'S MINOTAUR ✠ NEW YORK

DEAD BOYFRIENDS. Copyright © 2007 by David Housewright. All rights reserved. Printed in the United States of America. No part of this book may be used or reproduced in any manner whatsoever without written permission except in the case of brief quotations embodied in critical articles or reviews. For information, address St. Martin's Press, 175 Fifth Avenue, New York, N.Y. 10010.

www.minotaurbooks.com

ISBN-10: 0-312-34830-4
ISBN-13: 978-0-312-34830-4

First Edition: May 2007

10 9 8 7 6 5 4 3 2 1   .

For Renée and Renée
and Renée again

Acknowledgments

I would like to express my great appreciation to Coon Rapids City Attorney Tammi Fredrickson, whose aid and advice made this book possible.

I also would like to thank Susan Andre, the Anoka County Correctional Facility, the City of Coon Rapids Police Department, India Cooper, Jenness Crawford, Jennifer Denys, Cara Engler, Minneapolis Police Officer Robert Hipple, Dr. Butch Hudson of the Anoka County Coroner's Office, Phyllis Jaeger, Rhonda Martinson, Jean O'Donohue, Julie Ostergaard, Alison Picard, Lieutenant Richard Poirier of the Anoka County Sheriff's Office, Ben Sevier, Eddie "El Pato" Storch, Michael Sullivan, Dr. Jack Uecker, Chief Paul Wood of the City of Roseville Police Department, and Renée Valois.

Dead Boyfriends

I

The dream came back to haunt me the night they threw me in jail. No, not a dream. More like a Technicolor reenactment. There was nothing surreal or false about it; the facts were always the same, always accurate. It's night. I'm moving up on the scene. The armed suspect steps out of the convenience store. I see him. He sees me. I say, "Police. Drop the gun. Put your hands in the air." He raises his gun to shoot me. I fire first. The force of the 12-gauge hurls him back against the glass doors. Over and over and over again. I dreamed the dream quite often after the shooting, sometimes twice a night. Later, it became a couple of times a week, then a couple of times a month. I couldn't remember the last time I had the dream. Not for a few years anyway. Then they put me in jail.

What happened was I got lost. I was trying to navigate the residential streets of Coon Rapids, a third ring suburb north of Minneapolis. Meyer wanted to sell his seventy-five-year-old eight-chair, hand-carved dining room set with matching buffet, and I wanted to buy. I needed a dining room set. I liked throwing elaborate dinner parties for my friends, but I always had to squeeze them around a small kitchen table, and I wasn't so good a cook I could keep getting away with it. Only the directions Meyer gave me were confused. Either that or I was confused. It was hard to tell which.

I was cruising slowly, trying to find a street sign that would match the words written on the crumpled piece of paper in my hand, when a woman appeared in the street, waving her arms frantically. I stopped. Of course I stopped. I'm from Minnesota, and like most Minnesotans, I'm a helluva nice guy.

The woman staggered to my open window. She stood with both hands pressed against the side of my silver Audi. I powered the window down.

"Help me," she said.

"Help you?"

"Help me, please."

"Help you what?"

The woman was small and thin, in her forties, with dull brown eyes and long stringy hair that might have been brown. She looked like she hadn't bathed in weeks. Smelled like it, too.

"It's my boyfriend," she said.

"What about him?"

"He's dead."

"Really?" I couldn't believe she had said that. "Are you sure?"

"I don't know. I think so. Could you look for me?"

Hell, no! That's what my inner voice screamed. Usually I listen to it. This time I didn't. You know why? Besides being a helluva nice guy, sometimes I'm quite dim.

"Listen," I told the woman. "Just stay there, okay? Don't move. Just stay there."

I parked the Audi on the wrong side of the street in front of the house the woman pointed at.

"He was so good-looking," she said. "And charming. Very nice manners."

It was seventy-four degrees inside my car and ninety-seven degrees and humid outside. The difference snapped my head back.

"We were going to be married," the woman added. "I guess the wedding's off now."

"Where is your boyfriend?"

She sat down on the grass boulevard facing my vehicle and pulled her knees to her chest. "I thought he was the one."

"Miss?"

She began rocking from side to side while she stared at her distorted reflection in the door. She was wearing white pants and a white shirt. Both were stained with feces, urine, and, I was guessing, dried blood. There appeared to be feces and blood on her bare feet as well.

"Ma'am?"

She flung a hand over her shoulder toward the house. It was one of those $120,000 starter homes that people stay in for thirty years, a rambler with attached garage. I left her sitting by the Audi and followed the narrow, S-shaped concrete path to the front door. The door was open. A heavy odor of decaying garbage greeted me six paces before I reached it. I looked inside through the screen. A body dressed in blue jeans and a red T-shirt was sprawled in the center of the room in plain sight. No, it wasn't red. It was a white shirt soaked in dried blood. I had an unobstructed view of the man's bearded face. It seemed to be moving. I squinted. Maggots. And flies. Flies everywhere.

My gag reflex kicked in hard. I put my hand over my mouth and turned away.

The police cruiser came to a sudden halt behind my vehicle, the officer stomping on his brakes as if he were making a pit stop at Talladega. He was out of the car before his siren died away. The only thing that slowed him down was the immense wall of heat that smacked him upside the head the moment he opened the door. It had been only four minutes since I used my cell phone to call it in and already the back of my polo shirt was saturated with sweat.

"Baumbach, APD," he barked.

APD? my inner voice asked.

"I called the Coon Rapids Police Department," I said.

"This is Anoka, son."

No wonder I couldn't find Meyer's house. I was in the wrong city.

Baumbach swelled his chest and tugged at his gun belt. "What have you got?"

A cowboy, I told myself. *I need this, I really do.* Worse, he was young. He looked like a batboy for a minor league baseball team, yet he was calling me son?

"You have a first name?" I asked.

Baumbach glared at me as if I had just questioned his mother's occupation.

"Boyd," he snapped.

"Well, Boyd, it's like I told dispatch." I used my chin to point at the woman. "This woman wants to report a dead boyfriend."

The woman was still sitting on the grass, still staring at her reflection in my car door.

"Ma'am?" Baumbach asked tentatively.

The woman didn't answer.

"What's your name, ma'am? Ma'am? You reported a dead body, ma'am?"

No reply.

"Do you live here, ma'am? Is the body in the house?"

Still nothing.

Baumbach glanced up at me.

"I think she slipped into a fugue state," I said.

"A what?"

"A pathological condition in which a person is conscious of her actions yet has no real control over them. Kinda like sleepwalking."

"What do you know about it?"

"I read."

From Baumbach's expression, you'd think I had just confessed to downloading kiddie porn. He turned toward the house.

"I'm going in," he announced.

"Yeah? You do that. I'll see ya around."

"Where do you think you're going?"

"Hey, man. I've got places to go, people to see."

"No, no, no, no, no. You stay right here."

I was afraid he'd say that.

I attempted to lean against the Audi, but the surface was far too hot, so I just stood there, arms crossed in front of me, and waited while Baumbach followed the sidewalk to the woman's house. He opened the front door, stared for a few moments, then quickly closed it without going inside. A moment later he crossed the lawn, moving quickly in a straight line, stopping only when he reached his police cruiser. He braced himself against the hood with both hands, ignoring the heat. He seemed to have trouble catching his breath. Beads of sweat trickled from his hairline and down his jaw. I was willing to bet that the Kevlar vest he wore and the nineteen pounds of equipment he carried were beginning to feel very heavy indeed.

Officer Baumbach stood that way for a full thirty seconds, trying to fill his deflated lungs with air. Finally, he turned to look at the woman. His mouth worked as if he wanted to ask her something. She was still staring at her reflection. Silent. I watched a maggot slither across her bare foot. Baumbach saw it, too. It was too much for him. He moved between the police cruiser and the Audi. Using the bumpers for support, he hurled both his breakfast and lunch into the street.

"You okay?" I asked.

"No, I'm not okay." After he stopped retching, Baumbach wiped his mouth with the back of his hand. He glared at the woman. "What did you do?"

The woman glanced up at him, shielding her eyes from the bright sun with the flat of her hand.

Baumbach swooped down on her, grasped her shoulders, and yanked her to her feet. "What did you do?" he said.

"Hey," I said.

Baumbach shook the woman fiercely. "What did you do?" He shoved her backward. The back of her head thudded against the Audi, and she slid slowly to the ground. She didn't make a sound.

"What are you, nuts?" I pushed myself between them. "Stop it."

"Don't interfere," he shouted back, shoving me hard for emphasis.

"Do it by the book. Secure the scene. Call CID. Then get the hell out of the way. What's the matter with you?"

"Did you see that guy? Did you?" From the look on his face I guessed the closest Baumbach had come to real tragedy was watching driver's ed films in high school.

"He could have died of diphtheria, you don't know," I said.

Baumbach grabbed the woman's collar and dragged her away from the car.

"Why did you kill him?" he said.

The woman didn't say.

"Answer me!"

When she didn't, Baumbach gave her a quick backhand across the mouth. It wasn't a vicious blow, but it certainly got my attention.

"That's enough," I said.

I chopped hard at his wrist with the edge of my hand, and Baumbach released the woman. He stepped back and rubbed the spot where I hit him, his breath coming hard, an expression of utter astonishment on his face.

"I'm a cop," he said.

"Really? How long have you been on the job? Six minutes? Kid, you're out of control. Think about what you're doing."

Baumbach rested his hand on the butt of his gun.

"No one is going to hold it against you if you just sit tight and wait for the adults to arrive," I said.

"I'm the police officer," he said. "I'm in charge. Now turn around," he ordered.

"Look, pal, I'm trying to help you. I really am."

His fingers tightened around the butt, and for a moment I thought he was going to pull it.

"I said turn around."

I turned. He shoved me hard against the Audi.

"Assume the position."

I assumed, pressing my hands on the hot roof of the car.

"You're under arrest," he told me as he wound the cuffs around my wrists, pinning my arms behind me.

"What's the charge?"

"Assaulting a police officer. Obstruction of justice."

"Oh, for chrissake."

"You think this is funny?"

"A little bit, yeah."

"You won't think it's so funny when you're locked in a cell."

"Seriously, kid. How long have you been on the job?"

"Three weeks, if you must know."

"And they let you out alone?"

"Three weeks since my probation period ended."

Somehow I didn't think his field-training officers had given him a lot of sevens.

"Let me guess," I said. "You're bored, right? You thought the job was going to be like *Law & Order* or *CSI*, or maybe even *NYPD Blue*, right? Yet all you do most days is sit on the shoulder of 169, shooting your radar gun at passing motorists, hoping you can find just cause to make someone blow into the PBT. Right? Only now you have something worth doing. You're thinking, yeah, the guy in there, probably he's just a medical—someone who woke up dead—unless maybe, just maybe, you caught yourself an honest-to-God homicide. Only real homicides aren't like TV. They're not neat like TV. You weren't prepared for it. You blow chunks. That's embarrassing enough, but you do it in front of the woman and me and now you're pissed off. Well, welcome to the real world, kid, only stop behaving like a jerk. You don't touch the suspect. You don't violate her rights like that."

The woman was still sitting on the grass, watching us. I don't think she heard a word we said.

"She could confess to whacking the guy in there, to killing a hundred more, and most likely you won't be able to touch her because you violated her rights."

"Shuddup."

"Look, kid, be smart. You can still fix this, you can still make it go away. Start by removing the cuffs. Think about it."

He did. For about ten seconds. Then he said, "You're going to jail."

I tried to reason with him some more after he locked me in the back of his squad, but he wasn't listening. *Fine,* I decided. *I'll talk to whoever takes command.* That turned out to be a sergeant from the City of Anoka Police Department who looked too old for the job, thirty pounds over what the diet-hucksters consider his ideal weight, with hair that was more gray than brown. I watched him from the backseat as he moved about, directing his officers to secure the scene, something Baumbach had failed to do. We locked eyes a couple of times, but he never approached the car. I wished he would have. The engine—and thus the air conditioner—was off, and it was unbearably hot. I had to lean forward to avoid sticking to the seat. Sweat trickled from my brow into my eyes;

the cuffs prevented me from wiping it away. Baumbach had left a small crack at the top of the driver's side window, but it offered no relief. I felt like a small dog trapped in a locked vehicle in the parking lot of a shopping mall. It was all I could do to keep from panting.

The sergeant was soon supplanted by still another sergeant, this one in the uniform of the Anoka County Sheriff's Department. I wasn't surprised. Jurisdiction was always an iffy thing in a small community, and at about eighteen thousand people, Anoka was considered a small community. Its twenty-nine-man police department didn't have the resources to investigate a possible homicide even if it wanted to and readily gave way to the county's Criminal Investigation Division. Which didn't help me any. I was locked in a *City of Anoka* police car, and when the *Anoka County* deputy made a gesture in my direction and the sergeant shook his head, I knew I wasn't getting out anytime soon.

While the deputy directed his officers and a few plainclothes technicians, a couple of paramedics worked on the woman, checking her pulse, flashing a penlight in her eyes, asking her questions and receiving no answers. If they were curious about the swelling at the corner of her mouth, they kept it to themselves. Eventually, they loaded her in a car and drove away. I guessed that they were transporting her to the hospital, although it was a deputy that accompanied her, not a paramedic.

A few moments later, Baumbach returned to the squad and started it up. He switched on the air conditioner. It didn't work quickly enough for him, and he stepped back outside, waiting patiently for the interior to cool before he drove off. I didn't complain. What was the point? When he slid behind the wheel and put the car in gear I said, "Kinda odd that the deputy didn't want to interview me, seeing how I was the one who discovered the body."

"I told you. You're going to jail."

I swear to God that right up until they locked me in the holding cell, I thought he was bluffing.

————

The dream returned later that evening.

I didn't know what time it was. They had taken my watch along with my keys, my wallet, the cash in my pockets, my cell phone, my belt, and the laces to my Nikes. What they didn't do was book me. They didn't take my fingerprints or photograph; I couldn't even testify that they ran my name through CJIS or the NICS to check for wants and warrants, to learn if I had a record. This was payback, pure and simple. Supposedly, they're only allowed to imprison a suspect in a holding cell for up to four hours before transferring him to the county jail. When those ticked by, I figured I was in for the entire thirty-six— in Minnesota you can hold a suspect for thirty-six hours before you have to charge or release him.

Payback is a bitch, and I was plotting my own as I rested uncomfortably on a one-inch-thick blue mat stretched over a two-foot high concrete bed in an eight-by-six concrete room, my fingers locked behind my head, drifting in and out of sleep . . .

Twelve-fifteen P.M. I received the call. The two-second alert tone preceding the call told me it was trouble.

"Four forty."

"Four forty, go."

"Four forty, possible robbery in progress at the Food & Fuel convenience store."

The dispatcher gave the address at the same time as the information appeared on the squad's MDT screen, along with RE-MARKS: *alarm tripped, attempting callback at store.*

I fingered the button on my shoulder microphone. "Four forty, copy."

Eighty seconds later I slowly drove past the store, lights and siren off, hoping my arrival had gone undetected. I could see no one through the store windows. The parking lot was deserted. My own windows were rolled down, yet I heard nothing. I drove another fifty yards and parked where I could see both the store and the lot without being clearly visible myself, taking up a position of observance, just like I had been taught at the skills academy.

"Four forty, arriving." I spoke softly.

"Four fourty, copy," the receiver crackled.

I slipped out of the car, surprised by how quiet it was. The Food & Fuel was located kitty-corner to the campus of the College of St. Catherine, yet there was no traffic, no pedestrians, no music or TV sounds coming from the houses and apartment buildings. I could hear crickets, and in the distance a dog barked twice and then was silent. It was as if they were whispering to me.

I took a deep breath, let it out slowly. Now it was just a matter of staying put and watching until dispatch found a sergeant to call the store and determine if there was a robbery in progress or if some clumsy cashier had tripped the alarm with his knee, which happened only once a day and twice on Sundays. True, I could have ridden the hammer into the lot and kicked open the door, gun drawn, but then I would have been stupid. Probably dead, too. Always better to wait. Always better to take the bad guys outside instead of forcing a possible hostage situation inside. If there were bad guys.

"Four forty, the parking lot is empty, I see no movement inside the store."

"Four forty, copy."

I unholstered my nine-millimeter Glock, then thought better of it—I was never comfortable with the grip. Instead, I opened the door and leaned back inside the squad, hitting the button that released the standard-issue Remington 870 12-gauge shotgun from its rack. I liked the heft of it. That and its eight rounds of double-aught buck, four in the magazine. After activating the shotgun, I set it on the trunk lid of the car, the barrel pointing away from me, and waited some more.

Moments later, a late-model sedan turned into the parking lot of the convenience store, heading into harm's way.

"Oh, no." I lifted the shotgun from the trunk lid. "No, no, no."

I activated the radio.

"Four forty, we have a car heading into the lot. I'm moving up on the scene."

I jogged down the street and into the parking lot, carrying the shotgun in the port position.

The car stopped to the left of the entrance. Two doors opened. A couple emerged—a black man, maybe thirty, from the driver's side and a black woman, same age, from the passenger's side.

"Police. Get back in the car." My grip tightened on the shotgun. "Get back in the car."

The couple froze, deer in the headlights.

"Get back in the car."

The glass door of the convenience store swung open. A man was backing out fast, butt first, holding the door with his hip. His eyes were fixed on something inside the store, and he didn't see me. I pivoted toward him as he cleared the doorway. I was shouting before he could turn.

"Police. Police."

I braced the stock of the shotgun against my shoulder and sighted down the barrel. "Police. Drop the gun. Put your hands in the air."

The suspect turned his head just so. Then his body. He was

facing me now, and for the first time I noted the caramel color of his skin. I guessed his age at around twenty.

"Get your hands in the air, get your hands in the air, I want to see your hands!"

The suspect let his hands hang down below his hips. In his left was a paper bag with the store's logo. In his right was a Smith & Wesson .38. The man didn't move. He was considering his options.

"Don't think." I was surprised by how calm my voice sounded. "Drop the gun. Drop it now."

I had trained for hours and hours with the firearms training simulator, going over shoot/don't shoot scenarios until they all blurred together. This was different. My hands trembled. They had never done that with FATS. And my vision—I could see only what was directly in front of me. It was like looking down a long tunnel.

"For God's sake drop the gun."

The suspect raised his hands.

I fired once.

A spread of double-aught buck hit the suspect squarely in the chest. The impact from the blast lifted him off the pavement and hurled him against the glass door of the convenience store. He caromed off the glass. His legs folded and he pitched forward onto his face. He was still holding the gun and the bag shoulder high, away from his body.

The woman screamed.

The man shouted an obscenity.

I moved forward slowly, still pointing the shotgun at the suspect. When I reached his unmoving body, I kicked the Smith & Wesson out of his hand.

"Four forty, shots fired, suspect down, officer requires assistance." I was shouting. I didn't mean to shout. I simply couldn't help myself.

"You killed 'im, you killed 'im," the woman railed.

"He had his hands up," the man added.

"You killed 'im while he was trying to surrender."

"Racist pig."

They served breakfast, lunch, and dinner on thick brown plastic thermal trays. Each meal was nutritionally balanced, and the portions were certified by a registered dietitian to provide each inmate with approximately 2,200 calories per day, along with all the daily requirements of whatever it was the Minnesota Department of Corrections deemed necessary to a healthy diet. The meals were all quite good, better than some restaurants I could name, and obviously prepared by someone who took pride in his work. There were five meals in all—which is how I kept track of time, by the number of meals.

No one spoke to me, and I refused to give the cops the satisfaction of hearing me ranting and raving and demanding my rights. Instead, I was determined to remain quiet and still, to lie on my mat and stare at the ceiling and do nothing but sing softly to myself.

> *Nobody knows the trouble I've seen.*
> *Nobody knows my sorrow.*
> *Nobody knows the trouble I've seen.*
> *Glory hallelujah!*

I must have done that one thirty times. It seemed amusing at first.

My stomach was telling me that I was due for a sixth meal when the door swung open. I stayed on my back, staring at the ceiling, not moving until the officer announced, "You're free to go." I rolled off the concrete bed without speaking, taking my time, acting as if the officer had just told me that the dentist was ready to see me now. The officer led me to a desk in the booking station. The sergeant was leaning against the wall behind the desk. His name tag read J. MOORHEAD. I pretended not to see him.

The officer retrieved a large envelope and dumped the contents between us—my belongings. I slowly counted the cash. "It's all there," he insisted, so I made a big production of counting it a second time.

"Now then, what lesson have we learned?" the sergeant asked.

"What's the name of the woman—the one your officer beat up?"

The sergeant pushed himself off the wall. "Be careful what you say," he told me.

"Did you arrest her, too?"

"Let it go."

The officer behind the desk handed me a clipboard holding a single sheet of paper. "Sign here," he said.

I took the clipboard and flung it across the room.

I intended to say what I had to say quietly, only it came out loud. "I appreciate you standing up for your rookie, but I was doing you both a favor by keeping Baumbach from beating on a suspect—and you put me in jail for it? That's wrong. You should have checked me out first. You would have learned that I have eleven and a half years on the job with the St. Paul Police Department, five million bucks in the bank, and a bad attitude."

The sergeant smirked like a guy who'd heard it all before.

"Some people need more than one lesson," he said.

"Don't worry about it, Sarge. You're gonna get more than one."

It was three in the morning with the moon not shining when I stepped out of the City of Anoka Public Safety Center. I might as well have stepped into my own backyard for all the light and noise I found. The redbrick building, which housed both the police and fire departments, had been built in a residential section of the city well off the main drag and was as quiet as any of the old Victorians and English Colonials surrounding it. The only sound I heard was the scraping of my shoes on the concrete sidewalk as I skipped around a bronze statue of a child holding the hand of a benevolent police officer. I considered it yet another example of deceptive advertising.

I was just as lost as I had been the previous morning. Still, there were lights in the distance, and I followed them to East Main Street, which, surprisingly enough, actually was Anoka's main street. Unfortunately, nothing was open. No bars, restaurants, gas stations—ah, but a couple of blocks east I found the Anoka County Correctional Facility, which should not be confused with the City of Anoka Police Department. The Anoka County Correctional Facility—or jail, to use the politically incorrect term—is housed in the same building as the Anoka County Sheriff's Department and the Anoka County Court, the operative word being "County." It was located in the "City" of Anoka just to confuse outsiders. Like me.

The guard at the gate was stunned to see me at that hour. He took one look at my two-day beard and rumpled clothes and probably thought I was looking to break out one of the inmates. I asked him where the county would have towed my vehicle. He gave me directions to a lot off Highway 169. I asked him what the chances were of getting a cab. He thought I was kidding him. He laughed even harder when I assured him that I wasn't.

It was nearly 5:00 A.M. by the time I hoofed it to the lot. Naturally, it was closed. I waited. Rush hour traffic heading into the Cities was at its height when they finally got around to releasing my Audi—for about the price of a monthly payment—so you can imagine my frame of mind when I finally arrived home at eight forty-five.

Two editions of the *St. Paul Pioneer Press* were waiting on my porch along with a pile of day-old mail. I glanced through it while I listened to the eight messages left on my voice mail. The first was from Meyer, who wanted to know where in hell I was and did I still want the dining room set.

"You sorry bastard," I yelled at the recording. "If you could get your directions straight . . ."

The next message cheered me somewhat. Bobby Dunston's daughters wanted to come over and feed the ducks. For the past several years I've had a family of ducks living in the pond in my backyard. They arrive in the spring, leave in the fall, and return the following year, probably because my neighbor Margot and I feed them. Originally there were seven, then nine, then five. This year there were eleven. I used to name them but stopped because I lost track of who was who. Except for Maureen. Maureen was named after my mother, and I always recognized her. The girls seemed to be able to tell them apart, though, and they were always welcome.

The next four messages were left by Nina Truhler.

"Hey, McKenzie. Are you taking me to dinner before we go to the ball? You know a girl can't subsist solely on hors d'oeuvres and vodka martinis. If I can't get you on your cell, call me."

"McKenzie, you didn't forget we had a date, did you?"

"Dammit, McKenzie, where are you? If you stand me up—these tickets cost five hundred dollars a pop, and I bought a new dress."

"Forget it. You're not the only guy I know who owns a tuxedo, and you're sure as hell not the only guy who finds me attractive."

The Second Harvest Charity Ball. It had a James Bond theme that year. Nina bought the tickets. I had promised to take her. Only I had been unavoidably detained. Emphasis on "unavoidably."

She won't be angry once I explain, I told myself. Nina and I had been involved for nearly two years now. We've even discussed the M word on occasion. She was a reasonable woman. I reached for the receiver, hesitated. Nina owned and operated a jazz joint in St. Paul called Rickie's—named after her daughter, Erica. The hours she kept were more nocturnal than those the rest of us lived by. No way she'd be up yet. *Besides, it'd be better if you go to the club and see her in person,* my inner voice told me.

Except she didn't agree.

The phone rang while I was still standing there.

"Where have you been, McKenzie?"

"Nina? I was just thinking of calling you."

"Sure you were."

"No lie. I wanted to explain about the other night."

"Are you all right?"

"Yes, I'm—"

"Were you in an accident or something?"

"Accident? No, nothing like that."

"Did anyone shoot you?"

"No. What happened was—"

"Where were you? Did you forget about me?"

"Of course I didn't forget—"

"Then where were you?"

"I'm trying to explain."

"Then explain. Who's stopping you?"

"I was in jail."

"In jail?"

"I was in jail and they confiscated my phone."

"Why were you in jail?"

"There was this woman—"

"I'm sure there was."

"It wasn't like that, Nina."

"There was this woman who needed help and so you helped her."

"Okay, maybe it was like that."

"It's always something with you, you know?"

"I'm sorry."

"You're always sorry."

"Nina, it wasn't—"

"And it's never your fault."

"No, it's not. I mean, sometimes it is, but this time it really wasn't."

"Uh-huh."

"The Anoka cops threw me in jail."

"Uh-huh."

"Actually, it's kind of a funny story when you hear it."

"I bet."

"Tonight, let me come by and I'll—"

"I have a date tonight."

"A date."

"Yes."

"You have a date."

"Yes."

"Tonight."

"Yes."

"You have a date tonight."

"You're slow but sure, McKenzie."

"With who?"

"With whom."

"With whom do you have a date tonight?"

"The man who escorted me to the ball."

"You went anyway?"

"Of course I went anyway. Why wouldn't I?"

"I just thought . . . No, it's good that you went. Was it fun?"

"You would have liked it, McKenzie. Free vodka martinis, shaken, not stirred. Strippers, too. Very tasteful. They danced to songs from the James Bond movies—*Goldfinger, Diamonds Are Forever, Goldeneye*. Cheryl Tiegs ran the auction."

"Cheryl Tiegs the former supermodel?"

"She looked damned good for a woman her age. In fact, I'd say she looked damned good for a woman of any age. You would have liked her. You would have liked the purple dress I wore, too. But what is it you like to say? Oh, yeah—you snooze, you lose."

"Nina—"

"Anyway, I have a date tonight. With the man who was kind enough to drop everything and escort me to the ball—on very short notice, no less."

"I don't blame you for wanting to punish me, but if you let me explain—"

"I'm not punishing you, McKenzie. I'm moving on."

"Nina."

"Good-bye, McKenzie."

The *click* of the connection being severed sounded like a cannon going off in my ear. I kept calling Nina's name, even though I knew she was gone.

"This is not fair," I shouted at the wall.

Can you blame her for being angry? the wall replied.

"It's not my fault."

Whose fault is it?

"Baumbach and the Anoka fucking Police Department." I was still yelling.

I was too angry to sit, so I started stomping from one room to another, vengeance on my mind. I thought about it as I went into the "family room," slipped a Toots Thielemans CD on the machine, and listened to his jazz harmonica from nineteen speakers strategically placed in eight rooms and my basement. I thought about it as I ate a dish of leftover beef lo mein in the kitchen. I thought about it as I paced the empty living room and the dining room—at least it will be a dining room once I buy a table and a few chairs.

It occurred to me that I hadn't thrown a single dinner party in the past two years without inviting Nina.

"Dammit, I'm going to get those guys."

How?

I knew I couldn't bring myself to sue them. I couldn't sue cops—I used to be a cop. I couldn't file a complaint with the Justice Department for the same reason. *Besides,* my inner voice reminded me, *you and the FBI aren't exactly like this.*

I crossed fingers on two hands and held them up—and shook my head.

"Keep talking to yourself this way, the next thing you know you'll be collecting cats."

You could call the ACLU.

"Nah. I support most of what they do, but sometimes I just want to smack 'em upside the head. Dammit, stop talking to yourself."

Here, kitty, kitty.

"Arrggggggg!"

I was getting close to slapping myself silly when I decided to sleep it off. I showered, shaved, brushed my teeth, and went to bed. The dream came quickly.

> The glass door of the convenience store swung open. The suspect didn't see me. I tucked the recoil pad of the shotgun against my shoulder and sighted down the barrel.
>
> "Police. Drop the gun. Put your hands in the air."
>
> The suspect turned toward me. He was holding a paper bag in his left hand and an S&W .38 in his right.
>
> "For God's sake drop the gun."
>
> The suspect raised his hands.
>
> I fired once.

I was wide-awake when the phone rang.

It's Nina, calling to forgive you.

"Nina," I said into the receiver.

There was a slight pause, followed by a woman's voice I didn't recognize.

"Rushmore McKenzie?"

"Who's calling, please?" I was expecting a sales pitch.

"Mr. McKenzie, my name is G. K. Bonalay. I'm an attorney representing Merodie Davies."

"Who?"

The air conditioner was working hard, but my hair and pillow were matted with sweat. I swung my legs off the bed and sat on the edge.

"Merodie Davies," the voice said. "I understand you were present when the police arrived at Ms. Davies's home the other day."

"I didn't know her name. You are who, again?"

"G. K. Bonalay, her attorney. Were you present?"

"I was there."

"I understand you attempted to intervene when Officer Baumbach assaulted Ms. Davies."

"I wouldn't say 'assault' exactly, but, yeah, I did that."

"Mr. McKenzie, I am told that Officer Baumbach arrested you and held you prisoner in the Anoka Public Safety Center for thirty-five hours without charging you because you intervened. Is that correct?"

"Ms.—Bonalay, did you say?"

"G. K. Bonalay."

"My arrest was off the books. How did you hear about it?"

"Is it true?"

"Yes."

"Mr. McKenzie, can we meet?"

"For what purpose?"

Her reply didn't sound lawyerly at all.

"I'm going to get those guys," she said.

I didn't hesitate. I should have. I should have disconnected my phone. I should have left town. I should have done a lot of things. Instead, I said, "When and where?"

2

G. K. Bonalay was having a good day. She told me so to explain her dazzling smile. Seems the coke dealer she was defending was sentenced to eighteen months after pleading guilty to one count of possession. He could have earned ten years, probably should have, but she had muddied the waters sufficiently enough that the Hennepin County attorney cut her client some slack to get the case off his desk. Now she was giddy with success. 'Course, it's precisely because of deals like that that most cops have such a low opinion of defense attorneys. I'm not one of them. I reconciled myself a long time ago to the fact that they're a necessary evil. Besides, if they, the cops, prosecutor, jury, and judge all do their jobs properly, everybody gets exactly what they deserve—the bad guys go to prison, the good guys go home, and those in between get reduced sentences.

There was a lot of feline in G. K., in the easy grace of her movements, in her intelligent green eyes. I noticed it immediately when I saw her ascend the stairs leading to the second-story loft of the Dunn Bros.

coffeehouse on Third Avenue in downtown Minneapolis. She moved as though gravity were merely a suggestion, not a reality. She seemed so young that at first I thought she was a college girl, albeit a well-dressed one—red equestrian-style jacket, black pleated skirt, and black hose and pumps. She was deftly balancing a large ceramic mug filled with mocha on a saucer with one hand while carrying a heavy leather briefcase in the other. The loft was empty except for a man and woman, both dressed in suits, who sat across from each other at a small table, leaning in and talking low, their foreheads nearly touching, so it wasn't hard to pick me out. She walked to the table where I was nursing a French vanilla IceCrema.

"Rushmore McKenzie?"

"Yes."

"Thank you for meeting me." She set down her drink and briefcase and offered her hand. It was soft. "I'm G. K. Bonalay. I hope I haven't kept you waiting."

"Not at all."

We both sat.

"You're not what I expected," she said.

"What did you expect?"

She waved her hand as if it were an unimportant question.

"How do you like to be addressed? Rushmore? Rush?"

I cringed at both names. "Just McKenzie," I said. "How 'bout you?"

"Hmm?"

"What does the *G* stand for?"

"Oh. Genevieve. My friends call me Gen. Do you want to be my friend, McKenzie?"

"Is that a trick question, Genevieve?"

"Not at all. Today I'm everyone's friend."

"Why is that?"

She told me about her drug dealer. She assured me that the guy deserved prison time, but not ten years.

"The sentencing guidelines the legislature passed are so screwed up. Everyone's trying to prove they're tough on drugs, which means you can now get more time for possession of an eight-ball than you can for first degree sexual assault. That's nuts."

"How long have you been an attorney?" I asked.

"I passed the bar nearly eighteen months ago, but I've been practicing law for much longer."

"Can you do that?"

"With proper adult supervision, yes, you can, which is how I got this."

G. K. opened her briefcase and withdrew a sheaf of photocopies an inch and a half thick held together at the top with a two-hole metal clasp. She set the file in front of me. The top page read:

Case #07-080819
Merodie Anne Davies
Offense: Homicide

She smiled and patted the document as if it were the latest Nevada Barr mystery and she was recommending it highly.

"Everything Anoka County has on Merodie," she said. "Coroner's report, incident reports, supplementals, witness statements . . ."

"Am I missing something?"

"What?"

"It's been only a couple of days. How could the county generate that much paper in a couple of days? This is civil service work."

"The county attorney, David Tuseman. He lit a fire under everybody."

"Why?"

"He's running for the State Senate. He has a primary in a couple of weeks. Like most politicians, he wants to prove he's tough on crime."

"He's already indicted Merodie for murder?"

"No, Merodie hasn't even been charged yet. She's being held for violating her probation on a dis-con. Thirty days. I learned Tuseman is using the time to build a case. I'm trying to get it kicked before he brings it to the grand jury."

"Then how did you come by all of this?"

"I did an internship with the Anoka County attorney's office when I was in law school; I practically ran their misdemeanor division. After I graduated, I volunteered to work in the public defender's office while I was looking for a job. One of the cases I caught was Merodie's disorderly conduct. When they checked her sheet they noticed I had been her attorney of record and they gave me a call."

"No, no," I said. "I mean, why do you have these reports? These reports are supposed to be confidential. They aren't supposed to be released until charges have been filed."

"Like I said, I used to work in the county attorney's office. I still have friends there. Why? Since when do you care about the rules?"

"Excuse me?"

"I know you, McKenzie. I know all about you. You're not a play-by-the-rules kind of guy."

"Who says?"

"Clayton Rask in the Minneapolis Homicide Department. Brian Wilson with the FBI. The Feds don't like you very much, but Brian does."

"You're well connected. Especially for someone so young."

"I stopped being young a long time ago, McKenzie."

"What do you want from me?"

"First, when the time comes I need you to give a deposition stating that Officer Baumbach struck Merodie Davies repeatedly, that he demanded that she answer his questions, and that he did not advise her of her rights, and then testify to it again in court if it comes to that."

"I'll testify to exactly what happened. I won't embellish."

"I'm not asking you to."

"What else?"

"With your testimony I shouldn't have any trouble getting a judge to rule that all of Merodie's statements to the sheriff's department are inadmissible."

"What else, Gen?"

"I like it that you call me Gen."

"Gen?"

"I need a favor."

"A favor?"

"That's what you do, isn't it? Ever since you quit the cops and took the reward money for catching Thomas Teachwell, you do favors for people. There was the Entrepreneurs Club, and that thing for your friend Mr. Mosley that upset the Feds so much, and rumor has it that you did a favor for the governor's wife . . ."

"You got all this from Rask and Wilson?"

"Some of it."

"It's true, I suppose. Sometimes I'll do favors for friends. If they're good enough friends and there's a good enough reason."

"The law firm I work for doesn't mind that I'm working Merodie's case. They mark it down as pro bono. Except I'm still expected to put in my eighteen hundred billable hours, and they're not going to dedicate any resources to the case, they're not going to let me hire a private investigator, so . . ."

"So you want me to do it—all your legwork."

"Yes."

"I'm not licensed."

"Doesn't matter. You know your way around a police investigation, and I can give you a letter stating that you're acting on my behalf in case anyone hassles you. You can do the job."

"I can do the job, I just don't know why I should."

"Because I'm cute?"

"You're not that cute." *Besides,* my inner voice reminded me, *I have a girlfriend who's cuter. At least I hope she's still my girlfriend.*

"Because you want to see justice done?" G. K. said.

"Most of the time I don't know what that is."

"Because it'll give you a chance to stick it to the Anoka Police Department. Is that a good enough reason?"

"It's not a good reason," I admitted. "But it's enough."

G. K. asked, "How do you want to start?"

I picked up the file. "I want to read this and then talk to your client."

"Good. Let's go."

"Go where?"

"Anoka. We'll drive up and chat with Merodie. I need to speak with her anyway. I'll drive. You can read the file on the way."

Five minutes later I was in the passenger seat of an inferno red PT Cruiser taking Washington Avenue east to 35W. I was already on the third page of the report before we hit the ramp.

Office of

Anoka County Coroner

Final Summary

AC07-881

CID File 07-080819

DECEDENT: Eli Thomas Jefferson

AGE: 34

SEX: Male

PLACE OF DEATH: 1117 Deion Avenue, Anoka, MN

DATE AND TIME OF DEATH: Found August 14 (1300 hours)

Eli Thomas Jefferson was a 34-year-old never married, unemployed man who lived with his female roommate. He was reported to be a chronic alcoholic. A statement made by his roommate indicated that he had received a deep cut under his left arm and several smaller cuts to his face from a broken bottle. The body was in an advanced stage of decomposition and was insect infested with dried blood on most areas of the torso as well as arms and legs.

"How long was Merodie in the house with the body?" I asked.
"Two weeks," G. K. said.
"That's nuts."
"Yeah, it is."

The decedent had no significant past medical history.

A postmortem examination was performed which showed severe fatty metamorphosis of the liver with mild hepatic fibrosis. An alcohol analysis was performed on spleen tissue and was 0.333 GM/100 GM. Examination of the scalp after removal of hair revealed two areas of discoloration and laceration to the back of the head, each measuring between 4 CM and 6 CM. Areas are discolored reddish-blue and are characterized by a central contusion/laceration. In addition, there was a 2 MM laceration (partial transection) of the brachial artery within the left axilla (armpit). Clotting and inflammation around the wound would indicate that the victim lived 8–12 hours after the wound was received.

The death was classified as a Homicide-Accident-Undetermined and attributed to complications of acute blood loss, due to left axilla laceration. Acute chronic alcoholism and acute ethanol intoxication were listed as associated significant conditions.

"In other words, Jefferson died from a cut under his arm the length of my fingernail that he could have fixed with a Band-Aid," I said.

G. K. never lifted her eyes from the road.

"The blood wouldn't clot because of the alcohol," she said. "He passed out, and while he was out, he bled to death."

"If the sonuvabitch had been even close to sober . . ."

I didn't finish the thought, stopping instead to re-read the words

two areas of discoloration and laceration to the back of the head.

"Two areas," I said aloud.

G. K. caught my drift quickly. "One wound could be attributed to a fall," she said. "Not two."

"Someone beat this guy on the head, G. K. Which raises the question, did he bleed to death after passing out from the alcohol or from the beating?"

"Inconclusive. If the coroner knew for sure, it would be in the report."

She swung the Cruiser into the left lane and accelerated past a slower driver just as we entered the 35W–Highway 36 interchange.

"Tuseman has to have something that's not in the report," G. K. said. "As it stands, maybe he can make a case for assault one. Maybe he can make man three. Maybe, it's a stretch, but maybe he can get a grand jury to go along with unintentional murder in the third degree. Maybe. But murder two? He has to have more."

"Like what?"

"I was hoping you could tell me."

I kept reading. A Supplementary Investigation Report issued by the Anoka County Criminal Investigation Department deputy who had first responded to Officer Boyd Baumbach's call for assistance didn't tell me much, although there was one passage that did interest me.

The entire inside of the house was filthy. There was a large amount of feces on the floors and also smeared on the wall in places. Each room was littered with a large amount of empty beer cans and liquor bottles . . . The basement contains a family room that was equally as filthy as the upstairs of the home with blood pools and feces strewn about. However, a bedroom, which appeared to be set up for a small child, was immaculate. There was no blood or dirt of any kind.

The supplemental also listed an address for Eli Jefferson's next of kin—Evonne Louise Lowman—and Merodie's mother, Mrs. Sharon Davies.

We were on Highway 10 heading west by the time I finished the nineteen-page report—single spaced—issued by the Anoka County Sheriff's Office crime lab. The report described in minute detail every bloodstain, every shard of broken glass, every liquor bottle and beer can, and where they were located in the Merodie Davies residence. My eyes grew weary reading it all.

"Geez, you guys," I muttered. "There's conscientious and then there's anal retentive."

Only two entries from the summary made it into my notebook. The first described a Lady Thumper softball bat with blood smears on the barrel. The bat was discovered lying on the floor

exactly two feet, seven inches from the body (see photographs).

The second concerned one of the other thirty-eight items collected and tagged as evidence.

Found on right arm of sofa in living room, one white, number ten envelope, blank, containing one personal check dated Saturday, One August, in the amount of four thousand, one hundred sixty-six dollars and sixty-seven cents ($4,166.67) made out to Merodie Davies and drawn on an account owned by Priscilla St. Ana, Woodbury, MN.

"Who's Priscilla St. Ana?"

"That's another thing I'm hoping you can find out," G. K. said.

I moved to the Supplementary Investigation Report filed by Sergeant Doug Rios, Badge Number 191, of the Anoka County CID. It was he who had decided that Merodie Davies should be taken from her home to Mercy Hospital for evaluation. During the ride, Rios claimed, Davies had made several

> spontaneous statements

to him. Things like

> He was still bleeding yesterday.

and

> I didn't know I hit him so hard.

When they arrived at the hospital, Rios decided that since Merodie was in a talkative mood, they would hold off on any treatment until after she was interviewed.

"They withheld medical attention while they interrogated Merodie," I said.

"You noticed that, too," G. K. said.

I read the report on the interview carefully.

> Prior to questioning Davies, I advised her I was an investigator with the Anoka County Sheriff's Office. I advised her of her **MIRANDA RIGHTS** which she stated she understood. Davies agreed to talk with me.
>
> I advised Davies that Eli Jefferson had been found dead at her residence from apparent trauma and she told me that there were two separate incidents that happened Saturday two weeks

ago that could have caused those injuries. She told me that Jefferson had accidentally cut himself with a broken beer bottle in the kitchen and that is why there was blood in the house.

Davies then explained that on Saturday two weeks ago someone had broken into her home and started a fight with Jefferson. She indicated that she had been sleeping when the fight began. She woke up and saw the assailant hitting Jefferson. She said the assailant saw her and quickly left the house. She indicated that the assailant was a man with blond hair. I asked Davies who that might be and she told me that she felt it could have been a former boyfriend. I asked her for the name of the boyfriend but Davies claimed she could not remember.

Davies also informed me that she had been living downstairs for approximately two weeks and was unaware of Jefferson's activities during that time. A little later, Davies told me that she had brought food and several bottles of vodka downstairs with her. She told me that she did not want to go upstairs because she was frightened. I asked Davies who she was frightened of, but she said she could not remember.

I told her that I believed she was withholding information about the death of Jefferson and his fight with the former boyfriend. Davies denied any involvement in Jefferson's death and I concluded the interview.

According to the report, Merodie Davies was later examined by the hospital staff and physical evidence was taken—I took this to mean blood and hair samples. Sergeant Rios wrote that it was during these procedures that Merodie indicated to him that she had something to add to her previous statement.

I again advised her of her **MIRANDA RIGHTS** , which she stated she understood, and again she waived them . . . Davies was more coherent and spoke clearly during the entire interview.

Davies told me she had been drinking for two weeks but that she stopped drinking last night. She told me that she got up this morning and felt a little hungover and hungry. She walked upstairs and observed Jefferson lying in the living room. She said his body was bloated and cold to the touch.

I asked when she last saw Jefferson and Davies said that she recalled speaking to him the night before last while she was downstairs in the basement. She said he yelled at her and she yelled at him, but that she did not actually see him. She said Jefferson never came downstairs. Later, she said that Jefferson came downstairs once a few days ago and that he brought her a drink and they slept on the couch together. Still later, she claimed it might not have been a few days ago, that it could have been longer. She said she might have lost track of time.

When I asked her what could have caused Jefferson's injuries, Davies told me that she had thrown a beer bottle at him that shattered and cut him. She told me that she was angry at Jefferson over some remark he had made but she said she could not remember what he said. She denied ever intentionally inflicting any injuries on Jefferson with the broken glass, however. She also claimed that Jefferson had stopped the bleeding with a washcloth and refused to seek medical attention, claiming it was only a scratch.

When I asked how Jefferson hurt his head, she indicated that a man broke into her house and fought with Jefferson. I asked her if she witnessed the fight and she indicated that she had. I asked Davies if she could identify the man and she said no. I asked if the man had blond hair and she said yes, then corrected herself and said she couldn't remember . . .

I told her that a softball bat had been found at the scene.

Davies indicated that it was hers, that she played for Dimmer's Bar softball team until late July when the season ended. I told her that blood was found on the bat. I told her that we suspect that someone hit Jefferson with the bat. Davies denied hitting Jefferson with the bat. She said she only hit him with the bottle. I asked Davies if the man Jefferson fought with hit him with the bat. After a long pause, Davies said she did not see the man hit Jefferson with the bat.

I told her that many of her statements were inconsistent and Davies said she was trying as hard as she could. I asked her if she would take a polygraph test and she agreed. <u>See additional report for polygraph results.</u>

"They gave her a polygraph?"

"Oh, it gets better," G. K. assured me.

We had pulled off of 10 and were heading west on Main Street past the huge shopping center that Coon Rapids had built on Anoka's doorstep when I read the results.

Office of

ANOKA COUNTY SHERIFF

<u>CONFIDENTIAL</u>

<u>DO NOT RELEASE WITHOUT A RELEASE</u>

<u>OF INFORMATION FORM OR COURT ORDER</u>

<u>PURPOSE OF EXAMINATION</u>: To determine if Davies, Merodie Anne was being truthful when she denied killing Eli Jefferson.

A computerized polygraph exam was administered to Davies, Merodie Anne on 8/14 at 2100 hrs. at the C.I.D. Offices. Following the approved and recommended procedures, the polygraph questions were carefully reviewed with the subject prior to the examination. The questions consisted of control, neutral, symptomatic, and relevant questions. The following relevant questions were asked:

Question #1: Are you the one who caused those fatal injuries to Eli Jefferson?

Answer: No.

Question #2: Did you inflict those injuries which caused the death of Eli Jefferson?

Answer: No.

Results: In reference to the relevant questions, **DECEPTION WAS INDICATED.** The John Hopkins University Applied Physics Laboratory Computer Scoring Algorithm indicates that the probability of deception on the targeted issues is greater than 99%.

I closed the file and set it on my lap. I wanted to stick it to the Anoka cops, but I didn't want to help a killer go free for the privilege. G. K. seemed to have read my mind.

"No way Merodie could have understood the questions she was being asked," she said.

"You think?"

G. K. pulled off Main Street onto Fourth Avenue and into the parking ramp that served both the Anoka County Courthouse and the correctional facility.

"Talk to her yourself," she said. "You decide."

"They've revoked your probation on the disorderly conduct conviction from last May," G. K. Bonalay said. "They're going to make you serve the entire thirty days."

"They can't do that," Merodie Davies insisted. Her sharp words produced a disconcerting echo off the gray cinder-block walls of the eight-by-eight interview room.

"Yes, they can."

"Who's going to clean my house?"

"Your house?'

"My house is a mess. The blood. Who's going to clean up the blood?"

"Don't worry about your house."

"People are going to see it. After the funeral. After the funeral when, when . . ." Merodie dropped her chin against her chest. Her entire body began to tremble, and she gripped the small table so tightly that I was sure she would have overturned it if it hadn't been bolted to the floor. She grunted and groaned and cried out in unbridled anguish; she painted the walls with her suffering. Eli Jefferson might have been dead for two weeks, but the pain of it was fresh in Merodie's heart. G. K. patted her shoulder and said, "There, there." She looked at me like she wanted me to do something about it. I looked at the door and wished I could wait outside.

It took a while for Merodie to come back to us. She chanted, "I'm sorry, I'm sorry," as she wiped her tears with the sleeve of her olive-green jump suit.

"I know you're upset," G. K. told her, "but you must stop worrying about Eli and start worrying about yourself."

"I can't," Merodie said. "He was everything to me. He was my last chance."

"Last chance for what?"

Merodie didn't answer. She sniffed and dried her eyes and took several deep breaths, all while studying G. K. as if she were a curiosity, a new exhibit at the Minnesota Zoo. Then she turned her attention on me.

"Do I know you?" It was the second time she had asked the question.

"I was at your home the other day, the day you were arrested."

She nodded as if it were all coming back to her. I doubted that it was. Yet, while her mind couldn't quite wrap itself around me, it was becoming abundantly clear to her that she was in jail, specifically the Anoka County Correctional Facility, and that she was in deep trouble.

"They think I killed him, don't they?" Merodie said.

"Killed who?" G. K. was testing her. Merodie had been fading in and out all through our conversation. At one moment she was aware enough to answer G. K.'s questions clearly; at the next she was unsure who G. K. was.

"Eli," Merodie answered. "Eli Jefferson. They think I killed him. That wonderful man."

Merodie began pacing across the tiny room—four steps, turn, four steps, turn. When I first met her outside her home she had reminded me of the female lead in a zombie movie, *The Night of the Living Dead*—the original, not the remake—incoherent, oblivious even to where she was. Now, even though her eyes were red and blotchy and her face still had the same tint as the olive green jumpsuit that she wore, she moved like a woman alive with hope. More than that. Clean and sober, she was pretty, and I noticed for the first time that she was also young—no older than thirty-five—and that her features seemed delicate, as if she could be bruised by a hard wind.

It's amazing what a few hot meals and a good night's sleep can do, my inner voice concluded.

"Who is Eli Jefferson?" G. K. asked.

"My fiancé."

"Did you kill him?"

"I don't think so."

"No. Uh-uh. From now on, if someone asks you if you killed Eli Jefferson, you answer . . ."

"No." Merodie's shout bounced off the walls.

"Exactly."

"I mean it," Merodie insisted. "I didn't do it."

"What did you do?"

Merodie hesitated before answering in a low, childlike voice. "I hit him with a bottle."

"What did you say?"

"I hit him with a bottle."

"What kind of bottle?"

"What kind? I don't know. A bottle, you know, a beer bottle."

"How?"

"What do you mean, how?"

"Tell me what happened," G. K. said.

"I threw a bottle at him and I hit him."

"Where?"

"In the kitchen."

"No, I mean where did the bottle hit him?"

"In the kitch—. In the head. Not the head. He lifted his arm up in front of his head and the bottle hit him there and it broke to pieces. Pieces of glass from the bottle, they went everywhere."

"What happened next?" G. K. asked.

"He started bleeding here." Merodie touched the inside of her upper arm near the armpit.

"Badly?"

"I don't know. I guess."

"Then what did you do?"

"I told him to get a bandage for it. For the cut."

"Did he?"

"I guess not."

"Why did you throw the bottle at him?"

"I don't remember."

"Try."

"I can't." Merodie shook her head. "I can't be expected to remember every little thing."

"Listen." G. K. gave her the stock lawyer-client line, trying mightily to be patient. "I'm your lawyer. I'm not here to judge. I'm here to help. You can tell me everything. In fact, if you want me to defend you, you'd better tell me everything."

"But you said to shut up, already. You said not to say anything."

"To them," G. K. shouted, finally losing it, waving her hand vaguely at the gray metal door as her words reverberated through the room.

"Sorry." At first Merodie looked down at her gnarly fingers, a penitent schoolgirl, age thirty-five going on eight, then she perked up. "What about him?" she asked, pointing at me.

"He's on our side," G. K. assured her.

"Are you, mister?"

"Yes, I am," I said. "You can call me McKenzie."

"McKenzie? Do I know you?"

"We're close personal friends. Can I ask you a few questions?"

G. K. nodded.

"Do you play softball?"

"I do," Merodie said. She smiled broadly as if the memory of it brought her joy. "I play for Dimmer's. Second base, sometimes short."

"Can you hit?'

Merodie grinned at me. "I get my cuts."

"What kind of bat do you use?"

"Lady Thumper."

"Thirty-two ounces?"

"No, that's too heavy. Twenty-eight."

"Ever hit Eli with it?"

"With the Thumper? No. Why would I use . . . ?" She stopped speaking. For the first time she looked me in the eye. "No," she said. "I never did."

"Okay."

She smiled, and for a moment she actually looked innocent. It didn't last.

"Who is Priscilla St. Ana?" I asked.

Merodie erupted the way a volcano might—ferociously. She didn't call me anything I hadn't heard before, but she fitted the obscenities, profanities, and vulgarities together in such interesting combinations and with such a thrill in her voice that I felt she was creating a new art form. During her diatribe two points were made: Priscilla was the best friend Merodie ever had, and I should not dare to involve her in this mess if I knew what was good for me.

"It's okay, it's okay," G. K. said. She pulled Merodie back into her chair and patted her hand. "We won't bother her."

"You better not," Merodie said.

"It's okay."

"I mean it."

"Don't worry, Merodie."

"How long do I have to stay here?"

"You'll have to stay in here for thirty days, but you'll be safe."

And sober, my inner voice said.

"Everything will work out," G. K. said. "Only no more statements, okay, Merodie?"

Merodie nodded.

"I want you to promise not to talk to anyone except me and McKenzie here. Okay?"

"Okay."

G. K. leaned back in the plastic chair and studied her client from across the small wooden table. Merodie refused to meet her gaze, looking at everything but G. K.'s face.

Merodie was hiding something, I decided. Something about Priscilla St. Ana. Maybe about everything. I wanted to learn what it was, but not now. *Let her get straight first,* I told myself. A few days of sobriety have been known to work miracles.

"What about Eli?" Merodie asked, breaking the silence.

"If the county had enough to charge you, they would have done so by now," G. K. said. "Personally, I don't think they have much of a case, at least not for murder. I know the county attorney, though, and he's a sneaky little prick and he's up for reelection, so . . ."

"No, I mean the funeral. Who's going to take care of Eli?"

G. K. said she didn't know but would check on it for her.

"Can I be there for the funeral? I have to be there."

"I don't think they'll let you out."

Merodie hung her head again, and for a moment I thought she would begin weeping. Instead, she said, "He was such a good-looking man."

"I'm sure he was," said G. K.

"We were going to be married. Did I tell you that?"

"Yes, you did."

"Now he's gone. Like everyone else I've ever loved. Gone, gone, gone."

"Did you kill him?" G. K. was testing her one last time.

"I don't think so," Merodie replied.

G. K. slapped the table hard with the flat of her hand. The loud, unexpected noise not only startled the woman, it caused me to jump as well.

"Just say no," G. K. shouted. The walls repeated her words.

Merodie rose slowly to her feet and looked straight at G. K. Her voice was firm. "No, I didn't kill him." In a smaller voice she asked, "Why do these things always happen to me?"

G. K. fluffed her hair off the back of her neck with both hands, cooling it. We were both perspiring freely in the heat as we moved around the corner from the front door of the Anoka County Correctional Facility and made our way to the parking ramp. The weathergeeks said we could expect lows in the eighties and highs approaching a hundred degrees for the rest of the week without even a hint of rain. During winter, we actually long for this.

"About Priscilla St. Ana," G. K. said.

"I'll look into it."

"Thank you."

"I'll also talk to Merodie's and Eli's families, friends, neighbors, coworkers; examine their paper, you know, insurance, wills; try to get a handle on their relationship—everything a proper semiprofessional private investigator would do. Can you get me into her house?"

"When?"

"Tomorrow morning?"

"I'll make some calls."

We left the sidewalk and moved into the parking ramp. The shade didn't provide any comfort at all. G. K. had parked nose forward on the second level. We had just reached the Cruiser when another vehicle pulled up, blocking our way. It was a civilian car, a '93 Chevy Impala that looked like it had been left out in a hailstorm. Twice. City of Anoka Police Officer Boyd Baumbach, dressed in full uniform, was at the wheel.

"What are you doing here?" he asked.

"Excuse me?"

"I saw you on the sidewalk," Baumbach said. "You filing a complaint or somethin'?"

"You're blocking the way."

He pointed his chin at G. K. "Who's she?"

"Why? You looking for another woman to beat up?"

"Watch your mouth."

G. K. stepped around me. "Are you the police officer who assaulted my client?" she asked.

"Your client?"

"I'm G. K. Bonalay. I represent Merodie Davies. Does the county attorney know you assaulted my client, or do I have to tell him?"

"I didn't do nothing like that."

"That's not what I heard."

Baumbach looked hard at me. "I don't care what you heard," he said.

"Are you saying it's not true?" G. K. said.

"I never touched that woman."

"Will you testify to that under oath?"

"I ain't testifying to nothin'."

"We'll see."

"What's that supposed to mean?"

"You're very nervous, Officer," G. K. said. "Why are you nervous?"

"I ain't."

"Sure you are you, Boyd," I said. "I don't blame you, either. Sooner or later you'll have to answer questions under oath, and when you do, Ms. Bonalay is going to clean your clock. Then it'll be my turn."

"You want a piece of me? You want a piece of me right now, asshole?"

Normally I would have been offended, except after what Merodie Davies had called me, Baumbach's epithet sounded like a compliment.

"Oh, yeah. I want a piece. Why don't you get out of your car and give me some."

Baumbach came out of his car quickly. "Let's settle this like men," he said.

I took G. K. by the elbow and pulled her behind me. Baumbach moved close, well within striking distance, his hands stiff at his side.

"Let's go," he said.

I deliberately tucked my hands between my belt and the small of my back and leaned toward him.

"Take your best shot, woman-beater."

Baumbach brought his hands up, his face red with anger. But he hesitated. He wasn't as dumb as he looked.

"Go 'head," I told him. "The first one is free."

He glanced from me to G. K. and back again.

"Why are you doing this?" he asked.

"You chicken? C'mon."

Baumbach stepped backward until his butt was pressed against his car door. I brought my arms out and folded them across my chest again.

"What's going on?" G. K. asked.

"Cameras," I said.

"Cameras?"

I pointed at the boxes mounted high on the concrete walls at the top and bottom of the ramp.

"Security cameras. I provoke Boyd. He takes a shot. I bust his ass using the video as evidence, and he's the one who does time in a holding cell."

"I like it."

"You sonuvabitch," Baumbach called me.

"Ah, well. It was worth a try."

"You're trying to set me up," Baumbach said. "You're trying to set me up because—you ain't a man. You have a problem, you should settle it like a man."

"You're a bad cop, Boyd, and it's this childish notion of manhood you have that made you a bad cop. I'm going to take you off the board. It's my civic duty."

Baumbach clenched like a man about to throw a punch. "This ain't over," he said.

He flung a glance at G. K., pivoted, and climbed back into his Impala. The sound of his squealing tires echoed through the ramp.

G. K. grinned as she moved to the driver's door of her own car.

"Well, that was fun," she said.

3

To say Nina Truhler was smart and sexy was like saying the world was big and round—mere words simply didn't do her justice. I would have told her so, too. If only she had been at Rickie's when I arrived.

It took G. K. twenty-five minutes to drive from Anoka to Minneapolis even though, like me, she considered the posted speed limit to be more of a guideline than a law. She dropped me off at the Dunn Bros. coffeehouse after giving me her business card. On it she had written her personal cell and home numbers, as well as her home address. She told me to call her anytime. I pressed the card between the pages of my notebook and dropped it on the bucket seat on the passenger side of my Audi.

By then it was already late. Most of the people who weren't hopelessly tangled in rush hour traffic were probably sitting down to dinner by the time I drove I-94 from Minneapolis across the Mississippi River into St. Paul. Certainly, there were a great many people at Rickie's doing just that. The upstairs dining room, which featured live jazz starting at 9:00 P.M., was nearly filled with diners by the time I arrived, and most of the sofas, stuffed chairs, and small tables in the downstairs lounge were occupied.

I searched for Nina. I wanted to see her before she left on her date. I wasn't sure what I was going to tell her. "Please don't go" came to mind. Only I couldn't find her.

The bartender waved me over. "Hi, McKenzie," she said. "Looking for the boss?"

"I am."

"She left a few minutes ago."

"Did she go home?" I glanced at my watch. Maybe I still had time to intercept her.

"No, she left . . . Just a minute." She went to the beer taps and poured a Summit Ale, my usual. She set it in front of me.

"You're going to bad-news me, aren't you, Jenness?" I said, pronouncing the name Jen-*ness*, as she once instructed me.

"Nina left five minutes ago with the guy who took her to the charity ball."

I drank some of the beer.

"Sorry," she said.

"I already knew she had a date."

"I know."

"You know?"

"Nina's been grumbling about you for two days now."

"How bad has it been, her grumbling?"

"Pretty bad."

"It wasn't my fault."

"You mean about getting arrested?"

"She told you that, too?"

"When things are going well, Nina keeps her life pretty much private. When they're going bad, she kinda talks to herself out loud, if you know what I mean."

"I know."

I drank more beer.

"Did you meet this guy she's dating?" I asked.

"Daniel. Not Dan or Danny. Daniel. He's an architect. Has money if you go by his clothes and car."

Snob, my inner voice said.

"What does he look like?" I asked.

"He's about your size, your height and weight," Jenness said. "I figure he must work out because he's in good shape but, I don't know, he seems soft to me. Like he's never actually done any physical labor or played a contact sport."

Wuss.

"And he wears glasses."

Four-eyes.

"Where did they go?" I asked.

"I don't know. But if I did, McKenzie, I'd keep it to myself."

"Why?"

"Why? So you won't go over there and slap the guy around. I gotta tell you, that's not the way to a girl's heart, if you know what I mean."

"Jenness, would I do a thing like that?"

"I don't know. Would you?"

Good question.

I pushed the beer away.

"Bourbon," I said. "No ice."

Jenness frowned at me.

"Don't give up, McKenzie. So what if Nina dates this guy? It's a onetime deal. In a couple of days she'll cool off and the two of you will get back together."

"You think so?"

"I'm betting on it."

"Make it a double," I said.

———————

When people ask where I'm from, I answer St. Paul. If the question comes from someone who actually lives in St. Paul, I tell them I'm from Merriam Park and they know immediately what I'm talking about. True, I actually live in the suburbs. When I came into my money I bought a house for my father and me that I thought was in St. Paul's St. Anthony Park neighborhood, only to discover too late that I was on the wrong side of the street, that I had accidentally moved to Falcon Heights. Still, I'll always be a Merriam Park boy at heart.

St. Paul is a city of neighborhoods. There are seventeen in all not counting the neighborhoods within neighborhoods that are loosely defined by parks and churches, and the attitudes of the people who live in them can best be described as parochial. Take the Greater Eastside, an island between Interstate 35E and the City of Maplewood. It's a neighborhood of working-class people and immigrants who tend to stay close to home. The big joke there is that the city ends at Lexington Parkway, which cuts St. Paul roughly in half, because no Eastsider has any reason to go farther west. At the same time, you have the folks who live in the Macalester-Groveland neighborhood, just west of Lexington Parkway. They believe they're the intellectual and cultural center of the city for no better reason than that three liberal arts colleges—Macalester, St. Thomas, and St. Catherine—just happen to be located within its boundaries. And if you think these people like each other, you haven't been around for one of our more hotly contested mayoral races.

As for Merriam Park, it was developed in about 1885 by John Merriam as a commuter suburb since at the time it was located midway between what was then downtown St. Paul and Minneapolis. It attracted upper-middle-class residents because he insisted that every house built there cost at least $1,500. Many of those homes are still standing. So is Longfellow School, where I chipped a tooth falling off a playground slide, and Merriam Park Community Center, where I discovered hockey, baseball, and girls, not necessarily in that order. As for our attitude toward St. Paul's other sixteen neighborhoods, it's simple: If we ignore them, maybe they'll go away.

I had two more drinks at Rickie's—which, by the way, is located in the Summit Hill neighborhood—and drove to Bobby Dunston's house. Bobby lives directly across from Merriam Park Community Center in a home that he and Shelby bought from Bobby's parents when they retired, the house Bobby grew up in. I knew it as well as my own childhood home, an old Colonial with an open wraparound porch. Despite the heat, Bobby and Shelby were sitting on the porch when I drove up, sipping lemonade, looking like an old married couple in a Norman Rockwell painting.

We tend to lose our friends as we grow older. Without the glue of shared experiences—school, sports, the job—they drift away despite our best intentions to hold them close. Instead, we turn to family. Only I had no family, unless you count an aunt and uncle who send me Christmas cards from Colorado and a few distant cousins I've met maybe twice in the past three and a half decades. Bobby, Shelby, and their daughters were my family and my heirs.

I parked and made my way up the sidewalk. As I reached the porch Bobby said, "How's the Audi running?"

"Okay, but it hasn't been the same since the snowplow ran me off the highway."

"At least the insurance company paid for the damages."

Bobby was on his feet. I shook his hand.

"Those damages, sure, but they wouldn't pay to fix the bullet holes."

"I can't believe your policy didn't cover that."

Shelby was also standing. She winced at the word "bullets," but then she always was a worrier. I hugged her and kissed her cheek.

"Where were you the other day?" she asked. "The girls wanted to go over to your house and play with the ducks."

"Listen. You guys have a key. You're welcome to come over anytime. Feed the ducks. Feed yourselves. Use the mini-donut and sno-cone machines. Hell, if you're alone, use one of the bedrooms."

"Camp Rushmore McKenzie," said Bobby.

"Exactly what I'm saying. Same with the cabin up north. What's mine is yours."

They were both sitting now, and Shelby was pouring fresh-squeezed lemonade into an extra glass as if she had been expecting me. The sun was setting and it was growing cooler, but it was still hot enough for a man to sweat even while seated on a porch railing. Bobby and Shelby were both wearing shorts and T-shirts. Bobby's swore allegiance to the St. Paul Saints minor league baseball team, while Shelby's featured the logo of Buddy Guy's Legends, a blues club in Chicago. Bobby had taken her there in the spring while I babysat their two daughters.

"Where are the kids?" I asked.

As if on cue, Victoria and Katie appeared at a living room window that opened onto the porch just behind their mother's shoulder.

"McKenzie," they called through the screen.

"How're my girls?"

"Did you bring us something?" they asked in unison.

"Not this trip."

They both made disappointed noises, and I said, "Sorry."

"Is it because Mom threatened your life last time?" asked Victoria.

"You have to admit ten pounds of Tootsie Rolls is kind of excessive."

"It isn't," said Katie.

"Mom has been doling them out a few at a time for good behavior like we were prisoners in a Russian gulag," Victoria said.

"A gulag?"

"You know. Like where they kept Solzhenitsyn."

"How old are you again?"

"She's no fun," Katie insisted.

"Who?"

"Mom. Gol, McKenzie."

"Your mother was a lot of fun when I first met her."

"She was young then," Victoria said. "Now she's really old."

"That's it," Shelby announced. "The spankings will now commence."

"Oh puhleez, mother," Victoria said.

Shelby's eyes bore down hard on her daughter.

Victoria said, "I think I'll go upstairs and read."

"Good idea," Shelby said.

"Good night, all."

Victoria left the window. Katie followed her deep into the house.

Shelby sighed significantly.

"Victoria's almost a teenager," she said.

"Don't you just love that?" Bobby said.

"Have you ever spanked your children?" I asked.

"The threat of violence is usually sufficient, and when it's not, Bobby pulls his gun."

Bobby held up his hand, three fingers curled into his palm, his index finger extended, his thumb back, and made a clicking noise with his tongue.

"I can see how that might keep order."

"So, McKenzie," Bobby said. "I heard you were arrested the other day."

"Taken into custody, but not booked."

"Important difference."

"You heard this—how?"

"I had a conversation with an Anoka cop named Jerry Moorhead."

"No kidding. Why'd he call you?"

"He didn't. He knew a guy in the department. Moorhead asked about you, the officer knew we were tight, so I got the call. He was impressed that you had a friend who was a lieutenant in homicide."

"Aren't we all?"

"He was also impressed when I told him what a sterling example of law enforcement you were until you decided to take the price for Teachwell and live a life of undeserved luxury."

"What do you mean, undeserved?"

"He wants to arrange a sit-down, Mac. Buy you a few drinks."

"Does he?"

"That's what he said."

"I wonder why."

"The man made a mistake, he wants to apologize. What's the big deal?"

"Does he want to apologize because he was wrong or because he wants to get me out of his hair?"

"What are you talking about?"

"The woman Moorhead's deputy slapped around, they're trying to jam her up on what looks like a bogus murder charge. I told her lawyer that I'd look into it."

"Ahh geez," said Shelby. "Not again."

"What?"

"Why do you always get involved in these things?" she asked me. "If you're bored, go shopping."

We'd had this conversation before, and truth be told, I always came off looking silly defending myself. I decided to change the subject.

"Besides, is Moorhead going to call Nina, apologize to her? I was supposed to take her to that damn charity ball the other night, but I couldn't because I was in jail, so she went with some other guy and guess what? They have a date tonight."

"A date?" said Shelby.

"They went to dinner, la-de-da."

"How do you know?"

"I was over there."

"At Nina's?"

"No. At Rickie's. He picked her up at her place of business, do you believe that? Didn't even have the courtesy to call for her at home. The jerk."

"How do you know he's a jerk?"

"He's an architect. He wears glasses. His name is Daniel."

"Sounds like a jerk to me," said Bobby.

"If he wasn't a nice guy, Nina wouldn't date him," said Shelby.

"Oh, I don't know. She dates McKenzie."

"Way to stick up for me, Bobby," I said. "You're a real pal."

"Anytime."

"It's probably for the best," I said. "I should be moving on anyway."

Shelby stood abruptly, balled her hands into fists, and pressed them against her hips. She looked down at me and spoke without blinking.

"Don't. You. Dare."

"What?"

"Don't you dare. Every time you become involved with a woman you do this."

"Do what?"

"You start looking for something, anything, as an excuse to break up. 'Just didn't work out, time to move on'—you always say that."

"I do not."

"Always."

"Na-uh."

"You want a list? Should we start with Annie?"

"Whatever happened to her?" Bobby asked.

"She. Married. Someone. Else."

"Oh."

"Well, what am I supposed to do?" I asked. "Nina's dating this guy . . ."

"An architect," said Bobby.

"You can start by apologizing for standing her up," she told me.

"I did."

"Do it again."

"But it wasn't my fault."

"It. Doesn't. Matter."

"It really doesn't," said Bobby. "I've apologized to Shelby for a lot of things that weren't my fault, and . . ."

Shelby gave him that look. You know the one I mean. Bobby turned and stared past the porch toward Merriam Park as if there were something out there that was suddenly very interesting.

"McKenzie," Shelby said. "She's the best of them. Mary Beth, Annie, Judy, Theresa, Robin, Kirsten—Nina is the best of them."

"No, you're the best of them."

"Balderdash."

"Balderdash?"

"I'm just the excuse you use. You pretend to be in love with your best friend's wife, and since you can't have her, you won't marry anyone. 'Pity me, the poor lonely bachelor.' It's balderdash."

"There's that word again."

"If I were suddenly free—if Bobby got hit by a truck tomorrow— it'd be the same ol' thing. Just didn't work out, time to move on."

I looked at Bobby.

"It's true," he said. "If it wasn't, I would have blown your brains out back when we were in college."

"It's fear of commitment," Shelby said. "That's what we're talking about."

"Balderdash."

Shelby looked at me as if I were nuts.

"You said it first," I reminded her.

"We're trying to cut down on the cursing because of the girls."

"Yeah, but do you really want your kids to go around saying balderdash?"

Shelby refused to be distracted.

"She's the best of all the women you've known, McKenzie," she said. "She really is."

"I know."

"We'll make Moorhead buy drinks at Nina's place," Bobby said. "He can apologize to her at the same time. Whaddya say?"

"No."

"Why not?"

"Bobby, the dream came back."

"The dream? The shotgun dream?"

"It came back when I was in jail and then again last night."

"I thought you were done with that."

"So did I."

"You were supposed to get therapy," Shelby said.

"I did."

"You went three times and then you quit—pronounced yourself cured and started dating the therapist."

"Dr. Jillian DeMarais. She was a babe."

"She was a bitch," said Bobby.

"Nonetheless."

"McKenzie, the dream," said Shelby.

"It doesn't freak me out," I told her. "It wakes me up sometimes, but it's not like I can't sleep or I'm afraid to sleep. I don't shake, rattle, or roll—I can still function. It's just a dream. Like the one I used to have about not being able to find the classroom during finals. It'll go away just like it did before. Don't worry about it."

"What if it doesn't go away?"

"It will."

"You have to see someone, seriously this time."

"Not a bad idea," said Bobby. "It wouldn't hurt."

"I'd have to be nuts to go to a psychiatrist," I said.

No one laughed at the joke.

Lemonade was sipped.

Silent moments passed.

"What are you going to do?" Bobby asked.

"About what?"

"About Moorhead," Bobby said.

"About Nina," Shelby said.

They looked at each other. Shelby scowled and said, "First things first." Bobby surrendered without firing a shot.

"About Nina," Shelby repeated.

"I'll apologize. Again. I'll try to win her back. Will that make you happy?"

Shelby smiled like it would.

"About Moorhead?" asked Bobby.

"The bastard put me in jail. He gave me bad dreams. Fuck 'im."

"McKenzie," Shelby said.

"Balderdash."

It just didn't sound the same.

I looked at my watch. Eleven forty-seven. Eleven forty-seven at night and I was sweating in my car, the windows rolled down, crickets chirping all over the damn place. I could have closed the windows and used the AC, but that would have been a dead giveaway. A car parked along a residential street with the engine running—I might as well hang a sign from both bumpers reading UP TO NO GOOD. As it was, I was surprised the good folks in Mahtomedi weren't more observant. I was surprised someone hadn't already called the cops. I was surprised that the cops weren't shining their bright lights inside my Audi and demanding that I state my business.

"It's like this, Officer, I'm spying on my girlfriend."

Yeah, that would go over big.

What the hell are *you doing here?* my inner voice wanted to know.

Just curious, I told it.

What else?

Angry, excited, afraid, jealous, guilty, hopeful . . .

Hopeful?

Especially hopeful, although hopeful for what I couldn't say. I had been parked down the street from Nina's home for the better part of two hours, and I couldn't explain my motives to myself any better than when I first arrived. I guess I just wanted to see it for myself—Nina with another man. I could believe it if I saw it for myself.

What good would that do?

My God, you ask a lot of questions.

I looked at my watch again. Eleven forty-nine. How long does it take to eat dinner, anyway?

I turned on my radio and hit the scan button until it stopped at 89.3 FM, the Current, Minnesota Public Radio's new alternative rock station. Some people have labeled it the radio station for music connoisseurs, and it certainly is that. The first hour I listened to it I heard Otis Redding, Chet Baker, Johnny Cash, the Jayhawks, Little Eva, Blind Willie Johnson, the Byrds, Chaka Khan, the Red Hot Chili Peppers, and five bands that were new to me. I was hooked and remain so, although I must admit that as good as its selections usually are, sometimes the Current plays music of such stunning awfulness that I figure the DJ must have lost a bet. Like now. They were playing something I could only describe as Pakistani hip-hop.

I switched off the radio.

Where in hell was Nina? Didn't she know what time it was?

Eleven fifty-two by my watch.

A high-end Beamer captured my attention as it turned onto the street where Nina lived. I watched as it inched forward and turned into Nina's driveway. Its engine was switched off and its headlamps extinguished. Nothing moved for five minutes. I imagined what a couple could be doing in a parked car for five minutes and my hands tightened on my own steering wheel. Finally, the driver's door opened. A man slipped out of the car—Daniel the architect, if Jenness's description held true. He moved around the car and halted. His body language told me that he was disappointed Nina didn't wait for him to open her car door.

Atta girl, Nina.

He followed her to the front door and stood close to her while she worked the lock with her keys. The door opened. She turned to face him.

Don't kiss him!

She didn't. Instead, Nina took his hand and led him inside. The door closed behind them.

I stared at it for a long time.

You could kill him, my inner voice told me. *It would be easy.*

Yes, it would be easy. I'd get away with it, too. Simply wait for him to get into his car, follow him out of the neighborhood, pull up next to him when he stops at a light, roll down the window, say "Hey," and when he leans over put two rounds between his eyes and drive away. No muss, no fuss.

Yeah, but what about the next one? Or the one after that? If I started piling up dead boyfriends, Nina was bound to get suspicious. And how long could I get away with it before Bobby Dunston carted me off to Oak Park Heights?

I shook the idea from my head.

You could beat him up instead.

But what if he wasn't as soft as Jenness thought he was? There's nothing worse than picking a fight with a guy to impress a woman and getting your ass kicked.

What other options do you have?

A voodoo priestess once taught me a simple way to hex my enemies. She said I should write the evildoer's name nine times and insert the paper into the mouth of a snake.

Except you don't have a snake.

"Nina." I said the name out loud just to hear the sound of it. It didn't do me any good.

I started the Audi, flipped on the headlights, and put it in gear.

Well, you saw Nina with another man. Are you happy now?

4

I stood in the silent kitchen, doing a slow three-sixty, taking it all in. I loved my gadgets, and the counters and cupboards were loaded with them—pasta maker, bread maker, Cuisinart, blender, microwave oven, food dehydrator, deep fryer, rotisserie, ice cream churn, Macho Pop popcorn popper, mini-donut machine, sno-cone machine, pizza oven. Only it was my silver Vienna de Luxe coffee machine that I was searching for.

I had poured myself another drink before I went to bed. And another. And one more. Now I had awakened with a hangover that rocked my head and sent my stomach into a whirlpool of nausea. Still, I've had hangovers before, and I knew I would survive. Pepto-Bismol, toast, coffee, lots and lots of coffee, and I would function fine until noon, a respectable hour when I could have a stiff drink to help take the edge off.

Ingredients were already loaded into the machine. I pressed a button and a predetermined amount of French vanilla almond coffee beans was reduced to a fine powder in about six seconds and sprinkled into a filter; spring water was poured, and the coffee brewed.

I split a bagel and dropped the two halves into my toaster. While it was toasting I put on a CD, *Tosca*, by Giacomo Puccini. I don't have a lot of opera in my collection—normally, I'm a jazz guy—except I had been introduced to opera by Kirsten Sager Whitson, the very lovely, very wealthy woman who dumped me just before I met Nina, and somehow it seemed appropriate.

The opera was filled with heartache. It was all about Tosca, a beautiful singer who is forced to sacrifice her body and soul to the villainous Baron Scarpia in order to save the life of her boyfriend, Mario, whom the baron has imprisoned. Naturally, everyone dies in the end. Yet while I sipped my coffee and munched my bagel and listened to the incomparable Maria Callas sing the hell out of the lead, I had to wonder—when did I become Baron Scarpia?

Stalking Nina, lurking outside her home, contemplating the murder of her boyfriend even in jest—are you kidding me? I don't do things like that. I'm a good guy. Even the people who hate my guts would have to admit I'm a good guy, and where I come from, being a good guy isn't just a compliment. It's a responsibility. You're expected to step up. You're expected to take care of business. You're expected to *behave* like a man who can be trusted at all times.

I still had high hopes that I could win Nina back. After all, I'm rich, I'm good-looking, I can cook—I'm a helluva catch. Yet if I couldn't, certainly she must know she could trust me to take it like a man, like a good guy. Otherwise, I had no business dating in the first place.

I toasted Nina with my coffee cup at just about the moment in the opera when Tosca jumps off a parapet after first vowing to meet her tormentor in hell.

"Here's to you, sweetie," I said.

Then I went to work.

My PC was located in what my father used to call the "family room"—
one of the few rooms in my house that was actually furnished—where I
also kept my CD player and CD collection, my books, my DVDs, and
my big-screen plasma TV. I was using the PC to surf databases, gathering background information on both Merodie Davies and Priscilla St.
Ana of Woodbury, Minnesota. It wasn't difficult. Nor did the social
scans trouble my conscience.

The right-to-privacy zealots who fight tooth and nail to keep our
deepest darkest secrets from prying eyes don't get it. It has always been
possible for someone to learn an individual's employment, medical, and
credit history, as well as the schools he's attended, the addresses he's
lived at, his criminal record, whether or not he's married, whatever. It
merely demanded more effort. An investigator was required to actually
visit the sites where records were stored and physically sift through
mountains of paper to find the information he needed.

Now he can accomplish the task with just a few strategic cursor movements and keystrokes. The government is even helping us. County Web
sites list citizens' property tax information. The Department of Motor
Vehicles will happily reveal a driver's record for a mere nine dollars and
fifty cents. The Minnesota Court Information System allows anyone
with a PC to immediately access all orders, judgments, and appellate de-
cisions. If you want filings by private parties that aren't generated by the
courts, or charging documents such as criminal complaints, you're welcome to use the public access terminals available at the courthouse.

The depth and breadth of data available never ceases to amaze me.
So much of it is tied to the nine-digit number the government assigns
to each American shortly after birth. Yet even without a Social Security
number, I can easily zero in on a target, trapping him in a snare of computer printouts. It's just a matter of knowing where and how to look

and I know. I had been taught by a South Korean computer genius named Kim. Her massive tip sheet made the task easier—I had it laminated—along with other helpful hints on what to look for and how. Yet even without them, I was pretty adept at exposing an individual's history.

By ten fifteen I had learned nearly everything that was public record about Merodie Davies and Priscilla St. Ana, and a few phone calls gave me more. I arranged the information in a file folder and then made appointments to visit a few people. I was about to call G. K. to give her an update when the phone rang.

A recorded voice told me: *Qwest has a collect call from Merodie Davies, an inmate at the Anoka County Correctional Facility. To refuse this call, hang up. If you accept this call, do not use three-way or call-waiting features or you will be disconnected. To accept this call, press 1 now. Thank you.*

I pressed 1.

"Hello? Merodie?"

"Hi, McKenzie. Yeah, it's me. I'm still in jail."

"Are you okay?"

"I guess. I just got done with treatment. They make you go through treatment in here and—G. K. said I could talk to you. Can I talk to you?"

"Sure, but, Merodie, you need to be careful what you say. They tape these phone conversations, and anything you say can be used against you."

"I don't care."

"Maybe this isn't such a good idea."

"McKenzie—your first name is Rushmore, isn't it? What kind of name is Rushmore?"

"My parents once took a vacation in the Badlands of South Dakota. They told me I was conceived in a motor lodge near Mount Rushmore, so they named me after the monument. But it could have been worse. It could have been Deadwood."

I've told that story many times, and each time I got a laugh. Merodie didn't laugh. She said, "I'm so sorry."

"No, no, no—"

"It musta been hard on you."

"It's not that bad—"

"I understand what you've been through because, well, because of my name."

"Merodie?"

"Yeah. I'm probably the only woman in the world who has it. At least I hope so."

"Why's that?"

"Merodie is the name of a man's underwear manufacturer. I don't even know if it exists anymore."

"You're kidding."

"Uh-uh. My mom, she saw the name on a box in a store somewhere in South Dakota—same place your name comes from, isn't that a coincidence? Anyway, it was years and years ago when she saw the name. She always thought it was a good name for a girl, and when I was born . . ."

"I don't believe it."

"It's true. My mother named me after men's underwear. You know what? Like the guys say, I've been taking it in the shorts ever since."

She laughed when she said it, but there was no humor in her voice, and for a moment I thought the laughter would change to tears.

"I'm sorry, Merodie."

"It's okay. My mother's done worse to me than give me a crummy name. A lot of people have done worse. You kinda get used to it."

"I'm sorry." I didn't know what else to say.

"Hey, are you all right?" she asked me. "You sound funny."

"I'm good."

"You sound like you have a cold."

"Maybe a little one." Somehow, telling her about my hangover didn't seem like a good idea.

"It's this weather," she said. "It's been so hot everyone's got their air-conditioning running full out and you go from the real cool air to real hot air and then back to the cool air and you get a cold."

"I'm okay."

"You should put some Vicks on it."

"Vicks?"

"VapoRub. Put it on your chest and a little dab under your nose, it'll clear you right up."

"You're in jail, yet you're worried that I might have a cold. That's kind of amazing, Merodie."

"I don't know why. Just cuz you have problems doesn't mean you can't worry about your friends, right?"

"Right."

"You're my friend, aren't you, McKenzie?"

"Yes."

"That's good, cuz a girl, she can't have too many friends. But really, you gotta get some Vicks. You gonna get some?"

"I will. I promise."

"McKenzie?"

"Yes, Merodie?"

"I did therapy today. I think I told you. It was so early. You wouldn't believe how early. Up at six, shower at six fifteen, breakfast at seven. It's like—I know it's a jail but, my God. At seven thirty they bring me to this room, kinda like a classroom, you know, in school, and this woman was there, this chemical dependency counselor, a woman I've never seen before who was asking about my drinking problem. And I'm like, I don't know this woman, so I tell her, 'I don't have a drinking problem,' and she says, 'You were in a house for two weeks with a dead man and didn't even know it. That suggests you have a drinking problem,' which I guess is true enough. But I didn't kill him, McKenzie. I swear. I didn't kill Eli. That's what I told the counselor, and she just shakes her head and says, 'That's not my department,' and I'm like, 'What is your department?' "

"Merodie—"

"I know I have a problem, McKenzie. Okay? I've had this conversation before with other people. So many people. And I've tried. God knows I've tried. I've tried so hard to get straight, but . . . I don't know. I'm tryin' to explain it all to this woman and she's not listening, you know? Instead, she gives me this piece of chalk. I'm like, 'What's this?' And she says, 'Chalk.' I can see that, okay? And the woman, she points at this large blackboard mounted on wheels and she tells me to write down my history. She wanted to see my history of alcohol abuse, when I started drinking, how much I drank, the people I met while drinking, the things I did while drinking, the things that happened to me while drinking. And I'm laughing. I'm like, 'Got a few weeks?' And the counselor said she did, and so I start writing.

"At first my letters are tall and wide and I fill a whole line with only a few words, but then the letters become smaller cuz I'm trying to squeeze it all in. The counselor told me not to worry about chronological order, just write it down as it came to me, and I did, starting with a party in junior high school when I drank my first beer and the kegger at the river where I got drunk for the first time. And I kept at it, going through half a box of chalk, filling one side of the board and then the other, writing until my hand hurt—and that wasn't even half of it!

"The first time I had sex I was drunk. And the second time. And the third. And the fourth. I was drunk at the homecoming dance and at my junior prom and on the day I dropped out of high school. I was drunk when I fell down a flight of stairs and broke my collarbone. I was drunk when I drove my car into the fence that surrounded my mom's house. I was drunk when the doctor told me I was pregnant . . ."

Merodie began to weep. It should have been easy for me to say, "Hey, you brought it all on yourself." I couldn't manage it. Instead I found myself wishing I could reach through the phone and wrap my arms around her. That's what friends are for, right?

"McKenzie, you gotta help me. You gotta help get me out of here."

"We're trying, Merodie."

"I hafta get outta here so I can make it all right. Make it right for Eli. I was drunk, McKenzie, drunk when that beautiful man bled to death in my living room. I coulda done somethin' if I wasn't drunk."

"Don't say anything more, Merodie."

I had so many questions for her, but I was afraid to ask them for fear that the attorney-client privilege didn't extend to me, that anything she said over the phone really could be used against her.

"Please, McKenzie."

"It'll be all right. We'll get you out."

"Please."

One question I had to ask—nothing I had learned online had even hinted at it.

"Merodie? You said you were pregnant. When—"

"That's another reason you gotta get me out. I can make it all right, make it all right for everyone, I know I can. I can make it so no one else gets hurt, but I gotta be out to do it."

"Merodie . . . ?"

"I just gotta be."

"Tell me about the child, Merodie . . . Do you hear me . . . ? Merodie . . . ?"

The phone went dead.

G. K. Bonalay kept me on hold for nearly seventeen minutes, which was bad enough. Being forced to endure several Muzak versions of early 1970s bubble gum rock songs while I waited, that was just plain wrong. Trust me, you don't want to listen to an extended, all-strings cover of "Sugar, Sugar" with a hangover unless you have plenty of Pepto-Bismol at hand. I told G. K. so when she finally returned to the phone. She apologized profusely for making me wait—she was rushing from meeting to meeting. As for the music: "At my law firm, the Archies are considered cutting-edge."

I thought she might be joking, but since she didn't laugh, I didn't, either.

I told G. K. about my conversation with Merodie Davis, and she made a note to tell Merodie to stay off the goddamn phone, but said she wouldn't be able to deliver it until later. Her firm had saddled her with a number of billable meetings that promised to last until later that evening. However, she did manage to find time to get me access to Merodie's house.

"Someone will meet you at 1:00 P.M."

"That'll work fine."

"What can you tell me so far?" G. K. asked.

"Not much. We know that Merodie owned the house—"

"How do we know that?"

"I checked with the Anoka County Division of Property Records and Taxation. She's listed as fee owner. She owns the house, she pays the taxes, only here's the thing—as far as I can tell, she has no job, and she's not receiving welfare or unemployment."

"How do you know?"

"I asked."

"The county welfare department told you?"

"In a manner of speaking."

"They're not supposed to divulge that information."

"You're not supposed to have Merodie's file. Should we move on?"

G. K. took a deep breath and said, "Let's," with the exhale.

"Merodie has no income. However, there is this." I quoted the crime lab report. "'One white, number ten envelope, blank, containing one personal check dated Saturday, One August, in the amount of four thousand, one hundred sixty-six dollars and sixty-seven cents made out to Merodie Davies and drawn on an account owned by Priscilla St. Ana, Woodbury, MN.' "

"The envelope seized by the crime lab," G. K. said.

"Two things. The first is the date. August first. That's when most people get paid, the first and the fifteenth of the month. Second, the amount. Forty-one hundred sixty-six dollars and sixty-seven cents is an odd number. It doesn't really fit anything unless you multiply it by twelve, and then we have a nice round figure. Fifty thousand dollars."

"From that you deduce what?"

"Priscilla St. Ana is paying Merodie's way."

"Why?"

"I don't know, but I think we should find out, don't you?"

"Merodie won't like it."

"We won't tell her."

"What do we know about Priscilla so far?"

"We know that Ms. St. Ana has a master's degree in chemistry from the University of Minnesota and a master's in business from the University of St. Thomas. She's an active partner in a property acquisition and investment firm. Apparently, she and her partners identify underperforming businesses, buy a controlling interest, turn them around, and then sell them for obscene profits. Sometimes they're invited to do this by the company's directors; sometimes they're not. In addition, Priscilla is on the boards of several charities and nonprofit organizations. She's not married. However, she is the guardian of a sixteen-year-old niece named Silk St. Ana, who has a good shot to make the U.S. team in the next Summer Olympics as a diver. There's a nice piece about both of them in *Women's Business Minnesota* from a couple of months back."

I glanced at the magazine article while I spoke. In the photo I'd downloaded Priscilla appeared very regal, very proud, with golden hair piled high on her head like a crown. There was also a shot of the girl.

She was sitting on a diving board, hugging her knees to her chest. The cutline read *Olympic hopeful Silk St. Ana enjoys a quiet moment at the family's backyard swimming pool.*

"Apparently, Priscilla inherited St. Ana Medical, a pharmaceutical company, when her father drowned in his swimming pool about eighteen years ago. Her mother died a year before her father. Traffic accident. Priscilla took over the company and ran it for a couple of years. She sold it after her younger brother—what's his name? Here it is. Robert St. Ana. Priscilla sold the business after her brother died in another traffic accident."

"She's taken a beating, hasn't she?" G. K. said.

"Seems so. Anyway, she went back to school to get her MBA, helped found the investment firm, and is now flying high. Makes you wonder what you're doing with your own life, doesn't it?"

"No, but it does make me wonder why a woman like her is involved with the likes of Merodie Davies."

"I'm working on it," I told her.

People outside Minnesota think of the Twin Cities as just two municipalities—St. Paul and Minneapolis—sitting across the Mississippi River from each other. In reality, it's a sprawling amalgamation of 192 cities interwoven into a single tapestry by an intricate and occasionally overwhelming system of U.S., state, and county highways. There were over 2,950 miles in all the last time the Department of Transportation bothered to count, and the 2.7 million people who drive those roads slip from one city's limits to another so frequently and so casually that over the decades the borders have become blurred. It's the reason I became lost in Anoka while looking for an address in neighboring Coon Rapids; it's why I now live in Falcon Heights when I had vowed never to leave St. Paul.

It's also the reason why I carry a Hudson's Twin Cities atlas in my car. I know St. Paul and Minneapolis well enough, but when you start getting into our sprawling suburbs, you either use a map or suffer the indignity of stopping at gas stations for directions. I used the Hudson to find the address of Merodie's mother in Mounds View, and even then I got turned around.

As it turned out, Sharon Davies lived at the far end of a dead-end street in a one-story pale green stucco bungalow located on a bluff overlooking Highway 10. The house and a spotty, weed-infested lawn were both surrounded by a three-foot-high Cyclone fence. There was a front door, but there was no sidewalk leading to it, which was just as well since the only opening in the fence faced the back door. Before I could reach it, a voice rumbled out through the screened window.

"What do you want?"

"Mrs. Davies?"

"What do you want?" Her voice was louder than necessary.

"Mrs. Davies, my name is McKenzie. I work for the attorney who's helping your daughter."

There was no reply.

"Mrs. Davies?"

"Leave me alone."

"May I speak with you?"

"No."

"Your daughter, Mrs. Davies, she needs—"

The door opened abruptly. I was startled into taking a tentative step backward. The woman who opened it was six feet tall and so enormously broad she filled the doorway—I doubted she was able to squeeze through it. Her eyes were narrow and without color, and her hair was stringy and unwashed. She wore a garish housecoat fastened with a safety pin at the throat. The housecoat reminded me of one of my grandmother's quilts pieced together with whatever cloth was at hand.

"I don't want any part of that slut," Sharon Davies shouted. "I ain't had no part of that slut for sixteen years and I don't want no part of her now."

"She's your daughter."

Sharon Davies slammed the door and screamed, "Get out of here or I'll call the police," through the window.

My own mother died when I was twelve, and over the years my memories of her have become soft around the edges. I was no longer sure what was real about her and what might be what the psychologists call a false memory. Nor did I remember what she looked like. I only remembered what the photos I have of her look like, and that's not the same thing. Still, I always knew I was loved. I felt it in the brief years before her death and the long years after. I feel it even today. It has always been a comfort to me; there have been times in my life when I drew on it the way a thirsty man draws water from a well.

That's why seeing a mother or father disown a child, degrade a child, or abuse a child, do anything but love a child totally and unconditionally, leaves me feeling both angry and sad and thoroughly helpless. You can take children out of an abusive environment. You can force parents to obey the law. When no one is looking you can even beat hell out of them. But you cannot make parents love the people they should love the most, who need their love the most, and nothing is ever going to change that.

I got in my Audi and drove away without looking back and prayed what I always pray when I meet someone like Sharon Davies—that one day she will get exactly what she deserves. That she'll die alone.

I met Eli Jefferson's sister—her name was Evonne Louise Lowman—at the Mueller Funeral Home in Coon Rapids. The building seemed unnaturally cool and still. The ruby-colored carpet was thick, and I could barely hear the sound of my own footsteps. They piped organ music throughout the place, but somehow that made it seem even more silent. In the distance I heard voices speaking softly. I followed them, stopping outside a small conference room that was adorned with examples of flower arrangements, headstones, and urns.

Evonne and the director of the Mueller Funeral Home were inside. Listening to their conversation, I learned that Evonne had decided to have her brother cremated. Considering the condition of Eli's body, what with the autopsy and all, an open coffin just didn't seem like the way to go. The funeral director agreed even though he muttered something about losing money on the disposition—immediate cremation, no services, no obituary, just the minimum that the state required, you're talking seven hundred bucks compared to the average disposition of five thousand.

"What do you wish done with your brother's ashes?" he asked.

Evonne didn't care. What did he suggest?

"There's some vacant property owned by the crematorium. We could just scatter his ashes there."

"Sold," Evonne said, slapping the tabletop like an auctioneer.

The director produced some forms. Evonne signed them. She was in and out in ten minutes flat, which suited me right down to my toes. Funeral homes made me nervous. On the other hand, Vonnie Lou—she told me to call her Vonnie Lou—found the place quite comforting. Nice tunes, she said.

Vonnie Lou was a tall woman with coarse, disorganized hair and a woodenish body, all straight angles and no curves. Her eyes were small and dark, and she spoke with a pleasant, melodic voice, her sentences going up and down the scale.

"I'm an office temp," she told me. "That's why I asked you to meet me here during my lunch hour. I really can't afford to take the time from my job."

I told her I appreciated her agreeing to meet with me.

"Anything new on Merodie?" she asked as we moved from the sedately lit funeral home into bright August sunlight.

"What do you mean?" I asked

Vonnie Lou shielded her eyes with her hand. "Has she been charged with murder yet?"

"I don't think so."

"Good."

"Good?" I was surprised by her reaction. "You don't want them to lock her up and throw away the key for killing your brother?"

"Oh, I don't know. I kinda feel sorry for her. I've known Merodie a lot of years, going way back before she even met my brother. The sweetest woman you'd ever want to know. Kind. Generous to a fault. When I was going through my divorce—I was married for about a week to a loser named Mike Lowman—you know what she did? She brought me chicken soup. Do you believe that? Poor girl never seems to catch a break, especially with men. She's just the nicest person, too."

"Nicest person? The cops think she killed your brother."

"Yeah, but it's not like he didn't deserve it."

That stopped me.

Vonnie Lou took two more steps and pivoted on the asphalt toward me. "He was cheating on her," she said. "Didn't you know that?"

"No."

"Merodie didn't tell you?"

I shook my head.

"Huh. I figured she would."

"Did you tell the police?"

"Tell the police what?"

"That Eli was cheating on Merodie."

"No."

"Why not?"

"For one thing, they didn't ask. For another, I don't want to get Merodie into trouble."

"Will you talk to me?"

"You work for Merodie's attorney, right? You're trying to help her, right?"

"Right."

"What do you want to know?"

"Was he cheating on her?" I asked. "Do you know that for a fact?"

"He was using my home." Vonnie Lou shook her head as if she still couldn't believe it. "Something you have to know about my brother Eli. When he was drinking, every woman looked good to him, he wanted every one he saw, and for a few months before he died, it seemed like he was drinking nearly all the time. It didn't matter if the woman was pretty, ugly, married, single, young, old—Eli, he'd see her, he'd have to hit on her. It was like a compulsion. He didn't have much trouble picking up the women he went after, either. He was so good-looking. Charming. He'd say these incredibly goofy things and women would laugh. They loved him. Especially young women, if you know what I mean."

"You said he used your house?"

"I came home early from a job. Eli had a key to my place, so I wasn't surprised when I found his car there. I come inside and there he was, doing it with this, this slut, on my bed. My bed. I was pretty upset."

"I can imagine."

"So I threw the two of them out. My bed. God. This was, I don't know, a month or so ago."

"Do you think Merodie found out?"

"If not about her, then about someone else, yeah."

"Tell me about the woman."

"I don't know, some bimbo. Good-looking, I suppose. College age."

"What was her name?"

"We weren't formally introduced. Besides, what did I care what the bimbo's name was? I just wanted her out of my house."

"Did she give you an argument?"

"Eli gave me one, that's for sure. Kept saying, 'Ten more minutes, ten more minutes.' I guess he hadn't actually done it yet. Like I cared. The woman, she just gathered up her clothes and left. Never said a word, which was fine with me cuz I kinda had my hands full screaming at Eli." Vonnie Lou shook her head, smiling slightly. "Eli could be such a piece of work. I gotta be honest, though. If he hadn't been my brother, I probably would have been hot for him, too."

"Tell me about Merodie."

"We go back some," Vonnie Lou said. "We met, I don't know, years ago. We met at a joint called Dimmer's off Highway 169. We used to play softball, and Dimmer's was the sponsor. We'd start playing at six, finish around seven, be at Dimmer's by seven fifteen and close the place down. God, I still don't believe I survived those days."

"You don't play anymore?"

"No, I quit a couple of years ago when I tore up my knee. Merodie still plays, though."

"Do you see much of her?"

"On and off. It kinda goes in streaks. I'd see her a couple of times a week and then not for a few months. We started drifting apart after I quit softball. We lost most of what we had in common. Softball and drinking. I don't do much of either anymore."

"How did Merodie meet your brother?"

"I introduced them, I don't know, maybe a year ago. It was at Dimmer's. Eli and I walked in and there was Merodie and there you go. They started living together about a month later. Listen, McKenzie, I have to get back to my job."

"I appreciate your talking to me."

"If you have any more questions, just call or drop by the house. I'm in the book."

I thanked her and opened her car door. She slid inside and looked up at me.

"My brother. You wouldn't believe what a good-looking guy he was. Right up until Merodie bashed his brains in.'"

The street where Merodie Davies lived was teeming with young children enjoying their final weeks of summer vacation. I also saw a few stay-at-home moms. Instead of minding the kids, nearly all of them seemed to be intently watching me as I made my way to the Anoka police cruiser parked in Merodie's driveway. I didn't actually hear the words, but I could see them passed from one set of lips to another: "Now what?"

Officer Boyd Baumbach sat alone inside the cruiser, the windows and doors shut tight, the motor running. I tapped on his window, startling him. He quickly lowered it. Cool air lapped against my chest and face.

"McKenzie," he said.

"What are you doing here?"

"Rollie Briggs, he's the assistant county attorney, he said someone should let you look through the house."

My inner voice took notice. *Rollie Briggs—is he G. K.'s pal in the county attorney's office?*

"Why you?" I asked.

Baumbach silenced the car engine and stepped out. He looked directly into my eyes when he spoke. "I apologize for the other day. I had no right getting rough with you, and I should not have abused my authority by arresting you. I apologize. I hope you will forgive me."

"Wow." I was so shocked by his words that I nearly laughed in his face. "Moorhead must have really put the screws to you."

The straight line of Baumbach's mouth told me that it sure wasn't his idea.

"Do you accept my apology?"

"Sure," I said, although I knew his heart wasn't in it.

"Are you going to report me?"

"Report you to who?"

Baumbach brushed past me and moved to the front door of the house. "The assistant county attorney, Mr. Briggs, he said that the tech guys have been through it a couple of times. So has Human Services, so there's nothing you can foul up for us."

"Fine."

Baumbach unlocked the door and opened it. He waited for me to pass him. He took hold of my elbow when I did.

"Is there anything else, Officer?" I asked.

He released my elbow and stepped back.

"Nothing," he said.

"Are you coming inside?"

"If it's all the same to you, I'll wait out here."

"Sure."

Baumbach tried to smile, but it was too much effort, so he stopped. "I've been in the house before," he said.

"Sure."

I stepped inside and was immediately met by a punishing wave of warm, stale, fetid air that smelled strongly of rotting meat. It literally pushed me back against the door.

"Oh, God," I said, clamping a hand over my mouth.

The Anoka Fire Department had used its enormous fans to pull much of the odor from the house, and the county's Human Services Department had made an honest effort to clean the dwelling of the feces and garbage. Yet the stench, compounded by the August heat, was still so strong that I seriously doubted anyone would ever live there again.

I fished a handkerchief from my back pocket and cupped it over my nose and mouth. I inspected the nearly empty living room. A faded white chalk outline on the carpet represented the body of Eli Jefferson as he lay in death. Red chalk was used to outline the softball bat. I examined both outlines from several angles, using the CID's Photo Report as a guide. I didn't have any of the actual 147 photographs taken at the scene by the Criminal Investigation Division; however, I did have a sheaf of about fifty photocopies, plus the investigator's narrative describing in sequential order each photo that was taken. By using both, I was able to stand in the exact spot where each photo was taken and see what the camera saw.

Photo #18–22. These are overall photos showing the position and condition of the body as it was found.

Photo #29–31. These three photographs depict a softball bat that was found near the body. Note in particular the blood smear that is clearly visible in Photo #31.

Except for the missing body and softball bat, the living room looked exactly as it had in the photos. Cream-colored drapes were open to let in shafts of sunlight swimming with dust motes. Forest green carpet flecked with blue was stained in more places than I could count. A sofa was shoved against the wall; a floor lamp with a dirty white shade sat next to the sofa; a chair was hiding in the corner. The pieces of furniture seemed unrelated to each other and all had a secondhand shabbiness. A black velvet painting of a clown framed in gold hung on the wall, a solitary tear on the clown's cheek. That was it. I checked the report again. Apparently, nothing had been moved, removed, or added to the house since the photos were taken.

I pushed on.

Photo #34. This is an overall photo taken at the top of the stairway showing the condition of the top landing as well as partially looking into the kitchen. The hallway would be to the right, leading into the living room area.

Photo #42. This is looking through the open doorway of the kitchen off the hallway. Note the bloodstains on the kitchen floor and, in particular, in front of the stove, which is visible to the left center.

Photo #59–81. Overall and close-up photos depicting the condition of the master bedroom. Note in Photo #72 the close-up of the waterbed and, in particular, the rolled-up blanket found on the waterbed. In examining the blanket, it was found to contain what we believe to be human feces.

Photo #90. This is a photo looking down the steps into the basement level.

I found nothing that the police had overlooked, but I was moving quickly, driven onward by the foul odor and the lack of air-conditioning. I lingered only at a small bedroom made up for a young child on the downstairs level. Just one photo had been taken of the room, Photo #96. The narrative said simply:

This bedroom is referred to as a child's bedroom in my previous report.

The room was well cared for. There was no dirt or stains of any kind, only surface dust. It contained one bed, made up with a bedspread featuring characters from a Disney film. The bed was in the corner. Above it, a net was strung from wall to wall, supporting dozens of stuffed animals of every shape and kind. Across from the bed was a white wood dresser. The drawers were empty. I found half a dozen dolls on top of the dresser, along with three photographs of a girl I judged to be eight or nine years old. The girl was dressed all in white and standing next to a tree in one photograph, sitting in a chair holding a teddy bear in the second, and standing on a diving board, her arms stretched toward heaven, in the third. There were no names or dates written on the photographs. A fourth photograph framed in silver hung from the bedroom wall next to the door. It featured a truly beautiful young woman with chocolate-colored eyes and auburn hair, holding an infant. The young woman was about sixteen. Someone had written across the bottom left corner of the photograph:

The two of us forever.

"You wouldn't think something like this could happen here," the woman said.

It seemed to be a recurring theme among the neighbors I had interviewed up and down the street where Merodie Davies lived.

I had started my canvass shortly after Officer Baumbach, having satisfied himself that I hadn't swiped Merodie's silverware, drove away. The stay-at-home moms were still out in force. They all seemed a little bit frightened for their children and for themselves. Out in the far suburbs, they figured they were safe—isolated from "big-city" violent crime. I couldn't imagine why they felt that way. After all, Anoka was a twenty-five-minute drive from downtown Minneapolis, and the bad guys have cars, too.

I didn't want to quote crime statistics, though. I wanted to talk about Merodie Davies. Unfortunately, most of the neighbors hadn't even known her name until she was arrested. They saw her coming and going, and for a while it seemed the cops were camped on her doorstep every other night, but during the last year or so, they weren't even sure Merodie still lived there. The mother of four across the street was convinced that Merodie had moved out. Only the neighbor living next door to Merodie had a story to tell. She was home, nursing a broken ankle that kept her from her job.

"I broke it yesterday falling off a curb, do you believe it? I fell off a curb."

"Sorry to hear that," I said.

"Not as sorry as I am."

The woman ushered me into her overfurnished living room.

"Been living here long?" I asked.

"Two years. Moved in right before I divorced my husband, the prick. God, it's warm."

"I think the word is hot."

"I think the word is sweltering. Would you like something to drink? Pepsi? Beer?"

I declined.

"You sure? It's cold."

In Minnesota, it's considered impolite to accept food or beverage until it's offered at least three times, but I was thirsty.

"Pepsi," I said.

The woman said, "I'm going to have a beer."

"Well, in that case . . ."

Her name was Mollie Pratt, and she served Grain Belt Premium, brewed in New Ulm. It went down smooth, and I had to keep myself from gulping it.

"Yeah," said Mollie, "I moved in two years ago next week. Paid for the house out of my settlement. I had married poorly, but I divorced real well. Anyway, at first I wondered what I was getting into, all the cops and such."

"What do you mean?"

"That first year, seemed like the Anoka cops practically lived next door. People kept calling them because of the loud music, the loud arguments—it was always so loud. Merodie and Richard were fighting all the time, fighting and drinking, drinking and fighting. I even called my real estate agent and said, 'Hey, you told me this was a quiet neighborhood.' It was crazy."

I took out my notebook.

"Tell me about Richard," I said.

There's no special trick to conducting an interview. All it requires is a little patience, an ear for the important utterance, and the simple knowledge that to most people the sweetest possible music is the sound of their own voice.

"Richard was Merodie's boyfriend," Mollie said. "That's all I really know about him. I don't think he had a job. He was always around, always entertaining friends. Must have been a million people in and out of his driveway. My ex, the prick, he figured Richard was dealing drugs. Sure, dealing drugs out of a split-level in Anoka. What a laugh."

"Hysterical."

Mollie's eyes grew wide. "You think?"

"It's certainly possible."

Mollie didn't like the sound of that at all. She left her chair and limped to the window, fighting her cast all the way. She gazed out at Merodie's empty driveway. "You think he might have been a drug dealer?"

"You said a year?"

After a brief pause, Mollie answered, "Huh? A year? Yeah. Richard left after about a year. I didn't see him no more. Things got real quiet. You wouldn't have known anyone was even living next door."

"Where did Richard go?"

Mollie shrugged her ignorance.

"Do you know his last name?"

Mollie shook her head.

"Richard is all I know," she said. "I only heard it during the arguments."

"Did you have any contact with Merodie after Richard left?"

"I never had any contact with Merodie before Richard left. Not really. It was like, 'Hi, how you doing?' when we met on the street, which wasn't often. We didn't sit around the kitchen table drinking coffee or anything."

"You saw her come and go."

"Not lately. As near as I can tell, she was always in her house. She never left it."

"Not to go shopping?"

"Well, she must go shopping, for food and stuff, you know? I just never see her."

"The mail gets picked up."

Mollie didn't know what to say to that.

"The lawn gets cut."

"She must do that stuff when I'm at work. Truth is, I don't remember the last time I saw Merodie. Or Eli."

"Eli Jefferson? The deceased?"

"Yeah. I was really bummed when I heard he died. He seemed like a nice enough guy."

"You knew him?"

"I'll say. He hit on me. Couple of times." Mollie smiled at the memory. "The first time was in winter. He helped me shovel the driveway, then invited himself in for hot chocolate, and then tried to invite himself into my bed. I'm saying, 'What about Merodie,' and he's saying real dumb-ass things like, 'What Merodie doesn't know won't hurt her.' Guy was a jerk. Charming, though. Real charming. The next time, I'm in the backyard working on my tan. I look up and there he is, grinning. He starts talking about Minnesota's scenic wonders, meaning me, right? He asks if I've seen the Split Rock Lighthouse. I say, 'You mean up by Duluth?' He says, 'Oh, it's much closer than that,' and then looks down at himself. I say it now and I think, God, what a jerk.

Only at the time it made me laugh. I'll tell you, though. Something I learned from my ex-husband, the prick. For some people, charm is a weapon."

"How long did Jefferson live with Merodie?"

"I don't know. Six months?"

"Have you seen any activity at the house in the past two weeks?"

"Cops asked me the same thing. I really haven't. Last I saw of anyone over there was two weeks ago Saturday."

"That would be . . ."

"August first, but even then all I saw was a car drive up and then leave a few minutes later."

"What kind of car?"

"It's like I told the cops, I don't know from cars except it was black, a sports car. Now my ex, the prick, he knows cars. If he treated me as well as he treated his car . . ."

"Did you see who drove the car?"

"Not really. It could have been anyone."

"What time did you see the car?"

"Around noon?"

"Is that a guess?"

"I remember eating lunch and that's when I saw the car, so I figured it was around noon. It could've been later."

We talked some more, but nothing new came of it. Mollie offered another Grain Belt, and I was tempted. Instead, I passed, telling myself that a semiprofessional private investigator wouldn't drink while on the job. I gave Mollie one of the cards I had made up. It read R. MCKENZIE and had my phone numbers printed on it. Mollie set the card on her table and promised if she thought of anything more, she'd call.

I returned to my Audi, still parked in front of Merodie's house. The car was broiling. The AC worked well but took time to cool the interior, so after I started the engine and turned the air-conditioning on full, I slid out of the car and shut the door behind me. While waiting for the

Audi to become habitable, I glared at Merodie's house. The stench of death was still in my nostrils, hair, and clothes and probably would be for some time to come.

I turned away from the house and looked across the lawn toward Mollie Pratt's place. For a moment I thought I saw her watching me from behind her living room drapes, but then she disappeared.

5

Woodbury, located southeast of St. Paul, was nearly an hour's drive from Anoka. Yet more than distance separated the two cities. Anoka was old, with a history and traditions that stretched back to 1680. Woodbury, on the other hand, was brand-spanking new—I had a Carl Yastrzemski autographed baseball that was older. It wasn't even a city when Yaz won the Triple Crown in 1967, yet it was now home to over sixty thousand residents.

The private street where Priscilla St. Ana lived served a quintet of estates that somehow all bordered on different holes of the Prestwick Golf Course. Like most of Woodbury, the five houses looked like they had all been built yesterday. I parked in front of the one with red brick, white trim, and a slate gray roof set way back from the street, only a little more pretentious than its four neighbors. It reminded me of an Italian villa, or at least what I supposed an Italian villa to look like, having never actually seen one.

I hurried along the tile walkway to the front door of the estate—I couldn't think of it as a house—and used the bell. A doughlike woman of indeterminate age answered. She was dressed in a fawn-colored uniform and demonstrated no emotion or interest when I announced that I had an appointment to meet Priscilla St. Ana. With a curt "Wait here," she closed the door, leaving me outside with no way of looking in. She returned a few moments later with instructions.

"Follow me, please."

I trailed the maid into the immense house, moving through sumptuous, decorator-perfect rooms that would have caused my father to faint dead away at the excess. 'Course, my father was a man who used the same toaster for thirty years and believed the automatic icemaker that came with the refrigerator I bought when we moved to Falcon Heights was an unnecessary luxury. I told him that since I was now filthy, stinking rich I intended to surround him with a lot of unnecessary luxuries. He fought it every day of the six months he had left to live.

The maid guided me through French doors and onto a sprawling patio of red tile and salmon-colored marble that was surrounded by lush garden flowers, a low hedge, and several trees that couldn't have been more than a few years old. In the center of the patio was a huge swimming pool, its walls and floor painted sky blue. Deck furniture of rich redwood with wide arms and lacquered patio furniture with thick cushions were mixed together and scattered around the pool in no discernible pattern.

I heard the thumping sound of a diving board and looked up just in time to see a young woman wearing a bright yellow one-piece swimsuit twisting, turning, somersaulting, straightening, and slicing into the water. An ice cube dropped into a tumbler of scotch made a bigger splash than she did.

Between the pool and the house was a round table with a glass top, an immense opened umbrella protruding from the center of it. On top of the table was a half-filled pitcher of fresh-squeezed orange juice and a single glass, also half filled. An enormous white towel was draped over one of the chairs. The maid stopped in the shadow of the umbrella and announced, "Ms. St. Ana will be with you in a moment."

I sat down and watched the young woman climb out of the pool. She went back to the board and made another dive and then another and another. Not once did she acknowledge my presence. After her fifth dive, she used the ladder to pull herself out of the pool and walked to the table. She reached for the towel, moving close enough for me to see that her sun-drenched skin was flawless and to smell the chlorine in her fine auburn hair. I watched her use the towel to buff her body; the swimsuit stretched tight over taunt muscles and gentle curves.

She glanced at me with chocolate-colored eyes that glittered with intelligence.

"I'm Silk," she said.

"Yes, you are."

"You're here to see Priscilla."

It wasn't a question, but I answered yes just the same.

She squeezed her long tresses between the folds of the towel, breathing lightly with the effort. Beyond question, she was a lovely girl, and she looked almost exactly like her mother had in the photograph I discovered in Merodie's house—the one of Merodie holding an infant.

Silk casually tossed the towel over her shoulder and reached for the pitcher, performing each task with a fluid grace and sensuality that I usually associate with music, something by Gershwin perhaps. She filled the glass with orange juice and drank it down slowly, but I had stopped watching her long before then, turning my attention instead to a foursome of golfers lofting their second shots toward an elevated green beyond St. Ana's backyard. I knew when I was being played, and while I usually didn't mind, my inner voice kept repeating, *She's only a child.*

A few minutes later a woman stepped through the French doors onto the patio. Priscilla St. Ana was handsomely approaching forty-five. Not quite as young and attractive as her air-brushed photo would suggest, I thought, but pretty enough that she could pass for younger. The fact that she had changed her hairstyle helped. Piled high in the photo I had downloaded, it was now cut short. She was dressed in a crisp white shirt, tailored to accentuate her generous bosom and slender waist, and a long, thin black skirt with a silver buckle—two swans with necks intertwined. The skirt's front slit revealed a graceful leg.

Silk took her towel and her orange juice and moved past her as she approached the table. "Your guest," she said as she passed.

"So I see," Priscilla said. "Mr. McKenzie." She extended her hand. Her eyes were neither warm nor cold, and they didn't give much away—a poker player's eyes. I shook her hand.

"Can I offer you something?" The maid seemed to materialize out of thin air behind Priscilla's shoulder. "Caroline makes an outstanding iced tea."

"Tea will be fine."

"Thank you, Caroline," Priscilla said.

The maid disappeared into the house.

"I appreciate your taking the time to see me," I said.

"Not at all. Please, sit."

I sat. "You have a lovely home, Ms. St. Ana."

"Thank you. Please, call me Cilla. I was christened Priscilla by my parents, but I prefer Cilla, the name of my favorite character in *Johnny Tremain*. No one would call me that while my father was alive. Now everyone does."

A moment later, Caroline reappeared carrying a silver tray with both hands. The tray supported a glass pitcher filled with tea, a bowl of ice, a dish of sliced lemons, a sugar bowl, and two crystal tumblers.

"Thank you, Caroline," Cilla said.

The maid departed, leaving Cilla to fill both glasses herself, offering me one. The umbrella protected us from the hard afternoon sun but not from the heat, and I found myself drinking the tea much too fast.

"Please, help yourself," Cilla said in a voice that was more polite than friendly.

I poured another glass.

Cilla tossed her head a little so that her blond hair swung and I could see the auburn under the chemicals, close to the scalp. She smiled easily. The heat didn't seem to bother her at all.

"I was pleased before to notice you not noticing my niece," she said.

"Oh, I noticed her."

"You weren't ogling. Most men do. I find it distasteful."

"I make it a point not to ogle women who haven't voted in at least three presidential elections."

"Then you are an exception to most men."

"No doubt about it."

She regarded me carefully over the rim of her glass. "How may I help you?" she asked. Her tone reminded me of my high school math teacher—not antagonistic, merely commanding. I refused to be intimated, as I had been by the math teacher.

"I want to talk about Merodie Davies."

"So you said over the phone. I knew, of course, that Merodie was in trouble. I assumed she would seek my help. I am a bit bewildered that she hasn't." Cilla topped off my glass with iced tea. "What would you like to know?"

I gestured toward the pool.

"Silk is Merodie's daughter."

"Yes. How did you guess?"

"I saw a photo of her mother when she was about Silk's age."

"There is a resemblance."

"What exactly is your relationship with Merodie Davies?"

"Simple question. The answer is a bit more complicated. Why is it important that you know?"

"Ms. St. Ana, your personal check in the amount of forty-one hundred dollars and change was discovered in Merodie's house."

Cilla's eyebrows seemed to knit together as she gazed past the patio and adjacent pool toward the golf course, not seeing any of it. She said nothing.

"Cilla?" I said.

More nothing.

"Cilla. The check."

"I have been paying Merodie an allowance for quite some time now," she said. "Why does that matter?"

"Can you tell me why you've been paying her an allowance?"

"She is the mother of my niece. I can't just let her go homeless, can I?"

"Is that what you told the Anoka County Sheriff's Department when they questioned you?"

"They haven't questioned me. Why would they?"

My inner voice was shouting at me. *The cops haven't pressed Vonnie Lou Lowman or questioned Priscilla St. Ana? What gives?*

"Cilla, the check was dated August first."

"That is correct."

"It wasn't mailed; the envelope had no postmark. You must have hand-delivered it."

"Yes."

"On August first."

"Probably. Why is that significant?"

"That's the day Eli Jefferson was killed."

Cilla's voice rose in protest. "Are you suggesting . . . ?" She stopped herself. A puzzled expression crossed her face.

"What time did you take the check to Merodie's?" I asked.

Cilla hesitated before answering. "I honestly don't recall." She might have said more, except a voice coming from behind startled her.

"Aunt Cil, I'm taking off now."

"Silk." Cilla nearly shouted the name. She gestured for her niece to join us at the table.

Silk St. Ana was now wearing a navy blue one-piece swimsuit under blue shorts; red letters with a white border spelled USA across her chest. She was carrying a gold and maroon equipment bag with UNIVERSITY OF MINNESOTA GOLDEN GOPHERS stamped on it.

"Have you met Mr. McKenzie?"

"Not formally," Silk said.

I offered my hand. She squeezed it just enough to be polite.

"My niece, Silk," Cilla said by way of introduction. "She's going to be an Olympic diving champion."

"Aunt Cil," Silk said between gritted teeth. "She's always bragging to people about that," she told me.

"Are you going to be an Olympic diving champion?"

"Yes."

"Then it's not bragging."

"We'll see."

"Mr. McKenzie is a private detective," Cilla added. It wasn't true, but I didn't correct her.

"Really? That is so cool."

"It sounds more exciting than it is," I said without actually knowing if it was or wasn't.

"Mr. McKenzie is helping our investment firm on a land acquisition project."

"Really? I thought maybe he was involved in my mother's murder case."

Cilla sighed heavily, slumping in her chair. "I was lying," she admitted. "I'm sorry."

Silk gripped Cilla's shoulder reassuringly. "My aunt still thinks I'm four years old," Silk told me. "She still thinks I need to be protected from the truth."

"What truth?"

"Who and what my mother is."

"Who and what is that?"

"A selfish drunk."

Silk looked into my eyes when she spoke, deliberately trying to make me feel as uncomfortable as she did.

"When did you last see your mother?" I asked.

"I don't know. Eons ago. I doubt she would even recognize me."

She didn't so much as blink when she said that, but Cilla sure did.

"I'm sure you're wrong," I said.

"Maybe."

"Aren't you awfully young to be an Olympic diving champion?" I asked.

"Actually, no. The Chinese girl who won gold in '92 was thirteen. She won again in '96 and 2000."

"How long have you been diving?"

"I started when I was four years old—on the same day I came to live with my aunt. She had a swimming pool, and I couldn't get enough of it."

"This one?" I gestured at the pool in the center of the patio.

"No. We were living in Andover up in Anoka County back then. Actually, I think it's hereditary. I inherited my love of swimming from my aunt."

Silk was standing directly behind Cilla now, her hands resting on the older woman's shoulders.

"She set a state high school record for women in the breaststroke that stood for six years," Silk said. "How long ago was that, Aunt Cil?"

"Never mind how long ago that was. Don't you have practice?"

"I'm going to work off the ten-meter diving platform at the university aquatic center. Coach is going to videotape me again."

"Is that helping?"

Silk nodded. "Helps with visualization. I'm getting much better control of my take-offs."

"My niece, the Olympian." Cilla smiled.

Silk smiled right back. "If I keep progressing, if I don't get hurt, if I do well at the nationals . . ."

"No problem."

"Whatever you say, Aunt Cilla. May I take the Mazda?"

"You always do."

"That's because I look so good in it."

Silk pecked her aunt's cheek, said, "See ya," then added, "It was a pleasure to meet you, Mr. McKenzie."

She moved away from the table, hesitated, and turned back, her smile fading. "How much trouble is my mother in?"

"I'm not sure," I said. "The fact she hasn't been charged yet is a good sign. It means the county attorney's case isn't even strong enough to take before a grand jury."

Cilla reached up from her chair and stroked the girl's bare arm. "It'll be all right," she said softly.

"I know, I know."

The girl nodded another good-bye and moved across the patio toward the French doors. "Oh, by the way," she called over her shoulder. "I won't be home for dinner. I'm meeting Mark."

"Wait a minute." Cilla was on her feet now. "Excuse me," she said before crossing the patio. Both her face and her voice were stern while she spoke to her niece. I pretended not to listen.

"Who's Mark?" Cilla asked.

"A junior at the University of St. Thomas."

"Diver?"

Silk shook her head.

"JO major. Remember when I did that exhibition last spring, the school newspaper ran a story about me? He wrote it."

"College junior. That makes him what, twenty, twenty-one?"

"Twenty."

"You're sixteen."

"I look twenty."

"A fact that has kept me sleepless many a night."

"Don't worry, Auntie Cil. I'm not my mother." Silk bussed her aunt's cheek. "Something I want you to remember." She backed toward the French doors. "You know how athletes are always waving at TV cameras and saying, 'Hi, Mom'? If I ever get the chance to say 'Hi, Mom,' I'll be talking to you."

A few moments later Cilla returned to the table, but not before brushing both eyes with a knuckle, leaving a nearly imperceptible smear of mascara behind.

"Raising children," she said. "You try to do the best you can. You worry that you're making mistakes."

"How long have you been raising Silk?" I asked.

"Twelve years."

"From what I can see, you've done a pretty fair job."

"With all due respect, Mr. McKenzie, how would you know?"

"She doesn't act dreary and tired and hopeless, as if her life were already behind her, like so many teenagers do. She smiles as if she has a lot to smile about, and when she speaks she looks you in the eye."

The way she nodded, I got the impression that Cilla was pleased with my answer.

"We should find out soon, in any case," she said. She tapped the top of the glass table with a fingernail. "Now is when you learn what kind of parent you are. Now, when your children are fifteen, sixteen, seventeen and they're faced with real choices—when they have to decide for themselves what's right and wrong, what's important and what isn't, what they'll do and what they won't. Now, when they have to decide what kind of people they're going to be."

I took a sip of tea. *What did my choices say about my own parents?* I wondered.

"Sorry," Cilla said. "I don't mean to sound so . . ."

"Maternal?"

She nodded. "I'm not worried. Silk's a good kid. A smart kid. She'll do the right thing. Still, you try to protect her. All parents feel that way, I suppose."

"Tell me about Merodie. Silk is *her* daughter."

Cilla drank more tea and slowly set her glass down as if she were afraid it might shatter. "Mr. McKenzie, I do not believe things happen accidentally. I believe you earn the life you live. Merodie . . . Where do we begin? Before the alcohol took its toll, she was stunningly beautiful. The most beautiful young woman I have ever known, with the possible exception of her daughter. Unlike her daughter, however, Merodie had no self-esteem, no sense of self-worth. None. If you've met her parents . . ."

"I've met her mother."

"Then you know some of the reason why. Something else happened, as well. I believe behaviorists refer to it as a significant emotional event. When Merodie was far too young to make sense of it, she met a man—a man with good manners, a pleasant appearance, and plenty of money. This man took her to exclusive restaurants and smuggled her into elegant bars. He gave her expensive gifts. He not only told her that she was beautiful and special, he treated her as if she were. I know because the man was my brother, Robert. He was twenty-four and she was fifteen. My brother didn't care about the age difference. Nor did he care about Merodie. Not really. My brother cared only about what was pretty. He used it and abused it and often he broke it. The fact that he was corrupting a minor, that he was making love to a child, meant nothing to him. Eventually, Merodie became pregnant. She went to him with thoughts of marriage. My brother rejected her without a moment's hesitation. It's an old story, I'm afraid, and not particularly interesting.

"Like a lot of men, my brother thought doing the right thing meant offering money for a doctor. However, before arrangements could be made, Robert was killed in an accident. He drove his car off River Road in a snowstorm while under the influence of alcohol.

"I met Merodie at Robert's funeral," Cilla continued. "I admit I disliked her immediately, and not just because she was so preternaturally beautiful. I detest weakness, and Merodie was weak—physically, mentally, emotionally. Like my brother, she was a drunk, although I don't believe alcohol gripped her quite as tightly then as it would in later years. She told me about the pregnancy, told me that her parents had disowned her and barred her from her home. She begged for help. I gave it to her. Not because I felt sympathy for her, which I suppose is a failing on my part. I did it for the baby who probably would be the last of the St. Ana line—Lord knows I have no intention of ever marrying and having children.

"I gave Merodie money. I helped her hire an attorney so she could file suit against the bar where Robert became drunk the night he died. I arranged to pay for her hospital care when the child was delivered. A few months later, not long after Merodie herself had turned a mere sixteen, the child was born. Merodie's labor was surprisingly quick and painless. Fifty-seven minutes. Exactly. She had barely made it to the hospital in time. The doctor said it was the smoothest delivery in which he had ever been involved. He said it was 'smooth as silk,' and thus Silk was christened.

"Afterward, I helped Merodie buy a house in Anoka," Cilla went on. "I would check in on the two of them from time to time. Merodie soon spent all the money she earned in the lawsuit. She had become a fullblown alcoholic. Several times over the years I forced Merodie into treatment. Unfortunately, it never took. She'd go to two, perhaps three meetings and quit. I tried to intervene several times to protect Silk. Unfortunately, there was only so much I could do legally. Eventually, Merodie became involved with a man who abused her. I believe Eli Jefferson abused her as well. She seemed to attract that kind of man.

"One night that man passed out behind the wheel of Merodie's car while it was parked inside her garage and died of carbon monoxide poisoning. The next day I took Silk home with me. She was four years old.

Merodie, to her everlasting credit, never challenged this. Not once in twelve years. I believe she understood that Silk was better off with me. That's my only explanation for her actions, or rather, I should say, her lack of action. In any case, I've been raising Silk ever since."

"You've been paying Merodie fifty thousand dollars a year for the privilege of raising her daughter," I said.

Cilla managed a smile. "It is a privilege," she said. "I'd pay a great deal more, believe me. Would you care for more iced tea?"

"I'm not sure how it works," I said, "but when your brother died, wouldn't his daughter inherit his share of the St. Ana fortune?"

"My goodness, McKenzie, but you're cynical."

"Just asking."

"My brother didn't share in the estate. My father disinherited him shortly before he died. It wasn't punishment. Father was merely afraid that Robert would ruin the company once he was gone. It was a fear I shared. In any case, it's a moot question."

"How so?"

"Because Silk will get everything. She became my heir the moment I first set eyes on her."

"And Merodie?"

"I'll always take care of Merodie."

"Is that a privilege as well?"

"It is a small price to pay. Besides, over the years I have become rather fond of Merodie. Despite her many faults, she has a truly generous and caring soul."

I pulled a notebook from my pocket. "The man who died in Merodie's garage, what was his name?" I said.

Cilla closed her eyes, scrunched her face and said, "Becker? Yes, Becker. Something Becker. I can't remember his first name. Sorry."

I wrote "Becker" in my notebook.

"When did you last see Merodie?"

"A month ago."

"You didn't see her on August first?"

"When I delivered the check? No. I knocked on the front door, but no one answered. I went inside, called her name. No one answered. I left the check and departed. I was there for less than two minutes."

"When did you arrive at Merodie's house?"

"Early afternoon."

"How early?"

"One thirty, two."

"Huh."

"What does 'huh' mean?" Cilla asked.

"A few minutes ago you didn't remember when you delivered the check."

"Times change."

"What kind of car do you drive?" I asked.

"A Saab—an Aero sedan."

"Not very sporty."

"I like it."

"What color?"

"Black."

I studied Cilla for a moment. *The time doesn't match what Mollie Pratt told you,* my inner voice reminded me. *The vehicle—that's a stretch, too. On the other hand, Cilla is probably lying.*

"Did you see anything unusual?"

"Such as?"

"Such as a body lying on the living room floor."

"I saw nothing amiss."

I liked that word—amiss.

"Where did you leave the check?" I asked.

"On the table."

I closed my notebook and thanked her for her time and the tea. Cilla seemed relieved that I had stopped asking questions. She escorted me back through her sumptuous home.

"Do you believe that anything I've told you might help Merodie?" she asked when we reached the front door.

"It's hard to say."

Cilla rested her hand on my wrist and stepped close enough to kiss me. It was not an intimate moment, yet I felt a thrill just the same.

She said, "I do not believe it would be to Silk's advantage, especially at this point in her diving career, for her relationship with her mother to become common knowledge. However, having said that, I would very much like to help Merodie."

"In what way?"

"In any way possible. You'd be astonished, Mr. McKenzie, at what money can buy."

"I always am."

"We have good news and we have bad news," I said.

G. K. said, "Start with the bad news, but make it quick. I'm already five minutes late for a meeting."

I switched my cell phone from my right ear to my left. "Merodie had means and opportunity to kill Eli," I said. "Turns out she also had a strong motive. I found at least two witnesses who claim that Eli was cheating on her."

"What's the good news?"

"We can place Priscilla St. Ana at the scene. Her brother was the father of Merodie's daughter, the brother who died in a car accident sixteen years ago. Priscilla has been raising the girl."

"The girl that you told me about? Silk?"

"Yes. St. Ana admits that she was at the house, says she dropped off Merodie's check, says she saw nothing amiss. But here's the thing. In her original statement, Merodie claimed that a man broke into her house and had a fight with Eli, a man with blond hair. Priscilla St. Ana has short blond hair."

"Could she be confused with a man?"

"Not by anyone who's sober."

"Merodie wasn't sober. Or maybe she was. It would certainly explain why Merodie insisted we leave St. Ana alone. She's protecting her."

"Something else," I said. "St. Ana said that she's willing to open her considerable checkbook if it'll help Merodie's cause."

"Why?"

"Could be guilt. Could be she wants to stay close to the investigation in case it turns her way. Could be she wants to shield Silk against bad publicity."

"Which might be the reason Merodie wants us to lay off Priscilla—to protect Silk."

"Could be. One more thing. You said that the Anoka County attorney was trying to build a case against Merodie. Well, if he is, he's doing a damn poor job of it."

"What do you mean?"

"The only people asking questions about Merodie are us."

"That doesn't make sense."

"I don't know what to tell you, Gen. Maybe your information is wrong."

"No. No, my sources are solid."

"Assistant County Attorney Rollie Briggs, is he your source?"

G. K. chuckled. "You're very clever, Mr. McKenzie," she said.

"Could Briggs be wrong?"

"I don't think so." G. K. paused for a few moments. She said, "McKenzie, did you ever read *Alice in Wonderland?*"

"Curiouser and curiouser."

"That's the line."

Twenty minutes later, Daniel the architect was standing between Nina Truhler and me in the downstairs lounge of Rickie's. They were walking out while I was walking in. My intention had been to apologize to Nina. Apologize for not taking her to the charity ball. Apologize for conducting surveillance at her home the previous evening. Apologize for all of my faults and for every slight, real or imagined, that I had ever committed. Apologize up the ying-yang, as Shelby suggested, if that was what it would take to get her back on my side. Now I wasn't so sure. She was dating this loser two nights in a row? Hell, I only stood her up once!

Daniel said, "Can I help you?" He was over six feet tall and knew from exercise, but Jenness had been right about him. He was soft. Slap him in the mouth and he'd call his lawyer to ask what happened.

"I'd like a moment alone with the lady," I said.

"Would the lady like a moment with you?"

Daniel directed the question at Nina. She shook her head.

"I'll call you later," Nina told me.

"You heard the lady," Daniel said. He set a hand flat against my chest and pushed.

Behind the bar, Jenness made a hissing sound as if she had seen something that frightened her.

My inner voice screamed, *Is this guy suicidal?* My hands came up slowly as I debated which of Daniel's body parts I would damage first. I decided to go with the hand that was still pressing against my chest. *Let's see if he can draw blueprints with five broken fingers.*

Give him credit, Daniel stood his ground. Behind him, Nina gave me a quick headshake. Her eyes were both hard and unyielding, and the message they sent was unmistakable. *Don't even think about it!*

I lowered my hands and let Daniel ease me out of his way.

Daniel grunted in triumph—actually grunted. *Are you kidding me!* His smile was mocking, and his eyes were filled with condescension. I never wanted to punch someone so badly in my life.

He brushed past me and led Nina out the door. He didn't look back. I have no idea what I would have done if he had.

I went to the bar.

"I know you won't believe me," Jenness said, "but not kicking Daniel's ass, that was the smartest thing you could have done."

She was right. I didn't believe her.

I had had a lot to drink that night, but apparently not enough, because the dream returned—with extras. In the past it had nearly always ended with the actual shooting. This time it replayed the aftermath.

It began with my commanding officer shaking my hand and telling me, "The Ramsey County grand jury refused to indict. It ruled that you had acted properly and within the scope and range of your duties."

The scene then shifted abruptly and I was watching TV in my apartment. I had been placed on administrative leave—with pay—as was the custom whenever an a St. Paul PD officer discharged his or her weapon. WCCO-TV *News at Noon* was showing an excerpt of a press conference filmed at city hall just an hour before.

The minister who stood behind a makeshift podium was tall and severe-looking and reminded me of Denzel Washington when he played Malcolm X, yet his voice had a pleasant rhythm to it, and when he said "This assassin, this slayer of children," the words sounded like poetry. It took a while for their meaning to sink in.

"Did he just call me a murderer?" I asked the TV set.

Behind the minister stood the black man and woman who had driven into the convenience store parking lot that evening. They stood like statues, looking neither right nor left, up nor down. The minister said these good folks witnessed Rushmore McKenzie's cold-blooded execution of nineteen-year-old Benjamin

Simbi—for that was the brother's name—while he was raising his hands to surrender. He claimed it was yet another example of racism in the police department. He said the grand jury's verdict was just another example of what they already knew—"it is impossible for the black man to get justice in a white man's court"—adding that "there is no hope in the system."

"This is nuts," I told the TV set.

When I woke up, I said the same thing. "This is nuts."

6

I have known Clayton Rask for many years. He has been to my home. I've fed him cherry sno-cones and mini-donuts that he claimed were better than the ones you can get at the Minnesota State Fair. Today he wasn't talking to me like a friend. He was talking to me like the commander of the Minneapolis Police Department's Homicide Unit.

He said, "Meet me at the Anoka County Sheriff's Office. Do you know where it is?"

"I know where it is."

"Meet me at 9:00 A.M. Don't be late."

"Why? What's going on?"

"I'll tell you when you get here."

"Tell me now."

"McKenzie, you'll be doing us both a favor if you just show up. You really don't want me to come looking for you."

He hung up the phone before I could protest further.

———————

Rask had given me plenty of time to get to Anoka, but first I needed another toasted bagel with cream cheese and a second cup of coffee, which I consumed while reading the *St. Paul Pioneer Press* sports page. The Twins and the hated White Sox (at least I hate them) were slugging it out yet again for the Central Division title, and I decided that their statistics required careful examination. Once on the road, I stopped at a service station to top off my gas tank, and since I was there, I had my Audi washed. After I reached Anoka, it took a few minutes to locate a parking space in the shade. That's why it was 9:23 A.M. when I entered 325 East Main Street.

Rask was waiting for me in the lobby. His clothes were rumpled, his face was unshaved, and his eyes looked like they hadn't been shut for a while. That should have told me something, but it didn't. He shook his head and said, "You are such an asshole."

"Didn't you say nine thirty?"

"You think you're funny?"

For a moment, the man made me nervous—but no more than freeway traffic.

"C'mon," he barked.

Rask led me through the labyrinth of offices and corridors that was the Anoka County Sheriff's Department like a man who actually worked there until we reached a large corner office. A sign next to the door frame read LT. JOHN WEINER, CRIMINAL INVESTIGATION DIVISION. The door was open, but Rask knocked just the same before entering.

Lieutenant Weiner was sitting behind a polished desk; silver-framed reading glasses were perched on the tip of his nose. He was wearing a white shirt with a black tie, black epaulets, black flaps over his shirt pockets, an American flag over his right breast, a silver five-pointed star over his left breast, and a large blue patch on his left shoulder that screamed ANOKA COUNTY SHERIFF'S DEPARTMENT in case anyone was confused. The creases in his shirt and pants were sharp enough to cut butter.

He glanced up from the file folder he was reading. "McKenzie, you're late."

"I've been called worse," I told him.

He stared at me with an expression that was harder than calculus. Apparently, he didn't think I was funny, but then why should he be different from everyone else?

Rask sat on a comfortable-looking chair next to Weiner's desk without being asked, leaving me standing alone in the center of the room.

"It's your case," Weiner told him.

"So, McKenzie," Rask said. "Where were you last night?"

"Breaking up with my girlfriend."

"Nina? Really?"

"Yeah."

"That's too bad."

"Just didn't work out," I said. "It was time to move on anyway."

I winced at the words even as I spoke them. Weiner yawned.

"About what time was that?" Rask asked.

"Are you asking me if I have an alibi?"

"Yes."

"For what?"

Weiner dealt a black-and-white glossy from the folder and slid it across the desk. I took three steps forward, glanced down at it, and turned away. It was a photograph of Mollie Pratt's broken body, naked except for the cast on her ankle.

"Between 9:00 P.M. and midnight," Weiner said. "That's a rough estimate."

"You gotta be kidding me."

He took another item from the folder, a plastic sandwich bag containing my business card, and set it on the photograph.

"Jesus Christ," I said.

"Talk to us," Weiner said. "With the minimum of hysterics."

"I don't have an alibi for between nine and midnight. I was home. Alone. Watching the ball game."

"Are you willing to take a polygraph?" Weiner asked.

"Like Merodie Davies did?" The lieutenant seemed to flinch at the sound of the woman's name. "Polygraphs are a joke."

"I'll take that as a no."

"Take it any way you want." I stepped toward Rask and glared down at him. "What the hell is going on? Why did you bring me here?"

Rask spoke smoothly and carefully. He always did. "Mollie Pratt was beaten, raped, and murdered last night between 9:00 P.M. and midnight, when her body was discovered in an empty lot on Chicago Avenue off Lake Street in Minneapolis. That's why it's my case. Evidence suggests that she was killed somewhere else and her body dumped along with her belongings."

Weiner slipped another photograph from his deck and set it on the desktop, but I deliberately ignored it.

"We began the investigation here with the assistance of the Anoka CID"—Rask gestured toward Weiner—"by searching Mollie's home. That's when we came across your card. Imagine my surprise."

"You assumed from that that I'm involved."

"I don't assume anything, you know that, McKenzie."

"Would you be willing to give us a blood sample?" Weiner asked.

"Why?"

Weiner dealt still another photograph. Mollie's face had been badly beaten, and there were bruises around her throat.

"The killer left his DNA all over the victim," he said.

"Yes, I'll give you a blood sample."

"That won't be necessary," Rask said.

I was looking into Weiner's eyes when I said, "I'll do it anyway."

Weiner yawned again.

"Talk to me, Mac," Rask said. "Tell me what you know."

I started with Merodie Davies, explaining that I was helping her and G. K. Bonalay. I showed them the copy of the letter G. K. had given me. Both lieutenants read it without comment. I explained that Mollie was Merodie's next-door neighbor, that I had spoken to her, and that I had left my card on the off chance that she might have more to tell me. "She was drinking beer when I left her," I said.

"Beer?" asked Weiner.

"Grain Belt Premium."

"She must have been warming up, then, because a preliminary drug screen says she had ingested methamphetamine."

"That doesn't make sense."

"Why doesn't it make sense?" Rask asked.

"She wasn't sophisticated enough to do meth," I said.

"Any moron can buy meth," Weiner said.

"If the moron knows what to buy, where to buy. Mollie would have had to have a connection, and she didn't. Unless . . ."

"Unless what?" said Weiner.

"Unless she was lying," Rask said. "Could she have been lying, McKenzie?"

"Why would she?"

"I don't know. Why would she?"

I remembered Mollie peeking at me from the other side of her living room drapes.

"Richard," I said. "She might have been protecting Merodie's ex-boyfriend Richard." I told him how Mollie had reacted when I agreed with her ex-husband that Richard might have been dealing drugs out of Merodie's house. "Maybe she was Richard's best customer and didn't want me to know."

"Richard who?" Rask asked.

"I don't know his last name, but the Anoka city cops do. They were called to Merodie's address enough times when he was with her. They must have his name in their incident reports."

"Thank you for your time, Mr. McKenzie," Weiner said. "We'll be in touch."

"Excuse me?"

I glanced at Rask. He seemed as surprised by Weiner's behavior as I was, but he said nothing—he was in Weiner's house.

"That's it?" I asked.

Weiner came from behind his desk and took my elbow in his hand. He led me to the door. "We can forgo the blood test for now." He literally shoved me into the corridor.

"Hey."

"Good morning, Mr. McKenzie."

The sun had shifted while I was in Lieutenant Weiner's office, and instead of shade, now my Audi was bathed in sunlight. I left it where I had parked it and walked along Main Street toward the Rum River. I was still upset about both Mollie Pratt's murder and Weiner's behavior, and I wanted to think it over. I passed the Avant Garden because I thought it was a damn silly name for a coffeehouse and instead crossed the street and strolled a couple more blocks to Body of Art. It was a tanning salon and tattoo parlor as well as a coffeehouse, which appealed to me for reasons I didn't want to explore. I bought a frozen concoction topped with whipped cream. I ate it with a plastic spoon at a small table in front of the window. I looked across the street at the Anoka City Hall and the dam built across the Rum River just beyond. Outside the city hall, an electronic sign flashed the time, date, and place of various community events. BRUNCH WITH COUNTY ATTORNEY DAVID TUSEMAN 10:30 A.M. TODAY GREENHAVEN GOLF COURSE read one of the messages.

I glanced at my watch. If I hurried, I figured I just might make it before they ran out of hash browns.

The banquet hall of the Greenhaven Golf Course had been set for four hundred people, yet only about three hundred sat around the large round tables covered with white linen. A long, straight table had been set near the far wall between two large windows. Tuseman, wearing khakis and a blue shirt with the creases ironed in, stood at a podium mounted at the center of the table. His red, white, and blue campaign sign—DAVID TUSEMAN STATE SENATE FOR A BRIGHTER TOMORROW—was taped to the podium.

A microphone had been placed on a stand in the center of the room for supporters who wanted to ask the candidate a question. A half dozen lined up behind the microphone. I was hoping someone would ask how Tuseman had the nerve to charge fifty bucks for a plate of cold scrambled eggs, three strips of bacon, soggy hash browns, and a blueberry muffin the size of the Hubert H. Humphrey Metrodome, but no one did. (There was also a plate laden with fresh fruit, but I ignored it.)

Tuseman had a microphone, although he didn't need it. He spoke as though someone had taught him how, with a deep, hard baritone that gave polished nuance to every word and carried easily across the room. Sometimes he actually answered the question. More often, he recited a short, biting position on an issue that had only a nodding acquaintance with the subject the supporter had asked about.

I didn't know what Tuseman was for. However, in the course of about fifteen minutes, I learned that there were a lot of things that Tuseman was against. He was against taxes. He was against more funding for the public school system without accountability. He was against both abortion and sex education that didn't stress abstinence. He was against increasing the minimum wage. Mostly, however, he was against crime. When asked why he should be elected to the State Senate, Tuseman bragged about Anoka County's low crime figures, his high conviction rate, and the fact that people convicted of crimes in Anoka served longer prison sentences than the state average. The supporters liked hearing that. Truth be told, so did I. But then some smart-ass asked, "Are you prosecuting Merodie Davies to help your reelection chances?"

Tuseman's smile gave away nothing except how careful he was with his teeth. "I take exception to your insinuation, sir."

"I don't mind," I told him.

An anxious murmur spread across the room. The man sitting immediately to Tuseman's right motioned for a server. He whispered something into the young man's ear, and the server departed, moving swiftly toward an exit. I figured I had about two minutes, tops.

"I am not prosecuting Merodie Davies for personal benefit of any kind," Tuseman said.

"I'm only telling you what I heard."

"From who?"

"People. You know, around the courthouse."

"They're wrong," Tuseman replied. His raised his hand as if he wanted to brush something off his forehead, thought better of it, and let his hand fall to his side.

"That's what they're saying," I told him.

"Tell you what. Next time someone says that, remind him that this is not a high-profile case. Court TV is not going to cover Merodie Davies's murder trial."

"The *Anoka County Union* and the *Coon Rapids Herald* will. So will the *Minneapolis Star Tribune* if it's juicy enough."

"What makes you think so?"

"How many murders have been committed in Anoka County in the past decade? A dozen?"

"Probably less."

"The Merodie Davies murder case—it's the only one you've got."

"Crime is the cancer of our society," Tuseman declared. "Like cancer, it must be eradicated completely if we are to survive. We cannot live with even a little bit of cancer."

That brought a lot of applause.

"I'm not above trying to get some good publicity to further my career. I understand how politics works. But I will be damned if I'll make a prosecutorial decision based on whether or not it'll get votes."

More applause.

"Merodie Davies is guilty of murder, and I'm going to see that she spends the rest of her life in prison. Why? Because she's guilty. Not because it makes me a more desirable candidate. If she weren't guilty, I would release her, and I wouldn't care how it looked to the voters."

A heavy hand fell on my shoulder as Tuseman's supporters erupted into even louder applause.

"Well, it was nice chatting with you," I said, but Tuseman didn't hear me. The microphone had been switched off.

I turned. City of Anoka Police Officer Boyd Baumbach was smiling at me.

"This way," he said.

Baumbach hustled me out of the banquet hall, out of the clubhouse, and into the parking lot as if he had done it a dozen times before. He was pushing me forcefully toward his police cruiser when I broke his grip and spun him around.

"We going somewhere?" I asked.

"Resisting arrest," he told me. "You're in for it now."

"Arrest for what?"

"Trespassing. Disorderly conduct."

"Really? I thought I was exercising my right to free speech. Or are you as dumb about the Constitution as you are about the law?"

Baumbach smiled like a kid with a secret. "We can make all this go away," he said. "Isn't that what you told me the other day?"

"I was trying to do you a favor."

"Now I'm trying to do a favor for you. If you promise to shuddup about what happened . . ."

"Have I signed a complaint? Have I gone to IAD? Have I done any of that shit?"

"You told the sarge, and now he's on me."

"I hope he fires your ass."

"That's it. You're going to jail for keeps this time. Now we can do this the easy way"—Baumbach held his cuffs out for me to see—"or we can do it the hard way." He slid his sixteen-inch-long flashlight out of the loop on his belt and tapped the tip of his shoulder with it. "You choose."

"Let me guess. You're a manly man who does manly things in a manly way."

"Choose."

I surprised him by stepping in close.

He raised his flashlight over his head.

I hit him with two left-hand jabs and at least six straight rights, the last two as he was falling to the asphalt.

Baumbach wasn't unconscious, yet he might as well have been. He opened his mouth, but no sounds came out, and his eyes wouldn't focus. I grabbed the handcuffs from where they had fallen and clamped them on his wrists. I took the flashlight and reattached it to his belt.

An older gentleman pulling his golf clubs in a three-wheel cart across the parking lot stopped to watch.

"How you doing?" I asked him.

"He's a police officer," he told me.

"Appearances can be deceiving."

I grabbed Baumbach by the collar of his thick shirt and dragged him across the asphalt to his car. It was hard work in oppressive heat. By the time I reached the police cruiser, the back of my own shirt was saturated. I propped Baumbach against the front tire and wiped sweat out of my eyes.

"Boyd." I slapped him gently on both cheeks. "Boyd. Hey, Boyd. Are you still with me?"

"What are you going to do?" There was genuine fear in his voice. I liked that.

"What's your call sign?"

"My what?"

"Your handle. What's your handle?"

"Bravo-three. What do you—"

I leaned in and activated the microphone attached to the epaulet of his shirt.

"Bravo-three," I said.

"Bravo-three, go."

"Bravo-three requires a supervisor at the parking lot of the Greenhaven Golf Course. Is Sergeant Moorhead available?"

"Bravo-three. Boyd, you sound funny."

"Bravo-three. Let's pretend that we're a professional police organization, shall we? Is Sergeant Moorhead available?"

"Bravo-three. Yes, but—"

"Dispatch him to the parking lot of the Greenhaven Golf Course immediately. Bravo-three, out."

I straightened up and gazed toward the private road that led to the golf course, half expecting to see Moorhead racing toward me.

"You're in trouble," Baumbach said, yet there wasn't much vigor in his words.

"One of us is," I said.

Sergeant Moorhead's hand was resting on the butt of his gun when he slipped out of his cruiser. I held up my empty hands and turned slowly, proving that I was unarmed. He moved closer.

"Do you want to hear my story first, or his?" I asked.

Moorhead used his thumb to direct me toward his cruiser. I went and stood next to the driver's door while he lifted Baumbach to his feet and uncuffed his hands. Baumbach was talking earnestly. I couldn't hear what he had to say, and quite frankly, my dear, I didn't give a damn. Instead, I was debating which lawyer to call and wondering how much it would cost me—no way I was going back to jail. Not for thirty-six hours. Not for thirty-six minutes.

The conversation lasted over five minutes. At no time did either officer raise his voice or look at me. It ended with Sergeant Moorhead putting his arm around Baumbach and leading him to the door of his car. He slapped his officer on the back. Baumbach slipped inside and started up the cruiser. He said something through the window, and Moorhead smiled. A moment later, Baumbach drove off. Moorhead watched him go. He didn't turn toward me until Baumbach was out of sight.

"Say something funny, McKenzie. Any smart-ass remark will do."

"I'm innocent?"

"Fuck you."

"So I take it we're not going out for coffee and donuts."

"You mess with one of my officers, you're lucky I don't kick your ass up and down this parking lot and throw you in jail for a thousand years."

"Why don't you?"

"I owe you a favor."

"Not that big a favor."

"Then let's say I'm doing it for Baumbach. Believe it or not, the kid has a chance to be a decent cop. The only blemish on his record was when he screwed up at the Davies's residence. If I had known about it at the time I would have fallen on him and that would have been the end of it, but he lied to me. That's two strikes against him, and he knows it. Ever since he's been trying to prove that he was justified for what he did. That's what this was all about. You resist a dis-con, he has to use his light—it makes his story that you got rough with him before sound more plausible. Question is, now what?"

"That's a good question," I told him.

"If we forget the whole thing, pretend it's a foul ball instead of strike three, I can extend his probation, give him a chance to grow into his badge. If I arrest your sorry ass—man, that'll give me a lot of personal pleasure, but Baumbach will probably lose his career."

"He deserves to lose his career."

"Yeah? You deserve to spend a year in the county workhouse. I don't give a damn about your time on the job. I don't care about your money. You are way out of line, McKenzie. I should take a club to you myself."

"I was—"

"You were what? Trying to show a kid how smart you are? Give him the benefit of your years of experience? You're not a cop anymore. It wasn't your place."

He had me there.

"So, what's it going to be?" Moorhead asked.

"Why the hell are you protecting this kid? He's a bad cop and you're not. You should flush his ass."

"He's my nephew."

"So what?"

"So, so . . . so maybe I owe him something. He always looked up to me when he was a kid. He wanted to be like me. And I encouraged him. I helped him get his law enforcement degree. I helped him get through the academy. I picked his field training officers, made sure they nursed him along. If he's not ready, if he doesn't know how to behave yet, that's on me."

"Be that as it may . . ."

"Boyd just needs another chance."

"Sarge, what if he screws up again?" I asked. "Next time it could be serious. Do you know what I mean by serious?"

"He'll be all right. I'll take care of him."

"Sure you will."

"So, what's it going to be, McKenzie?"

"I don't have a problem if you don't have a problem," I said.

"Let's keep it that way, shall we?"

"Am I free to go?"

"Yes. Please go. Go as far away as possible."

"I can't go too far. I'm kind of involved in this Merodie Davies thing."

"So I've heard. I hate kibitzers, McKenzie."

"I don't blame you. Listen, do I have any credit with you at all?"

"Are you serious?"

"About a year ago, you used to make a regular run to Merodie Davies's house because of noise complaints, I don't know what else, involving her and her boyfriend Richard something. What's Richard's last name? How can I find him?"

"You just don't know when to quit, do you? Look, McKenzie, this is way bigger than Merodie Davies. Way bigger. Let it go. Walk away while you still can."

"I can't. I gave my word."

"You think this is a fucking game? There's no place for playground honor out here. People are going to get hurt."

"What people? What do you mean by way bigger?"

Moorhead shook his head as if he felt sorry for me. "I got nothing more to say to you."

He brushed past me and moved to his cruiser, slid inside, started it up, and drove off without so much as a backward glance.

A few moments later I reached my own car. The brunch had finally broken up. David Tuseman was among the first to leave the clubhouse. I thought he might linger outside the door and hobnob with his supporters. Instead, he moved quickly toward two cars parked in the first row of the parking lot, his staff fast on his heels. I threw him a wave. He didn't acknowledge it.

"I liked the way you handled the cops."

The voice startled me, and I spun toward it.

A man I knew only as Norman stood ten feet away.

I immediately drew my hand to the place on my hip where I would have holstered my gun if I had thought to carry one. The last time I saw Norman, he was drilling holes into my Audi with a stainless steel Charter Arms .38 wheel gun. In return, I put a nine-millimeter slug into his shoulder. I was pretty sure he was still nursing a grudge.

"Norman," I said.

"McKenzie."

"How's the shoulder?"

"Hmm? Shoulder? It's fine. Why do you ask?"

"No reason."

He was wearing a black sports jacket over a slate gray polo shirt. His hands were hidden behind his back. It worried me that I couldn't see them. I edged toward the Audi, trying to put it between us as I had during our last encounter.

Norman grinned. He brought his hands out slowly to show that they were empty.

"Our personal business can wait until another day," he said.

My sentiments exactly.

"Mr. Muehlenhaus would like to see you."

Seven words. That's all it took to convince me that Sergeant Moorhead was correct. This was bigger than Merodie Davies.

Mr. Muehlenhaus was sitting alone in the backseat of a black limousine, the car's engine running and the air-conditioning up full. He was so pale that I wondered if he survived on transfusions of milk.

Norman held the door open, and I slipped inside.

"Nice ride," I said. "I didn't know you were a limo guy."

"My granddaughter's idea," he said. "I prefer my old Park Avenue."

"Less ostentatious," I said.

"Yes, but it doesn't have this." Muehlenhaus leaned forward and opened a refrigerator built into the back of the driver's seat. There were several soft drinks and bottles of water there—Muehlenhaus was not a drinker. "May I offer you something?"

"Do you have ice?"

"Of course."

Why wasn't I surprised? I declined a beverage, and Muehlenhaus closed the refrigerator.

"It seems, Mr. McKenzie, that once again we find ourselves on the same side."

"I know I'm going to regret asking this, but what side would that be?"

"Should we give it a name? How about the Anti–David Tuseman League?"

"I have nothing against Tuseman."

"Tuseman wants to prosecute Merodie Davies for murder to further his political ambitions. You wish to stop him from doing so."

"How do you know?"

Muehlenhaus sat back in his seat, spread his hands wide, palms up, and said, "Mr. McKenzie. Please," as if I should have known better than to ask. He was right. I should have known better.

To suggest that Muehlenhaus was a mover and a shaker would be belittling. He was more like the village wise man—if you think of greater Minnesota as a village. It was he who told people what to move, what to shake. He possessed immense wealth, power, and the desire to meddle in the lives of other people. Yet he was no zealot. From what I was able to observe, he had no desire to shape the world into one of his own liking. He had no agenda beyond proving that he was smarter than everyone else.

"Genevieve Bonalay," I said. "She's one of yours."

"A lovely young woman, not that it matters to a man my age."

"Who's kidding who, Mr. Muehlenhaus?" He might have been on the other side of eighty, but he wasn't dead.

He grinned, and suddenly his face was transformed from the stoic puppet-master to the gregarious uncle that your parents didn't want you spending too much time with.

"What's your angle, Mr. Muehlenhaus?"

"Angle, Mr. McKenzie?"

"You juggle governors and U.S. senators. A state senator—that's beneath your notice."

Muehlenhaus's grin broadened into a full-fledged smile.

"For decades now, the Democrats have controlled the Minnesota State Senate," he said. "However, lately their margin has been thinning. A few wins in key districts in the coming election, and the Republicans might take over. If they do, they will have control of both houses of the state legislature as well as the executive branch for the first time in a generation. With that power, they can transform the state. That is decidedly not beneath my notice."

"Check me if I'm wrong, but I thought Tuseman was a Republican."

"Not the right Republican, if you'll excuse the pun. I do not believe he can defeat the incumbent. My candidate will, if we can remove Tuseman in the September primaries. You can help."

"Why would I want to do that?"

"The enemy of my enemy is my friend."

"Mr. Muehlenhaus, the last time you spoke those words to me, people got killed."

"You didn't kill them. Neither did I."

"You tried to have me killed."

"A simple misunderstanding that fortunately was rectified."

"Yeah? Tell Norman that."

"I have, Mr. McKenzie. Several times."

I didn't like where the conversation was going. In fact, I didn't like any of my conversations with Muehlenhaus.

"Mr. Muehlenhaus, I'm going to try to get Merodie Davies out of jail. If that helps you, swell. If not, tough titty, said the kitty, but the milk tastes fine."

"I like you, Mr. McKenzie. You're so colloquial."

"I'm just trying to do a favor for a woman who could use one."

"Truth be told, that is all I am doing, as well. A favor for friends. In so many ways we are very much alike, Mr. McKenzie. If there is a significant difference, it is merely at the level on which we grant our little favors."

"Now you're just being nasty."

The smile on Muehlenhaus's face changed with my remark. It looked the same as it had, yet the mood behind it was different. I supposed that he thought he was paying me a compliment and was angry now that I didn't see it his way.

"Thank you for your time, Mr. McKenzie." Somehow Norman knew I was being dismissed, because the car door opened abruptly. "I will be following your progress with great interest."

I stepped out of the air-conditioned car. The midday heat hit me like a brick, and I actually lost my balance for a few beats. The asphalt beneath my feet was soft; I could cut into it with a butter knife. Norman, in his black sports coat, didn't seem to notice. He skipped around the limo and opened the driver's door. He glared at me over the roof of the car, yet said nothing.

A moment later I was standing alone in the nearly empty parking lot. There were only a few golfers hardy enough to take on eighteen holes in that heat. I figured the smartest thing I could do was get my clubs and join them. I didn't. Pity.

7

I doubted I'd be welcomed at the Anoka County Records Division, so I drove all the way to the public library off Hennepin Avenue in downtown Minneapolis and made use of the bank of personal computers available to the library's many patrons. I used one to surf the Web for something, anything, on a man named Becker who died of carbon monoxide poisoning twelve years ago in Anoka and another named Richard who might or might not have been dealing drugs from the same address. Nothing. I even tried Googling Richard Becker and discovered a sculptor, an illustrator, a bird-watcher, a film director, and a winemaker, all very much alive.

Robert St. Ana, however, was a different matter. I had a number of hits on his name, nearly all of them tied to Cilla. None of them told me much about the man's life or death, probably because he had died so long ago, but I did learn the exact date he died.

Fortunately, the library had preserved every copy of the *Minneapolis Star Tribune* ever printed on microfiche and stored the rolls in a bank of gray metal file cabinets. Next to the cabinets were a number of viewers, provided free. I threaded the appropriate reel of microfiche into a viewer and hit the fast-forward button. About a month's worth of news events and advertisements whirred past. I slowed the deluge of newspaper pages as I approached the correct date.

Andover man's death ruled alcohol related

A man whose body was found in his snow-covered car at the bottom of a ravine by cross-country skiers Thursday died of carbon monoxide poisoning, according to the Anoka County Medical Examiner's Office.

Robert St. Ana, 24, of Andover, died from breathing the deadly fumes after falling asleep as a result of "acute alcohol intoxication," the autopsy report said. St. Ana's blood alcohol level was measured at .187, nearly twice the legal limit.

St. Ana's vehicle was found in a ravine near Coon Rapids Dam Park. Evidence at the scene suggests that he drove off of East River Road and plunged 30 feet into the ravine during Tuesday's record snowfall.

It is not known if St. Ana lost consciousness before or after his car left the road. The car stayed hidden until discovered Thursday morning by a family of cross-country skiers.

Authorities believe that the car continued to run even after it came to a halt. An examination of the vehicle revealed that the keys were locked in the "on" position when the car was found, yet the gas tank was empty.

Sources at the Anoka County Sheriff's Department reported that several witnesses saw St. Ana drinking heavily at the Ski Shack, a popular

restaurant and bar in Coon Rapids, the evening
the accident occurred.

St. Ana is the son of Donald St. Ana, founder of
St. Ana Medical Co. Donald St. Ana died two years
earlier, drowning in his backyard swimming pool. It
was reported at the time that he had also been in-
toxicated when he died, with a blood alcohol level
of .163.

"Carbon monoxide poisoning?" I said aloud, much to the dismay of the other library patrons.

"Shhhh," a woman hissed.

Coincidences do happen, as my pal Bobby Dunston likes to tell me. Still, what were the odds that St. Ana and what's-his-name Becker both died of carbon monoxide poisoning? I needed more information and decided that Vonnie Lou Lowman would be a good source. A quick glance at my watch told me that no way would she be back from work yet. I decided to pay a visit to the Ski Shack, but first I slid a quarter into the printer. A moment later I had an $8\frac{1}{2} \times 11$ copy of the newspaper story. I folded it and slipped it into my pocket.

After returning the microfiche, I was out the door, my car keys in hand, and heading across the street toward the nearly full parking lot where my Audi was parked. Along the way I was forced to dodge a knot of young children disembarking from an enormous green van, some of them holding hands. One of the children announced with a mixture of awe and glee, "This is bigger than our school library."

In that moment the dream returned.

There was no sound track, only images moving in ultra slow motion, moving the way they did on NFL replays so the announcer could point out the exact moment when the play went terribly, terribly wrong.

The glass door of the convenience store swings open. Benjamin Simbi backs out slowly, his attention drawn to something in the store. I shout at him. He turns to face me. He is carrying a Smith & Wesson .38 in his right hand and a bag of loot in the left. I calmly tell him to drop the gun. He raises his hands slowly—slowly—slowly—slowly. They are level with his chest when I squeeze the trigger of the shotgun. The blast catches him in the chest and throws him against the glass door of the convenience store.

Then the dream repeated itself, starting with Simbi raising his hands slowly—slowly—slowly, raising his gun to shoot me except I shoot him first.

I had kept walking, stopped, tried again, finally slumped against an SUV—a blind man groping for support. I bowed my head, held it with both hands, closed my eyes, and waited for the memory to pass the way you would a bout of dizziness after getting up too quickly. This had never happened before. Dreaming in broad daylight. It was the first time the memory had crept up like that, and it startled me. I couldn't imagine what triggered it, either. Certainly not the children laughing; that made no sense. If searching Merodie's house, breathing the stench of death, or fighting with Officer Baumbach hadn't initiated a flashback, how could a child's laugh? What did that have to do with it?

Maybe you really should think about therapy again, I told myself silently.

"I could use a drink," I said out loud.

I was a half dozen steps away from my Audi when I realized that I no longer held my keys in my hand. I checked my pockets. I checked the ground around me. I retraced my steps.

The sudden change from the air-conditioned coolness of the library to the hot, humid air outside had brought a shock to my skin. It was at least ninety-five now and still six degrees below what the newspaper had predicted. In those conditions, the slightest physical exertion produced a great deal of perspiration, and just walking through the library's parking lot, my eyes examining everything that was even remotely shiny, was enough to cause rivulets of sweat to trickle from my armpits down my sides.

I found the iron grate of a storm drain built against the curb approximately where I had crossed the street after leaving the library. I didn't even have to look. I knew that my car keys, house keys, firebox key, boat key, everything had gone down the drain.

I stood there, muttering short, Anglo-Saxon words that attracted the attention of a young, anorexic-looking woman who was crossing the street. She smiled knowingly.

"Dropped your keys into the storm sewer?"

I nodded helplessly.

"Happens all the time," she said, and motioned for me to follow her.

I didn't believe her, but I trailed the woman into the library just the same. She led me to the information desk, leaned over the top, and plucked a telephone from a shelf. She punched in a number without looking it up, calling the Minneapolis Department of Public Works. The woman did all the talking. After she hung up the phone, she told me, "It'll be a little bit before they can get a guy out here."

"Thanks."

"Happens all the time," she said.

I told her I wanted to reward her for her kindness, but she brushed me off. Instead I stuffed a twenty into a box that sought donations for the Friends of the Public Library and returned to the parking lot.

I waited for fifteen minutes. It seemed longer. Finally, a panel truck with CITY OF MINNEAPOLIS painted on the side arrived. I walked quickly to the driver's door. A woman with enormous brown eyes peered out at me.

"I lost my keys," I announced.

"Other than that, how are you?" she asked.

"Down there," I gestured toward the storm drain.

"Let's take a look."

The sewer worker took a long, yellow, rubber-coated flashlight from the cab of the truck and moved to the drain. She squatted next to it and shone the powerful light through the grate. The beams illuminated something silver below, but it was a good fifteen feet away, and neither I nor the sewer worker could testify that the reflection was my keys.

The sewer worker flicked off the flash and stood up. "I don't suppose you could call your wife to bring you a spare key," she said. There was Hispanic blood somewhere in her family tree, but her voice had the flat twang of America's northern states.

"I'm not married," I told her.

"Girlfriend?"

"Not at the present time."

"Really?"

The sewer worker smiled again; her face lit up like a hundred-watt bulb, and I said, "Hey."

She was in her late twenties, a little more than five foot six, about 120 pounds. Her hair was the same color as her eyes; a bandanna kept it off her neck and shoulders.

"What's your name?" she asked.

"Why do you need to know my name?"

"It's only fair since I'm about to risk my life for you."

She was putting me on, yet she spoke in such an earnest manner that for a moment I couldn't be sure.

"What do you mean, risk your life?"

The sewer worker gave her head a small, sad shake and moved toward her truck.

"Wait a minute." I followed her. "What do you mean, risk your life?"

The sewer worker opened the back of the truck and retrieved a pair of coveralls that she quickly slipped into. The name on the coveralls read BENNY. She put on a pair of knee-high rubber boots and heavy gloves. She said, "If anything happens, my name is Benita. Benita Rosas. Tell them . . ." She bowed his head as if the words were simply too painful to speak.

"What are you talking about?"

Benita gently placed her hand on my shoulder. "This is his sewer," she said.

"*His* sewer?"

"I don't mind the raccoons," Benita said. "The bats, the cockroaches, the spiders—I can live with them, as well. And the rats."

"Rats? There are rats down there?"

"Of course there are rats down there," she replied somberly. "It's okay. The rats are our friends. Where there are rats, there's air. It's just *him* we need to worry about."

"Who's him?"

"He doesn't have a name. We just call him—*him*."

"All right, then. What is him?"

"A twelve-foot alligator."

"An alligator?"

"A twelve-foot alligator," she corrected me.

"There are no twelve-foot alligators in the sewer system."

"Ten-foot, then. You know how people exaggerate."

"There are no alligators, period, in the sewer system."

Benita looked at me with such an expression of sadness that for a moment I felt compelled to apologize for doubting her. But only for a moment.

"Seriously," I said.

"We're not supposed to tell the public. The authorities are afraid of panic."

"Cut it out."

Benita averted her eyes, looking out toward the people moving in and out of the library entrance, many of them children. "See them," she said, gesturing with her hand. "Kids." She sighed heavily. "We need to protect the kids."

"Oh, brother."

Benita took a measuring wheel from the truck. She went to the sewer drain opening and set the wheel at the edge of the metal grate. Without a word, she started walking in a more or less straight line. I followed.

"Three hundred sixty feet," she announced when we came to the nearest entryway to the sewer system. "That's 360 feet through the tunnel to where you dropped your keys and another 360 feet back. That's a long way—with *him* down there."

"Honest to God, Benita, I wish you'd stop saying that. I know you're joking."

"Call me Benny," she said, and smiled.

I liked her smile. I liked her face. She wasn't so attractive that I would have noticed her in a crowded room, yet the more I looked into her soft brown eyes, the more I liked what I saw.

"Benny," I said.

She smiled some more.

Using a metal rod with a handle on one end and a curl on the other, Benny pulled the heavy iron lid off the sewer pipe and slid it away. She checked her flashlight by shining it into the palm of her hand.

"Here goes," she said.

She stepped on the rungs of a ladder that led to the entrance of the sewer tunnel and began her descent. Her body was halfway into the sewer when she stopped and gazed into my eyes.

"Wait," she said

"Yes?"

"It's all right," she smiled. "If your face is the last thing I see—that's good enough for me."

That caused me to laugh. I couldn't believe this woman.

She climbed down the ladder. I watched her. When she got halfway, I called to her.

"Hey, Benny?"

She looked up.

What the hell, I thought.

"My name is McKenzie."

"Thank you," she said, and continued her journey. A few moments later, she was crawling through the tunnel, using the measuring wheel to mark her journey. Her voice echoed up to me. She was singing.

"McKenzie, I just met a boy named McKenzie, and nothing in the worrrrrld will ever be the saaaaame—again."

I laughed some more. After her voice faded, I ran to the storm drain opening where I had lost my keys and waited for Benny to appear. The wait seemed interminable.

"Benny," I called into the sewer. "Benny, can you hear me?"

There was no reply.

"There are no alligators in the sewer system," I called. "That's just an urban myth."

A few moments later, Benny appeared beneath the grate.

"What took you so long?" I asked.

"I thought I heard . . . I thought I heard—something—but it must have been the rats."

"I wish you'd stop talking like that."

"Like what?"

"You know."

"You're not worried about me, are you, McKenzie?"

"Why would I be worried? There are no alligators in the sewer system, and I don't even know you. Now would you get the hell out of there."

"You are worried."

"Stop it."

"In a minute."

"And stop smiling."

Only Benny couldn't help herself. She continued to smile even as the foul liquid she was digging in flowed over the top of her gloves and around her fingers. After a few moments of searching, she snagged my keys.

"Found 'em," she announced, holding them above her head. "Meet you at the other end."

I watched her disappear into the pipe. A moment later I heard the echo of a loud scream that might have been bloodcurling if it hadn't been so obviously exaggerated. I waited, looking through the sewer grate, until Benny poked her head back out the tunnel.

"Let me guess,' I said. "It was *him*."

"No," said Benny. "It was *her*."

"Her?"

"Haven't you heard about the giant anaconda that lives down here?"

"Well, of course. The sewer snake. It was in all the papers."

A few minutes later I met Benny at the sewer entrance. She held the keys out for me. They were dripping with a brown liquid.

"Eww," I said.

"Ahh, wait," said Benny. She removed the bandanna from her hair.

"Don't do that," I said, but Benny wiped off the keys anyway and handed them to me. "Terrific," I said. I actually thought of giving her a hug, but Benny's boots, coveralls, and hands were smeared with brown sludge, and she smelled like, well, a sewer.

"I, ah, don't know how to thank you," I told her.

"Take me to dinner tonight," she blurted.

"Dinner?"

"I promise, I clean up real good."

"A date?"

"Sure."

"I don't think so," I said.

"You don't want to be seen with a woman who works in a sewer all day."

"Of course not," I said, then quickly corrected myself. "No, that's not what I meant." Benny was confusing me. I wished she'd stop smiling. "I mean I don't mind if I'm seen with a woman who works in a sewer."

"Then it's a date."

"No, Benny . . . Look, you seem like a nice girl."

"I am a nice girl."

"It wouldn't be fair to you. I'm just coming off this relationship—"

"The bitch."

"Who?"

"The woman who hurt you. Point her out. I'll kick her ass."

"You'll what?"

"Never mind. Violence never solved anything."

I started to laugh again. Just about everything Benny said made me laugh. There was something about her delivery.

"About dinner . . ."

"I can't," I said.

"Let me tell you what happened. This woman you were seeing, you dated her for how long? A year? Maybe more?"

"Yes."

"Then you discovered that you couldn't trust her. You discovered that she couldn't be depended on when the going got tough, that she wouldn't be there when you needed her, that she was putting her needs before yours, am I right?"

"Something like that."

"But with us—you and me—you already know that you can depend on me. McKenzie, you don't need a year to find out."

"I know this—how?"

"Think about it. How many women do you know would crawl through a filthy, stinking, alligator-infested sewer pipe for you?"

"You're the first."

"Well, then."

"Where do you live?"

"Near Lake Nokomis. Only you can pick me up at the Nash Gallery at the U. Do you know where it is?"

"No."

"In the Regis Art Center?"

"Sorry."

"Rarig Theater? It's on the West Bank."

"Rarig Theater? I'm not sure . . ."

"Okay, now you're scaring me. It's next to the Wilson Library."

"I remember the library. Why there?"

"You'll see," she said. "Eight o'clock?"

"Eight o'clock."

"Should I change, or do you think I can get by with what I have on?" she asked.

I thought the question was awfully funny.

The bartender at the Ski Shack liked what he saw—a good-looking woman in her early twenties, definitely not a working girl or junkie, with midnight hair and a face that looked like it had been exposed to books. At a distance her eyes were gray. They changed to a lovely pale green as she approached the bar and hoisted herself onto a stool three places down from where I sat.

"Excuse me," he said and hustled over to her without worrying whether I excused him or not. It took them a long time to decide that the woman wanted a vodka gimlet. Half a minute later, the bartender set the beverage in front of her and asked, "Do you want to run a tab?"

The woman said she did. I wasn't surprised that he didn't charge the drink to the house. After all, business was business.

"I should card you," the bartender said.

"Don't I look twenty-one?" the woman answered.

The bartender paused before answering. Perhaps he was distracted by her honeyed voice. The sound of it raised goose bumps on my flesh, and she wasn't even talking to me.

"You look like the snow-capped mountains of Tibet," he said. "You look like the Brazilian rain forest. Like the islands of coral off the shores of New Zealand."

"Oh, brother," I said.

The bartender turned toward me. From his expression, I doubted that he considered me a scenic wonder. He pointed his finger at the woman and said, "Hold that thought." To me he said, "What can I do for you?"

"Tap beer," I said. He listed some brands. I picked one. He poured the beer quickly and expertly and set it in front of me.

"I'm investigating an incident that occurred here a while back," I said. "Were you working here sixteen years ago?"

It was a silly question, and he quickly told me why.

"Sixteen years ago I was playing bantam hockey. How 'bout you?"

"Probably looking for a job."

"I was a Brownie," the woman said.

"Brownie?" asked the bartender.

"A very young Girl Scout."

"You don't look like a Girl Scout."

The bartender was flirting now, leaning on the stick, supporting his weight with his elbows. The woman was flirting back. She also put her elbows on the bar and leaned in.

"You don't look like a hockey player," she said.

"That's because I still have all my teeth," he answered, giving her a good look at all of them.

"Is the owner available?" I asked.

"Huh? No." The bartender stepped back from the bar.

"Do you expect him?"

"He went out for an early dinner. He should be back in a little bit. Ski. Michael Piotrowski. Everyone calls him Ski. He can answer your questions. Sixteen years ago he was here. Thirty years ago, too."

"I'll wait."

The bartender shrugged as if he couldn't care less what I did just as long as I stopped interrupting him. He turned all of his attention on the woman. For lack of anything better to do, I studied the bar. There weren't many customers. It was late afternoon, but still too early for the quick-drink-after-work crowd. The few people in the Ski Shack looked like they had been there all day and didn't plan to leave anytime soon. Some seemed interested in a rerun of a poker tournament on ESPN. The rest didn't seem to be interested in much of anything. Mostly they looked like people who needed the company of other people, even strangers. It was a phenomenon I understood quite well. When you're my age and single and essentially unemployed, you tend to spend a lot of time alone. Sometimes you get lonely.

I flashed on Nina Truhler—she had kept the alone feeling at bay for a long time now. Thinking about her made me regret my date with Benny Rosas. *You should be at Rickie's begging Nina's forgiveness, not chasing skirts at a U of M art gallery,* my inner voice told me.

"Benny—I bet she hasn't even voted in three presidential elections yet."

"Did you say something?" the bartender asked.

I pointed at my empty glass, and he refilled it with Summit Ale.

I forced myself to drink slowly. I had been hitting it too hard the past few days, and if I kept at it—it's like the man says, if you try to use booze to solve a problem, one day you're gonna discover that you have two problems. Still, I wasn't too concerned about it. Especially when I saw my reflection half hidden behind several rows of assorted bottles in the mirror that ran the length of the bar. I had the look of a man who knew what he was doing and was proud of himself for doing it. It was the same look I had when I was a member of the St. Paul Police Department.

Only they took that away from you, didn't they, I reminded myself.

I had become a public relations problem after the Simbi shooting, the cause célèbre of every anticop faction in the Twin Cities, a symbol of corruption and arrogance and everything that was wrong with police departments everywhere. Most of my fellow cops were on my side, and those that weren't—the politicians at the top who were worried about things like image—couldn't fire me because of the grievance procedures guaranteed in the union contract with the St. Paul Police Federation. They didn't have grounds. I hadn't done anything wrong; the grand jury cleared me. But I had been on the fast track toward sergeant stripes, toward a gold shield, and suddenly I was nudged into pit row, going nowhere fast. The department couldn't be perceived as rewarding a controversial officer that many citizens called a killer. So when I found Thomas Teachwell and the millions he embezzled from a national restaurant chain, I quit the department and took the reward offered by the insurance company.

I was leaning on my elbows and moving my glass in ever widening circles, enlarging a wet smear on the dark wood, when I heard a man's voice.

"Man, it's hot," he said. "I almost melted out there."

Michael Piotrowski leaned across the bar in front of me. He was sweating.

"You lookin' for me?" he asked.

Piotrowski was a big man, old and ugly, with a mouth twisted in a permanent frown. He had a harassed quality about him, as though he had many things to do and not enough time to do them.

I introduced myself, then asked, "Do you remember a man named Robert St. Ana? He died about—"

"Fuck yeah, I remember him. Fucker got hisself killed in a car accident and they blamed me for it just because he was drinking in my place."

I had met plenty of people like Piotrowski when I worked the streets of St. Paul, people who loved to give me both the play-by-play and color commentary. Accident, burglary, assault—it didn't matter. I'd ask a simple question, "What happened?" and get six pages' worth of answer in reply. Which wasn't necessarily a bad thing.

"Fucker was sitting right where you're sitting now, swear to God," Piotrowski recalled. "Kept hammering those Long Island teas—that was all the rage back then, Long Islands, and he sure liked 'em. Had a half dozen easy. Now, he was a young guy, but he could handle his booze. You could tell he had been drinking illegal for years. I tell him after six, 'Hey, you're done.' I cut him off. He said, 'No problem. I'll get a ride.' I said, 'I'll believe it when I see it,' and he goes over to that phone, right over there"—Piotrowski pointed at the pay phone on the wall between the two restrooms—"and he makes a call, comes back, says, 'It's okay, I have a ride.' Fine with me, so I keep serving. An hour later, less than an hour, a woman comes in. The two of them, they sit at a table right over there, start talkin'. I'm at the end of the bar tending to some paying customers, so I don't get a good look, okay? But the woman is kinda young-looking and I figure I'm gonna have to card her. That's what I need—a drunk and a' underage drinker. But when I look up, he's following her out the door. End of story, that's what I'm thinking.

"Only, couple days later they find the guy dead. Drove his car off the road in a snowstorm, passed out in the car. Fucker dies of carbon monoxide. Who's to blame? Him? Fuck no. The woman, whatever the fuck happened to her? No way. The goddamn blizzard? Uh-uh. Me." Piotrowski poked himself in the chest. "I'm the guy. I killed him. Shit."

During the brief pause that followed, I asked, "This was sixteen years ago. How come you remember it so well?"

"Cuz I got my ass sued, that's why. You want another one?" He was pointing at my empty glass. I had another one.

"Bitch sued me for wrongful death," Piotrowski continued after he poured my beer. "A kid. Fuck. A sixteen-year-old kid sued me, claimed that this St. Ana fucker was the father of her child. She's suing me on behalf of this child wasn't even born yet. I get pissed just thinking about it."

"Do you remember the woman who picked up St. Ana?"

"No, it was a busy night and I wasn't payin' attention. Christ, it would've saved my ass if I knew who she was."

"Do you remember what she looked like?"

"A looker—a looker with long dark reddish hair. That's all I 'member."

"Not Merodie Davies?"

"Know what? That was my first thought, cuz the kid, she had the hair. 'Cept my lawyers said it couldn't be, insisted the kid didn't even have a fucking driver's license. I mean, shit."

You were only fourteen when your father taught you how to drive a stick on the dirt roads Up North, my inner voice reminded me, but I didn't say.

Piotrowski paused for a moment to catch his breath, then started up again. "I wanted to fight, that's what I told my insurance company. 'Let's go to court,' I said. Not them pussies. They say, first, they only have my word that there really was a woman, like I made it up, right? Like I shoulda fucking asked her name, right? Shit. Then they say putting a sixteen-year-old unwed mother on the witness stand, crying all over the fucking place over this guy what was supposed to marry her and raise the baby, that's what they call a 'no-win proposition.' So they settle out of court. Eighty-five thousand bucks, and me with a twenty percent deductible. Fuck. That's all I can say. Why you want to know all this shit for, anyway?"

"The woman, the kid who sued you . . ."

"Merodie fucking Davies," Piotrowski said.

"She's in jail on a murder charge."

"Really?"

"Yes."

"Well, good," Piotrowski said.

———

Vonnie Lou Lowman, Eli Jefferson's sister, lived in a small, split-level house in New Brighton, a suburb just north of Minneapolis. The doors and windows of her house were closed and the drapes drawn, giving the place a murky look. Apparently, Vonnie Lou thought her efforts would keep the heat at bay. I admit, it was a few degrees cooler inside, yet the back of my shirt stuck to me just the same.

Vonnie Lou offered Dr. Pepper, which I accepted greedily. The beers I had at the Ski Shack were working on me, and I didn't want to be sloshed when I met Benny.

"No. No. No possible way." Vonnie Lou answered my first question. "I'm not just saying that because he's my brother, either. Eli would never have abused Merodie, would never have hit her. I don't know who told you that, but it's just not true. He was the most good-natured man you would ever hope to meet. Sweet as honey, I'm not kidding. He liked women. Believe me."

"Were you and your brother close?"

Vonnie Lou smiled at the thought. "We had our ups and downs," she said. "Like I told you, he was a sweet man. He liked his liquor though, and when he drank he did stupid things. Not mean things, or dangerous things. Just stupid."

"Like sleeping with other women?" I asked.

Vonnie Lou nodded her head then, sipped her pop. "This time I thought it would work out for Merodie," she said. "I really did. Merodie hasn't had a whole lot of luck with men."

"So I've been led to believe."

"They've either turned out to be assholes or they died on her."

"Let's talk about that. I know about St. Ana."

"Robert St. Ana, the guy who got her pregnant. That was before my time, before I met Merodie."

"Did Merodie ever talk about him?"

"Not really, although from what she did say, I guess he wasn't exactly the nicest guy in the world. Beat on her some, Merodie said. Did other things. Then he got her pregnant and wouldn't marry her. The way I figure it, the best thing that could have happened to Merodie was him dying like he did."

"What about Becker?"

"Brian Becker?"

"Is that his name?"

"If we're talking about the same guy, yeah. Brian Becker. Him I did know. He used to live with Merodie. He was—God, what a creep. You heard he abused Merodie? That's no lie. Slapped her around, called her names—he did it in public, too. We all told Merodie to get rid of him, told her he was no good, but she stood by him. I don't know why. He treated her place like it was his. Drove her car. Took money from her. The day he died—I'll tell you how much of a jerk he was. The day we heard that Becker died, we all went out and partied."

"How did he die?" I asked.

"He died from being stupid, that's how. You know what happened? He went out drinking without Merodie, but driving Merodie's car. He drove back to the house, pressed the button on the remote to open the garage door, drove into the garage, parked the car but didn't turn it off, closed the garage door, passed out, still in the car, and died of carbon monoxide poisoning. Merodie found him the next morning and called the police. The cops wrote it down as an accident. Personally, I think it was divine intervention. God decided Becker was just too stupid to live."

"What about Richard?" I asked.

"Richard Nye?" Vonnie Lou spat the name. "Another jerk. He used to live with Merodie, too. I swear, Merodie attracted them like ants to sugar, you know? This one, Nye, he sold crystal meth right out of Merodie's living room, I swear to God. Beat Merodie up when she told him to stop. Last I heard he was doing time."

"For dealing drugs?"

"Yeppers."

I made a note in my book and asked, "Did Merodie turn him in?"

"You're damn right, she did." There was pride in Vonnie Lou's voice. "I'll tell you what happened. Richard attacked Merodie in her own home, and in self-defense, Merodie hit him over the head with a softball bat."

The instant she said "softball bat" I recognized that this was the missing piece G. K. Bonalay had been looking for, the reason the Anoka County attorney was pushing a murder charge against Merodie. *It would seem to indicate*—my inner voice was choosing its words carefully—*a propensity toward violence and possibly even an MO since Merodie used the same weapon—the bat—on both victims.*

"Merodie hit him with the bat," Vonnie Lou continued, "and Richard broke her jaw. They both ended up in the hospital, only Richard was there for a night and Merodie was there for nearly a week. She complained to the cops, but it was one of those he said/she said deals. A domestic matter, one guy called it. As far as the cops were concerned, it was *both* of their faults."

"What did they fight over, do you recall?"

"Silk."

"Merodie's daughter?"

"Yeah. See, Merodie has this fantasy that Silk is coming back to live with her, that one day she's just going to just show up, suitcase in hand, or something like that, which is never, ever going to happen."

"Why not?"

"Silk has been living with her aunt all these years and she doesn't come by, not ever. Maybe it's the aunt's doing, I can't say. I've known Merodie for, God, at least ten years, probably more, and I've never met Silk, never even seen her except for these photographs that Merodie has that are really old. I mean, it's just not going to happen—Silk moving back. At least I can't see it. Only Merodie believes, okay? So when she learned that Richard had been dealin' out of her house, she freaked out, told him that she wouldn't allow drugs in the same house as Silk. Richard laughed at her, and one thing led to another.

"Anyway, there was no way Merodie was going to let Richard get away with what he did to her—laughing at her, beating her. Right before she left the hospital she called the cops and burned him. Burned him right down to the ground. He was already in custody by the time she got home."

Vonnie Lou was smiling—perhaps she always smiled—but her melodic voice suddenly grew hard and cold.

"Merodie, she's one of the nicest people you're ever going to meet," she said. "I love her to death. I mean it. She almost never gets angry at anyone or anything, but when she does get angry—you know what? You don't want to make Merodie angry."

8

The Katherine E. Nash Gallery was housed just inside the Regis Center for Art in the West Bank Arts Quarter—at least that's what the colorful banners hanging from the light posts along Twenty-first Avenue called the area. It was near O. Meredith Wilson Library as Benny had promised, on that part of the University of Minnesota campus known as the West Bank because it was located on the western shore of the Mississippi River. I had gone to the U, mostly on the East Bank. Graduated cum laude, thank you very much. Yet all this was new to me. I remembered the library and, now that I saw it, the Rarig Theater. I also remembered the Viking Bar on Nineteenth and Riverside. The rest—Barker Center for Dance, Ted Mann Concert Hall, Ferguson Hall, the parking ramp that I would have used if I had known it was there—when did all that happen?

You really should start paying attention to the alumni magazine, my inner voice told me.

A sign on an easel outside the entrance to the gallery read WELCOME

MFA SHOW. I presumed MFA meant master of fine art and this was an exhibit of the students' work. Probably Benny had a sibling or a friend in the show.

I didn't know what to expect when I entered the gallery—a handful of elegantly dressed patrons examining the exhibits while waiters passed among them with trays of champagne and hors d'oeuvres, I suppose. What I found was a pulsating throng of supporters, half kids around twenty-five and younger and the other half adults about fifty and older. Most were attired as if it were ninety-five degrees outside; I felt overdressed in black jeans and a black silk sports jacket. The crowd moved in a counterclockwise swirl, not unlike a hurricane, from one large room to another. I went with the flow.

There wasn't much that interested me. One artist—and I use the term loosely—had built a model of a very narrow building that had a facade like the State Capitol. There was a silhouette of a man painted on the wall at the end of a long corridor inside the building and another painted on the wall at the other end. A much shorter corridor intersected the building in the middle. I'm sure it all meant something, I just didn't know what.

Another artist exhibited a loop of photographs of ordinary women going about their everyday lives on a computer screen. I couldn't detect what linked them together except, well, they were all photographs of ordinary women going about their everyday lives.

The four walls of the next room each held a single huge photograph of—I'm not making this up—a wall. The walls in the photographs seemed to be from an empty motel room or possibly an efficiency apartment. Three of the walls were blank. The fourth framed a small window and an air conditioner. Taken together I suppose you could argue that the photographs were meant to depict the emptiness of our lives, yet all I saw was a room badly in need of furniture, not unlike my own house.

I was beginning to think that Benny had brought me there as a test of character. If I went screaming out of the gallery—and don't think I hadn't considered it—then I just wasn't the man for her. I sucked it up and kept moving, all the while searching for her.

I didn't find Benny, but I did find an exhibit that I actually enjoyed—a series of woodcuts printed on silk. The prints were thirty inches wide and five feet high and hung from the ceiling in pairs, the images overlapping each other. One in particular I found fascinating. Looking at it from the front, I saw a hungry wolf stalking a woman who was on her hands and knees and drinking from a mountain pool. Stepping around and studying it from behind, the woman appeared to be stalking the unsuspecting wolf. After examining it for a few moments, I noticed that the face of the wolf and the woman morphed into one.

I discovered a title card that accompanied the wolf-woman. It read PORNO WOLF GIVES ME A STOMACHACHE. B. ROSAS. I decided right then that artists should not be allow to title their own work.

An arm looped around my arm. Benny's voice said, "What do you think?"

"Beautiful," I said.

She stepped back and spun in a small circle. Her full red cotton skirt swirled around tanned legs; a black fitted linen jacket embroidered with red flowers was tight around her torso. The jacket had three buttons, but only the middle button was fastened.

"I told you I clean up real good," she said.

"Yes, you do. But I meant the silk screen." I pointed at the wolf-woman.

She slugged my arm playfully. "So where are you going to take me?"

"Do you like the blues? Big Walter Smith and the Groove Merchants are playing at a barbecue joint in Uptown. Otherwise . . ."

"That sounds like fun."

"Good." I continued to study the silk print.

"You really like this piece of junk?" Benny said.

"Yes. I like it very much."

"Why?"

"I'm not sure. Maybe because it asks questions that demand answers. Who's the hunter, who's the prey? It tells a story—I just haven't worked it out."

"The story could be different for everyone who looks at it," Benny said.

"Isn't that the definition of art? That it affects us all differently depending on what each of us brings to it?"

Benny shrugged. "What about the rest of the show?"

"That depends. Do you know these people?"

"Most of them."

"Then I think it's all just swell."

"I think it's mostly self-indulgent bullshit."

Something in my expression must have convinced her that I was surprised by her announcement.

"I'm a skeptic." Benny was speaking quietly so no one else could hear. "I'm skeptical about the place of visual art in society. Such a very small segment of the population will actually see it, and not necessarily the people I care about. It's a very insular world, the art world. All of the art in this show—it's for the artists. We love it, only I'm not sure what everyone else gets out of it.

"Personally, I don't want to have my stuff shown only in museums and galleries to this tiny group of people. I'd rather do stuff for people like me, people who have real lives, if you know what I mean. I want to do stuff for people who might pay two hundred bucks for a piece and take it home and get some pleasure out of owning it."

"Do you have something in the show?"

Benny pointed at the silk screens hanging from the ceiling.

"How is that possible?" I asked.

"Someone has to do it."

"No, I mean—this is wonderful, Benny."

"Thank you."

"It really is."

"Thank you."

"But isn't this for students?"

"Yes, part of their MFA thesis."

"At the risk of being insulting, you're what, twenty-eight, twenty-nine? How can you be a student?"

"I'm thirty-five, and I do not find you insulting in the least."

Which means she could have voted in four *presidential elections,* my inner voice told me.

"It's a three- or four-year program, and yes, most of the students are much younger," Benny said. "As for me—I took a few years off after I got my BA and then took the course part-time."

"While working in the sewers of Minneapolis," I said.

"Inspiration is where you find it."

"What are you gong to do now that you have your MFA?"

"Rent out a studio with a couple of friends. Buy an intaglio press—that's what I used to create the prints. Make art. Sell it."

"Are you going to quit your day job?"

"Eventually, if I can make enough money. Most people who get an MFA want to teach, or at least they want to make a steady living while they pursue their art. Some start applying for grants and support themselves that way, but you need to be a real go-getter to do that. I'm lucky because I work in the sewer."

Now there's eight words I never thought I'd hear, I told myself.

Benny nudged me along to another exhibit. This one featured two identical steel tracks that were twisted into an upward spiral not unlike a staircase. The steps consisted of thirty six-by-four-inch silk prints hung from the tracks by thread, starting with an image of a small child at the top and an old man at the bottom. In between there was a variety of images, some violent, some benign, some familiar, and some incomprehensible to me. The card on the wall read STAIRWAY TO HEAVEN. B. ROSAS.

"I have a question," I told Benny.

"What?"

"Shouldn't the child be at the bottom and the adult at the top?"

"The stairway to heaven doesn't go up," Benny said. "It goes down. As a baby, as a child, we are as close to heaven as we're likely to get. We slide away because of the choices we make during our lives."

"That's a cynical attitude."

"The images—Catholicism and religion run through the piece because that's a part of how I was raised. But mostly the images are about me and how things were passed down to me—values, ideas, possessions like my grandmother's brooch—and how all that influenced my life."

Based on the images, I decided Benny must have had an interesting thirty-five years. I was about to ask her about them when her hand tightened on my arm.

"Oops," she said.

"What is it?"

"My boyfriend."

A man, I placed him at midthirties, was waving as he plowed through the crowd. I assumed he was waving at Benny, but he was looking at me when he reached us. From his expression, he wasn't thrilled to see me. Benny maneuvered so that she was standing between us.

"Benita," he said.

She placed a hand solidly against his chest, stopping him. "Lorenzo," she said.

"Benita," he repeated. "May I speak with you for a moment?"

"No." Benita added a head shake to her words. "No, not now. We can talk some other time."

"Please."

Lorenzo reached out his hand, but I intercepted it before it could fall on Benny's arm.

He looked at me with surprise that turned quickly to anger.

"I was speaking to Benita, not you," he said.

"Like the lady said, some other time." I told him. At the same instant my inner voice asked, *When did you become Daniel the architect?*

From the expression on his face, I was convinced that Lorenzo was preparing to attack me. I took a step backward. His hands came up. I put myself into a balanced fighting stance. Lorenzo could see Benny standing next to me, though, and she must have passed a message because the fight quickly went out of him. He lowered his hands.

"Good-bye, Lorenzo," Benny said.

She tugged at my elbow, and I followed her through the crowd and out the door.

We stepped out of the Regis Center into suffocating heat—I was beginning to think that was the only kind there was—and began walking along the cobblestones of Twenty-first Avenue south toward Riverside. That was another thing. When did the University of Minnesota start paving its streets with cobblestones? It was something to think about the next time the regents pled poverty before the Minnesota state legislature, which only happens every two years.

I removed my sports jacket and carried it by the collar in my left hand. Benny walked with her hands behind her back and her head down.

I spoke first. "Back inside, with Lorenzo . . ."

"I'm sorry about that," Benita said.

"I noticed you called him your boyfriend. Not *ex*-boyfriend."

"He loves me," she said.

"You are lovable," I told her, trying to keep it light. "But that's not what I'm asking."

"I've known him for so long. We . . . He . . . Us . . ." She couldn't get the words out.

Behind us, footsteps echoed on the cobblestones.

"Benita." Lorenzo was shouting. "Benita, Benita."

I turned toward him, positioning myself between him and Benny.

He came at us in a hurry.

Benita called his name.

"Benita, please," he said.

"Whoa, pal," I said. I let my jacket fall to the ground.

"Leave us alone," Lorenzo shouted.

I didn't move.

When he got in close he threw a long, slow roundhouse right at my head—easily one of the most incompetent punches I had ever seen. I slapped it away and followed with a short right jab to his chin, putting my weight behind it. Lorenzo went down as if he had been hit with a surface-to-air missile, and in that instant I realized his punch wasn't incompetent at all. Lorenzo knew exactly what he was doing. I realized it because of the way Benny shouted his name and pushed past me.

"Lorenzo, Lorenzo," she chanted. There was no anger in her voice. Only concern. She knelt at his side on the concrete sidewalk. "Are you all right?"

She tried to caress his face, but Lorenzo pushed her hands away. She tried again. This time he let her succeed.

"I'm sorry," Lorenzo said.

"No, I'm sorry, I'm sorry," Benita said.

Somehow Lorenzo's head ended up in Benny's lap, and she stroked his hair.

Damn, my inner voice chided me. *If only you had let Daniel the architect punch you out.*

"Forgive me," said Lorenzo.

"Forgive me," said Benny.

"Forget this," said I.

Benny glanced up at me.

"I'm guessing our date is over," I said as I retrieved my jacket.

"I'm sorry, McKenzie," she said.

Everyone's sorry. Everyone's looking for forgiveness.

I didn't have anything to say, so I didn't say anything.

If I had been paying attention, I might have seen him, but I was upset as I made my way west to where I'd parked my car next to the trash bins outside the North County Co-op Grocery. First Nina, and now Benny, with Shelby Dunston giving advice to the lovelorn from the sidelines. "It shouldn't be this damn confusing," I said to no one in particular. Still, it all seemed to prove a theory that I had been advancing for years now. When it comes to love and romance, none of us ever really leaves high school.

I had unlocked the Audi with the key-chain remote, opened the passenger door, and draped my jacket over the seat when he hit me hard in the kidney. The pain rippled through my body and I nearly lost my legs. I had to grip the top of the door to keep from falling. He hit me again—and again—before moving to my head. I pivoted toward him, tried to get my hands up to fend off his blows. It was only a gesture, a suggestion that I knew how to defend myself. I don't think he noticed.

He was six inches taller than I was and at least fifty pounds heavier. His long hair and full mustache were jet black, and his features were Hispanic. The expression on his face told me only that it took some effort to beat me up, but nothing he couldn't handle.

He put a hard fist into my solar plexus and my legs melted beneath me. I slid into a sitting position, my back against the rocker panel, my legs drawn up to my chest. He hit me twice more with his fists and then a couple of times with the car door.

Is this about Benny? my inner voice wondered, but only briefly. I was losing focus fast. Two stinging slaps on both cheeks brought me back.

"I told the lawyer and now I'm telling you." His voice was calm but demanding. "You ain't helping that bitch Merodie Davies no more."

Merodie? Who's . . . Oh, her.

"Do you understand?"

Understand?

"Nod your head if you understand."

I nodded.

"Don't make me tell you again."

I might have nodded some more—I don't remember. I don't remember seeing him leave, either. Or if he had any parting words. *See you later, alligator. After a while, crocodile.* He was there and then he wasn't there. Maybe he left an instant ago. Maybe an hour. It was hard to tell. Possibly I had lost consciousness and that's why I had no sense of time. Yet if I was unconscious, why was I singing "What a Wonderful World"? Wait, that was Louis Armstrong. Jeezus, my head hurt.

It was growing increasingly difficult to see, and for a panicked moment I thought there was something wrong with my eyes, but it was only the gathering dusk. I wanted to stand and knew it was going to hurt, so I took my time getting ready for it. I unfolded my body and, using the car door, lifted myself high enough to fall onto my car seat. A tsunami of nausea told me that I had made an unwise decision. I hugged my knees until the convulsions subsided, proud that I kept the contents of my stomach to myself. Minutes passed, and the bright red light behind my eyes faded to a dull amber. I made a slow and careful inventory of body parts. Everything seemed to work more or less as designed, although if I were a used car, they'd have me in the "best offer" lot.

The loud chiming in my ears became the tinkle of a dinner bell. I could hear my own thoughts again.

He wasn't so tough, I told myself as I gingerly fingered my jaw, satisfied that it was still in one piece. *Bobby Dunston's girls can hit harder.*

Yeah, right. What was all that about, anyway?

Merodie. Someone wants you to lay off Merodie.

Merodie?

The man said, "I told the lawyer and now . . ."

"G. K.!"

The notebook I was using for the Merodie Davies investigation was in my glove compartment. Pressed between the pages was the business card Genevieve Bonalay had given me. I dialed the home phone number she had written on the back. After four rings a voice mail message kicked in.

"Dammit."

I hopped out of the passenger seat and jogged around the Audi to the driver's side without thinking about the pain that squeezed my head and body. I slipped behind the wheel and started up the engine. The address G. K. had scrawled below the phone number placed her residence on Xerxes Avenue North in the Cleveland neighborhood. That was on the far west side of Minneapolis. I estimated it would take me at least twenty minutes to reach it, assuming I obeyed the prevailing traffic laws, which, of course, I didn't.

Twice more I called G. K., and twice the phone was answered by voice mail. By the time I came to a skidding halt at her address on Xerxes sixteen minutes later, I was anticipating the worst. The two Minneapolis police cruisers parked out front of G. K.'s house confirmed my suspicions.

I left the Audi in a hurry and sprinted up the concrete walk toward the front door—or at least I ran as fast as I could, considering my legs seemed to belong to someone else. I passed a large clay planter that was broken into several pieces and the remains of what I thought were impatiens. A man watched me from his perch on a stepladder, the ladder leaning against the front wall of G. K.'s two-story brick house. He was using a battery-operated screwdriver to secure a sheet of plywood over what should have been a bay window. He kept watching while I rapped hard on the door. He could easily see all of me under the porch light. The only feature of his that I could make out was his bald head reflecting the street lamp.

"It's not locked," he said. I rapped on the door anyway. It was opened by a uniformed Minneapolis police officer.

"Genevieve Bonalay," I said.

"Here."

G. K. called to me from a living room sofa. She was wearing a white T-shirt and blue jeans. Her hair was damp and fell to her shoulders. She was sitting with her bare feet tucked beneath her. Another police officer sat next to her, his notebook out.

I moved around the cop at the door. "Are you all right?"

"God, McKenzie, what happened to you?"

"Are you all right?" I asked again.

"Yes, fine, but you . . ."

The cop spoke up. "Is he a friend of yours?"

"Yes," G. K. said.

I heard the screwdriver and turned toward the window. The sheet of plywood was covering a large hole. Someone had smashed G. K.'s window from the outside. I was willing to take bets on who.

"You're sure you're all right?" I asked G. K.

She left the sofa and moved toward me on her bare feet, and I said something about broken glass. She assured me all the glass had been cleaned up and nudged me toward a stuffed chair.

"Sit," she told me, and I did. "Tell me what happened."

"I met a man. We had a conversation. It was a trifle one-sided."

The cop spoke again. "Can you describe your assailant?"

I said I could and then proved it. He took notes while I spoke. When I finished, he said, "It's the same man."

"Yes," said G. K.

"What's going on?" I said.

"You tell us," said the cop.

I looked to G. K. for an indication of how to answer. Technically, I was working for her and her client. She said, "It's about Merodie Davis."

"Yes," I said. If she was going to tell the truth, so was I. "A large man attacked me from behind." I made sure I got that last part out in case the cop thought I was a wuss. "I was already down before I could see his face. He told me to lay off the Merodie Davies case or he would come back."

"Exactly what he told me," G. K. said.

"He said that he had already told the lawyer, meaning Ms. Bonalay. That's why I'm here. I called first, but your voice mail picked up."

G. K. glanced at her phone. "I've been letting it ring," she said.

"Would you like to file a complaint?" the cop asked.

"Sure, only who would I file it against?"

"Ms. Bonalay?"

We all turned toward the door. The man with the screwdriver was standing there. He appeared in his mid- to late sixties with a balding head and a strong weathered face.

"I got the plywood up. That'll keep the weather out and the air-conditioning in for a spell. Tomorrow we can call someone about fixing the window."

G. K. came off the sofa. She moved to the old man and hugged him close. "Thank you for everything," she said. "I'm so lucky to have you as a neighbor."

The interest she showed the old man made his heart pump too much blood to his face, and he turned away.

"It was nothing," he said. "Glad to help. I best be getting home now—tell Mary everything's all right."

"Excuse me, sir," said the cop. "Do you remember anything more about the man you saw?"

"No, sir," said the old man. "Only what I told you."

"His car?"

"Just what I said. It was a black car. Something small. I tried to get the license plate, but my eyes, they ain't what they once was."

"Thank you," said the cop.

The old man left, and a few minutes later, so did the officers. They promised to keep an eye on G. K.'s house for a few days, but I knew that wouldn't amount to much more than watching it when they drove past.

"You look like hell," G. K. said when they left.

"I don't feel much better."

She took me by the hand and led me to the bathroom and turned on the light.

The entire left side of my face was bright red and purple and swollen, including my ear. My eye was little more than a slit, and there was a visible knot on my forehead. Touching anything caused red explosions between my eyes. I lifted my shirt. My back on the right side of my spinal cord was the same color as my face—the man must have broken a thousand blood vessels. In a couple of days I was going to be just one giant black and blue bruise.

"I'll get ice," G. K. said.

A few minutes later I was sitting on her sofa, an ice pack pressed against my kidney. I held another against my face. "Thirty minutes on, thirty minutes off, repeat as needed," my hockey coach once told me.

"I'm impressed," G. K. said.

"By what? That I can take such an awful beating?"

"That you can take such an awful beating and then come rushing to my rescue."

She was sitting in a stuffed chair across from me, her feet again tucked beneath her. She was nursing what looked like a vodka and orange juice.

"If you had answered your phone I might not have," I told her.

"Yet you did come. Beat up like you were, all you could think of was me."

"I'm a helluva guy. Ask anyone."

"I can see that for myself."

"Tell me what happened to you."

G. K. took a long sip of her drink. "I took a shower when I came home from work—was taking a shower." She took another sip. "A lukewarm shower because it's been so hot. I was washing my hair, and I heard a pounding. I stopped and listened. The pounding stopped, and then it started again, and I . . . I left the bathroom. The upstairs bathroom. I threw on a nightshirt and came downstairs. The pounding was coming from my front door, and I looked through the peek hole and I saw him. He was—he looked awful. Frightening."

"Yes," I said, and shifted the ice pack to my forehead.

"I shouted through the door—no way I was going to open the door. I asked him what he wanted. He said he wanted to see me. I asked him who he was. He didn't answer, just kept pounding on the door. I told him to leave or I would call the police, and the pounding stopped. I went to my window"—she gestured with the glass at the plywood— "and looked out. He was watching me and smiling, and I realized that the nightshirt—I was still wet from the shower and the nightshirt was clinging to me and he could see my body outlined in the shirt, he could see . . ."

G. K. took another long pull of her drink.

"He said things to me. Vile things. And I . . . I just stood there listening. I couldn't move. I don't know why. I just . . . Then he shouted that I was to stay away from Merodie Davies or he would come back and he and I, we would have a party. He said he might come back anyway. That was when my neighbor came out of his house. When the man saw my neighbor, he picked up a planter I had outside my front door and threw it through the window."

"Were you hurt?"

"No, the planter, the glass—I wasn't hurt. But it made me— That's when I called the police and ran upstairs to put on clothes. He was gone by the time I came down again."

"It's over now."

"No, it's not," she said.

"I knew you were going to say that. So we're still on the case, then?"

"Of course we are. Aren't we?"

"We are if you say so. Just tell me one thing. Is it you talking or Mr. Muehlenhaus?"

"You know about him?"

"We're old friends."

G. K. finished her drink and made another. She had offered me one before, but I had turned it down. Mixing alcohol with a possible concussion didn't seem like a good idea. When she returned to her chair, she said, "Mr. Muehlenhaus told me to contact you."

"Why?"

"It's complicated."

"Yeah, well, try to make it simple. I have a headache."

G. K. drank more orange juice and vodka. "I became involved because I was Merodie Davies's attorney when she was busted for the discon. To be honest, I was going to blow her off. I didn't owe Merodie anything. Then Mr. Muehlenhaus called. I don't know who brought him into it or why. I think it might have been Rollie Briggs, but that's just a guess."

"Rollie Briggs," I said. "He's the assistant county attorney in Anoka County under David Tuseman."

"Yes."

"Considering how helpful he's been, he either hates his boss or likes you."

"Both, I think," G. K. said. "Anyway, Mr. Muehlenhaus asked me to get Merodie Davies off before her case came to trial. He didn't want Tuseman to get any traction from her trial at all. I told him we might have a good chance of getting it kicked because a cop roughed up Merodie and the man who tried to help her during questioning. I mentioned your name, and Mr. Muehlenhaus laughed."

"He would."

"He said some people have all the luck. I think he meant himself, not you. Anyway, he said we should try to recruit you to help, that you would help if we asked you the right way. He said you were resourceful. He said you were courageous—I guess you proved that tonight."

"Sure."

"He said you never quit."

"He's wrong about that."

"McKenzie."

"Genevieve. Did it ever occur to you that Merodie Davies might be guilty as sin?"

"That doesn't matter."

"Not to you—you're her attorney. It matters a great deal to me. Listen. Robert St. Ana abused her; he's dead. Brian Becker abused her; he's dead. Richard Nye abused her; he's doing time for drugs. Eli Jefferson cheats on her; he's dead. Do you see a pattern here? Then there's the softball bat."

I told her about it. G. K. turned the information over in her head.

"Tuseman will claim it supports a history of violence," she said. "He'll probably try to get it admitted under Spriegl."

"I'm not going to protect a murderer just because I'm miffed at the Anoka City Police Department," I said. "Muehlenhaus knows that. Which brings us to our friend tonight. Who do you think sent him?"

G. K. stared at me for a few beats before answering. "Not Mr. Muehlenhaus."

"He's done it to me before—kept me interested in a case by trying to scare me off of it."

"He wouldn't do that."

"Sure he would. The man's a master manipulator. He enjoys it."

G. K. stared at her drink for a few moments, took a sip, and said, "I don't believe that's true, and if it's not true, that means there's someone else at work here."

"There's always that possibility." I shifted the ice pack again.

"McKenzie, you can't quit. I need you. I need you to help me sort it all out."

"Okay."

"What?"

"I'll stick. For a while, anyway."

"But you said . . . You're confusing me."

"I think there's a good chance Merodie Davies is a serial killer," I said. "I think that Muehlenhaus knows it—he seems to know everything—and that he sent his thug to motivate me into helping Merodie get off anyway. The moment I can prove either for sure, I'm gone. Make no mistake about that, G. K. However, there's one small, nagging detail that makes me think, yeah, you could be right, there might be more to it than meets the eye."

"What detail?"

"Your neighbor said our visitor drove off in a small black car. It could be a sports car."

"Yes?"

"Yesterday Mollie Pratt told me that she saw a small black sports car parked in Merodie's driveway the day Eli Jefferson was killed."

"You mentioned that."

"Last night Mollie Pratt was murdered."

"Oh."

G. K. made a third vodka and orange juice. We talked some more while she drank it. I told her about Mollie Pratt; told her I had been convinced that she had seen Priscilla St. Ana's car even though the description and time didn't exactly match, only now I wasn't so sure. I told her about my adventures with Lieutenant Weiner that morning and everything else I had learned in the past few days. We talked for a long time. After a while it became just conversation.

I told G. K. it was time for me to leave. The news sent a visible shiver through her.

"McKenzie, I know I'm asking a lot, but . . . can you . . . can you stay here tonight?"

She didn't need to tell me she was frightened to be alone. I could see it in her eyes.

"Do you have more ice?"

I stretched out on G. K.'s downstairs sofa. The streetlights shone in every window save the one covered with plywood. It was nearing midnight. I was tired, yet each time I started to drift off to sleep I found another aching body part that demanded attention. After a few minutes I discovered G. K. standing at the foot of the sofa. She was dressed in a white lace nightgown that ended at her knees. I could barely make out her face in the dark.

She said, "Would you like to come upstairs?"

I said, "I would like that very much." She reached out her hand to me. "But not tonight." She let her hand fall slowly to her side. "You're frightened, Gen, and a little confused. Plus, you've had too much to drink. I don't want you to do anything now that will make you feel uncomfortable in the morning. Come to me tomorrow when you're sober, clear-headed, and feeling no pain. I'll still be here."

I couldn't read her expression; probably I had insulted her. She turned, moved toward the upstairs staircase, and paused.

"This is the second time tonight that you've impressed me," she said before floating silently up the carpeted steps.

Yeah, my inner voice told me. *You're a helluva guy.*

"Rushmore McKenzie, this assassin in blue, this killer of children," the minister chants from behind his podium.

Benjamin Simbi turns to face me. I brace the stock of the shotgun against my shoulder and sight down the barrel. "Police. Drop the gun. Put your hands in the air."

"This is just another example of the racism that is rampant in the St. Paul Police Department," the minister says.

There's a Smith & Wesson .38 in Simbi's hand. I beg him to drop it. Instead, he raises his hands slowly—slowly—slowly—slowly. The gun is nearly level with his chest when I squeeze the trigger.

"Proof—as if we need any further proof—that it is impossible for the black man to get justice in a white man's court."

The impact from the blast lifts Simbi off his feet and hurls him against the convenience store.

The woman screams.

The man shouts an obscenity.

"There is no hope in the system for people of color," the minister says.

9

I tried to wake up, but I was having a hard time managing it. I was flotsam—or is it jetsam—bobbing along on the lake Up North where I built my cabin. Each time I drifted close to shore, a wave would pull me away again. Finally, G. K. rested a gentle hand on my shoulder. I opened my eyes and they focused on her face, and for a moment I thought she was an angel.

"Are you all right?" she asked.

An ice pack, the contents melted long ago, slid to the hardwood floor as I pushed myself into a sitting position on G. K.'s sofa. I stretched, slowly, purposefully. Every muscle felt like a rubber band that was extended to the breaking point—a little more pressure and snap! There was a dull throbbing behind my eyes, and my stomach bobbed and pitched like a small boat on a large, unruly ocean. Yet as stiff and achy as I felt, I knew it would be much worse later. It's been my experience that the body doesn't hurt nearly as much the day after as it will the day after the day after.

"Are you all right?" G. K. said.

"You keep asking that question. Don't I look all right?"

"Not really."

"Swell."

"You were talking in your sleep."

"Did I say anything interesting?"

"You said, 'It's not my fault.'"

"Then it probably isn't."

"What were you dreaming of?"

"I don't remember. Maybe I was running for public office."

G. K. helped me to my feet. I was hoping for the white lace night-gown, but instead she was wearing a turquoise skirt suit and black pumps. Her hair was arranged in a pile on top of her head. She offered to feed me breakfast, but I declined and told her I should go home and get cleaned up. She said it was just as well, she needed to get to her office. I told her that there were a few things I would look into later that morning and that I'd call her. She said that would be fine. She did not repeat her offer from the previous evening.

Oh, well.

Ice for the first twenty-four hours, then heat—if you've been beaten up as much as I have, you learn things. One of the things you learn is that sitting around and nursing your wounds won't make them hurt less or go away sooner. Best thing to do is to be up and about. Stretch those muscles; ignore that pain. That's what I kept telling myself while I showered, shaved, dressed, ate my last bagel, and popped enough ibuprofen to boost the stock price for at least three pharmaceutical com-panies. Despite the heat, I wore a lightweight sports jacket—the better to conceal the nine-millimeter Beretta that I fetched from the safe built into my basement floor. True, carrying the gun probably wouldn't have helped much the day before, but it made me feel better. I also parked the Audi in the garage and switched to my Jeep Cherokee. It bothered me that my friend was able to find me at the Regis Art Center, and I decided the Audi must have had something to do with it.

I checked my voice mail. A message from Nina Truhler made my heart race, even though it wasn't much of a message. She didn't say why she called, or if she would call again, or if I should call her back. Nor did she attempt to reach me on my cell phone. Still, I took it as a good omen and tried all four of her phone numbers. Either she wasn't around or she wasn't picking up.

"You snooze, you lose, Nina," I said aloud.

Only I didn't mean it.

Thirty minutes later I was standing on the "police side" of the City of Anoka Public Safety Center. A plaque on the wall outside the administrative offices proclaimed that the Anoka Police Department had been accredited by the Commission on Accreditation for Law Enforcement Agencies. That meant it was rated among the top 3 percent of all police departments throughout the United States and Canada.

I shook my head at the wonder of it. Apparently, the CALEA didn't know these guys like I did.

I found the Records Unit. The female police technician who waited on me was six feet tall and blond, with pale skin, severe blue eyes, and a no-nonsense face—a Norse warrior in a pencil-thin skirt that reached to her ankles. The narrow plastic tag above her left breast read BARBARA ANDERSON.

I asked if it was possible to buy a copy of the police report on a death that occurred twelve years ago.

"Those records aren't on the computer," she told me.

"Can I get a copy just the same?"

"As long as the file you request doesn't begin with the letter *C*, you can."

"Why can't I get a *C*?"

"We lost them."

"Lost them?"

"The *C* files. We had an accident when we were switching to the computerized system and lost them all."

"All the *C*'s."

"Yes."

"What happened?"

"Does the name on the file you want begin with a *C*?"

"No."

"Then it doesn't really matter what happened, does it?"

She had me there.

"The name is Becker, first name Brian," I said.

Anderson wrote it on the top sheet of a notepad, then tore it off. "This will take some time," she said. "All of our paper files are stored in boxes down in the dungeon."

"The dungeon?"

"We have a couple of rooms set aside in the parking garage downstairs. We call it the dungeon."

"Colorful."

"I'll be back as soon as I can," she promised.

"I'll wait," I said, and watched as she disappeared into the labyrinth of halls and offices beyond. I wrote her name in my notebook for no other reason than I liked her.

She returned nearly a half hour later. There was a smudge of dust above her right eyebrow that I would have brushed away if I could have reached her over the counter.

"Ten dollars," she said.

I slid a Hamilton across the counter, and she slid back a stack of photocopies.

"Another file, if possible," I said. "This one I'm sure is on your computer. Nye, first name Richard. He's doing time for drugs."

Anderson worked a computer terminal while I watched.

"Nye, Richard Scott," she said.

"That's probably it."

"Hmmm."

"Hmmm, what?"

"The files are in the custody of the county attorney's office. They're not available for review."

"What does that mean?"

"That means if you want to see Richard Nye's records you need to get permission from Mr. Tuseman."

"Hmmm," I said.

I sat behind the wheel of the Cherokee with the big door open, my legs hanging over the rocker panels. The county coroner's Final Summary was attached to the police report.

> DECEDENT: Brian James Becker
> AGE: 27
> SEX: Male
> RESIDENCE: 1117 Deion Avenue, Anoka, MN
> PLACE OF DEATH: Residence
> DATE AND TIME OF DEATH: June 24 (Found) 0900 Hours
> CLASSIFICATION OF DEATH: Homicide-Accident-Undetermined
> PRIMARY CAUSE OF DEATH: Respiratory failure
> DUE TO: Carbon monoxide poisoning
> OTHER SIGNIFICANT CONDITIONS: Acute alcohol intoxication

With no indication of foul play, the authorities reached the same conclusion as Vonnie Lou Lowman—Becker died because he was too damn stupid to live—although they couched their verdict in much more diplomatic terms. The only one who seemed to disagree was Detective Walter Sochacki. His Supplementary Investigation Report ran twenty-seven pages, single spaced.

I returned to the Public Safety Center and located Barbara Anderson.

"Something more?" she asked.

"I'd like to speak with Detective Sochacki. Do you know if he's on duty?"

"Walter? No. He retired a couple of years ago. Back when we were still located down on the river."

"Do you know how I can find him?"

"Have you tried the phone book?"

The white pages told me that there was a Sochacki, Walter T., living on Grant Street. I found the address near Sunny Acres Pond. A woman pushing sixty answered the door as if it were a great imposition.

"You here for the car?" she asked.

"Car?"

"The car in the paper."

"No, ma'am. I'm here to speak with Walter Sochacki, if I can."

She pointed with her thumb more or less toward the back of the house.

"He's in the garage," she said. "You look like a pleasant, upstanding young man. Maybe he'll sell it to you."

"Sell what to me?"

"The car. He's seen at least a dozen potential buyers, but none of them has been worthy."

"Worthy of what?"

The way she shrugged her shoulders I guessed she didn't have a clue.

A few moments later I was standing in the open doorway of Sochacki's garage.

"Oh, my God," I said. "A 1965 Ford Mustang. And it's the same color."

The light blue sports car stood between Sochacki and me. I ran my fingers over the hood. He rounded the car and came toward me.

"Are you here about the ad?" he asked.

"May I?" I said, and popped the hood before he could refuse. "It is. It's the same car. One-seventy cubic inch straight-six engine, 101 horsepower, three-speed transmission on the floor—I know this car. My father taught me how to drive a stick in this car. I knocked out three transmissions before I caught on. Power steering, power brakes, bucket seats—it has a push-button AM radio, not even FM, am I right?"

Sochacki nodded. "I restored it with as many original parts as I could find."

"I even remember the tire pressure," I said. "Twenty-four psi front and back. You're selling this?"

"Yes."

"How much?"

"The ad said eight thousand . . ."

"I'll take it."

"Just like that?"

"It's a work of art. It should be in the Louvre."

"Actually, I think it's in the Smithsonian," Sochacki said. "I don't know. You said you owned a Mustang just like this one."

"Exactly like this one."

"What happened to it?"

"I spun it out on Mississippi Boulevard near the Lake Street Bridge and busted the A-frame."

Sochacki winced as I said it. His forehead furrowed and his eyes grew narrow. Suddenly I knew what his wife meant when she said none of the previous potential buyers were "worthy."

"I was a dumb kid," I said. "I've become much more responsible since then."

Sochacki nodded, but I don't think he believed me.

"What happened to your face?" he asked.

I almost told him I had been in a car accident, but caught myself in time. "I ran into a door," I said.

"Sure you did."

"Will it help that I was once a cop?"

"Was?" Sochacki said. "Why aren't you still a cop?"

"That's kind of a long story."

Sochacki nodded again.

I was losing ground fast.

"I promise to treat the Mustang with all the love and respect that she richly deserves," I said.

"Are you married?"

"No."

"Then you don't know much about love and respect, do you?"

I couldn't win with this guy.

"Only what my parents taught me," I said.

Sochacki gently closed the hood of the Mustang and gave it a loving pat. She wasn't going anywhere.

"Actually, I didn't come about the Mustang," I said.

"Oh?"

"I wanted to ask about a case you worked a dozen years ago."

"What case?"

"Brian Becker."

"Brian Becker . . ." He squeezed his eyes shut as if he could conjure an image of the man from behind the eyelids.

"Carbon monoxide poisoning," I said.

"Sure. Killed himself in his garage. It was eventually ruled an accident."

"Only you didn't believe it."

"What makes you say that?"

"I read your supplementals. You did everything to prove Becker was murdered but conduct a séance."

"If I had thought it would work, I would have tried it," Sochacki said.

"Why didn't you believe it was an accident?"

"You read the entire file?"

"Yes."

"Then you tell me."

"Two domestic assaults in nine days prior to Becker's death."

"Yeah. Plus the eleven contacts we'd had with him before that."

"Still . . ."

"I admit it, I couldn't prove anything," Sochacki said. "There was no insurance claim. No property changed hands. There was no money in joint accounts. Except for getting the asshole out of her life for good, Merodie Davies didn't profit at all from Becker's death. Neither did anyone else that I could find. There was no evidence of foul play—no bruises, no contusions on the body, no signs of a struggle; he wasn't anchored to anything. There was nothing there. Nothing. My partner knew it. The boss knew it. The county attorney knew it. I suppose I knew it, too. It just—it just didn't feel right. You said you were on the job."

"Eleven and a half years in St. Paul."

"Then you know what I mean."

"I know."

"At first I thought it was the woman in the bar. Maybe she slipped him something. 'Cept the ME said no way. There was nothing in Becker's blood but booze."

"Tell me about the woman in the bar."

"From what witnesses told me, she was drinking alone until Becker arrived. Then they drank alone together. After an hour or so they left. I never could get an ID on her. Witnesses said she had long auburn hair.

Said she was a beauty. Said they never saw her before or since. I had hoped she paid for her drinks with a credit card or personal check, but she was all cash."

"Was she waiting for him?"

"Witnesses said she was waiting for someone. Whether it was for Becker specifically or anyone who walked through the door, I can't say."

"Could it have been Merodie Davies?"

"That was my first guess, but no. Not a chance. Merodie had played softball that evening. Afterward she and her teammates closed down Dimmer's, then went to the house of one of them named"—Sochacki shut his eyes again—"Vonnie Lou Jefferson. Merodie stayed the night. Left at nine the next morning. By then Becker had been dead for at least six hours."

"What about the girl?"

"What girl?"

"Merodie's daughter?"

From the expression on his face, I gathered that Sochacki had no idea what I was talking about.

"Merodie Davies had a daughter living with her at the time Becker was killed," I said. "She must have been about four years old."

Sochacki shook his head. "There was no daughter. Merodie and Becker lived alone."

"Are you sure?"

"I was a very good investigator, Mr. McKenzie. I would have noticed a four-year-old girl."

Twenty minutes later I was standing in front of the counter at the Anoka County Correctional Facility. The woman on the other side of the inch-thick bulletproof glass partition was soft and doughy; she looked like someone Barbara Anderson might beat up for exercise.

"Merodie Davies," I said, repeating the name for the fifth time.

"Are you her lawyer?"

"I work for her lawyer." To prove it, I slipped the letter G. K. had given me from my pocket. The attendant couldn't even be bothered to read it.

"You aren't her lawyer, you don't get to see her."

"Why not? It's visiting hours."

"She's in isolation."

"For what?"

"Are you her lawyer?"

"No, but . . ."

The attendant turned her back to the glass partition. Suddenly, I wasn't there anymore.

I called G. K. on my cell, but she wasn't available. I left her a message: "Better check on Merodie."

Sitting idle in Priscilla St. Ana's concrete driveway was her elegant black four-door Saab. In the driveway across the street were a silver BMW convertible and a Lexus. Compared to them, my world-weary Jeep Cherokee looked like refuse someone had abandoned at the curb. No doubt the recyclables people would be around at any moment to cart it away. I longed for my Audi even as I admonished myself for the thought. *Damn, McKenzie. When did you become so shallow?* 'Course, if I could talk Sochacki into selling me the Mustang, I wouldn't care what anyone thought.

The maid, Caroline, met me at the door. This time she allowed me to wait in the foyer while she summoned her employer.

Cilla's heels made a loud tapping sound on her tile floor as she approached, and for a moment I wondered if she was going to or coming from a business meeting, or if she always dressed so exquisitely around the house. She was wearing a butter-colored dress under a matching jacket. The skirt on the dress was shorter than most high schools would allow.

A looker, Michael Piotrowski had said.

She was a beauty, said Detective Sochacki.

"My goodness, Mr. McKenzie, what happened to your face?" Cilla asked.

"I ran into a door," I told her.

"A door?"

"A car door."

"Did it hurt?"

A silly question, I thought.

"I've been hurt worse playing hockey," I said.

Cilla nodded, but I don't think she believed me any more than Sochacki had.

"What can I do for you?" she asked.

"Has the Anoka County Sheriff's Department contacted you yet?"

"Have you come all this way to ask that again?"

"Among other things."

"The answer is no. I have not spoken with anyone from the sheriff's department. Why would I?"

"The check."

"Why is the check so important?"

"It proves that someone was in the house other than Merodie when Eli Jefferson was killed."

"Apparently, the authorities haven't accorded it nearly as much importance as you have."

"Apparently."

"There's something else you wish to inquire about?" Cilla asked.

"When last we spoke, you explained how you came to take custody of Merodie's daughter."

"Yes."

"You took charge of Silk after Brian Becker was killed."

"Yes."

"According to my information, Silk was not living with Merodie when Becker died."

"No, she was here. Or rather she was with me."

"Imagine my confusion."

Cilla smiled, and for the first time I realized that there was no joy in it. Nor did it ever change. Cilla could be looking at a sunset or a plate of mashed potatoes or me—her smile was always the same.

"Silk would stay overnight with me on the evenings that Merodie played softball with her friends. It was my understanding that having a four-year-old daughter to care for cramped Merodie's—style, is that the correct word?"

"No, but it's close enough. So Silk was already with you when Becker died?"

"Yes. She was safe in my home in Andover."

"You're not a natural blonde, are you, Cilla?"

"McKenzie. What an impertinent question."

"I have a reason for asking."

Cilla studied me for a few moments and then smiled as if she could read my mind. "No," she said. "My hair is naturally auburn. I began coloring it when I turned forty, to hide the gray."

"You wore it long."

"Longer than it is now, yes."

"You had long auburn hair when Becker was killed."

"Yes."

"If I may be so bold . . ."

"Bolder than you've already been?"

"Back then most men would have described you as being a stone babe."

"They still do."

Cilla smiled her empty smile.

"Yes," I said. "They still do."

Cilla smiled some more, waiting.

Somewhere in the distance I heard the rumble of thunder. It was only after staring at Cilla for a few moments that I realized it was the sound of a vacuum cleaner overhead. Caroline had worked her way down the upstairs hall and was now on the staircase.

"An attractive woman with auburn hair was seen with Brian Becker the night he died. She hasn't been identified."

"That was me," Cilla said.

The fact that she admitted it so freely caught me by surprise, and my expression must have shown it. Cilla smiled again, but this time it reached her eyes. I had the distinct impression that she was enjoying herself.

She rested her hand on my arm. "Do you play chess, Mr. McKenzie?"

"Chess? Yes, I play . . . I used to play . . . Cilla, do you realize what you're telling me?"

She took my arm in both hands and gave it a squeeze. "Let's see what kind of game you have."

Cilla led me across her sprawling living room to a den. Inside the den was a fireplace so large I could have parked my Audi inside it. We sat in front of the fireplace in ornate wooden chairs carved in the Spanish style, facing each other across a matching table. A chessboard was on the table, the pieces already arranged in neat, orderly ranks.

"Would you like something to drink?" Cilla asked.

"Drink?"

"Yes."

"Iced tea?" I said.

"Nothing stronger?"

"Put a shot of gin in it."

Cilla smiled at that. "Caroline," she said.

The maid appeared at the doorway.

How did she do that?

"Two glasses of your special iced tea laced with gin."

"Ma'am," the maid said, and departed.

"So," said Cilla.

She moved her pawn to E4. I countered with the identical move to E5. Cilla slid her king's bishop to C4. The move was insulting. She was going for a Scholar's Mate. In four moves it was nearly the shortest checkmate possible—a strategy you'd only use against an amateur. I easily countered it by moving my king's knight to F6.

"I expected more," I said.

"I only wanted to see if you were paying attention, Mr. McKenzie. You seemed dazed."

"It's not often that I hear people confess to murder for no particular reason."

"Did I confess to murder, McKenzie? I don't think so. I will, how-ever, if you wish."

"Ms. St. Ana . . ."

"I told you, McKenzie—it's Cilla."

She moved another pawn.

"Would you like to hear it?" she asked. "The whole truth and noth-ing but the truth?"

I moved a pawn of my own.

"Please," I said.

"It's a long story." Cilla smiled her empty smile. "Perhaps we should wait for our drinks before we begin."

We sparred quietly on the chessboard, neither of us gaining an ad-vantage, until Caroline arrived. Cilla set her drink on a coaster without touching it. I took a stiff pull of mine.

"Where to begin," Cilla said. She studied the board for a moment and hid her knight behind a pawn. "It begins, I suppose, with the death of my mother. That's when I decided that I would never allow a man to abuse me in any way ever again.

"You see, McKenzie, my father was an evil degenerate. Corrupt. Depraved. He treated women, treated my mother, maids—as far as my father was concerned, women were a royal prerogative to do with as he wished, a natural entitlement of wealth and power. His specialty was live-in maids. It gave him immense pleasure to tease them, flirt with them, pursue them, and eventually abuse and terrorize them. And worse. Much worse. A lot of money was spent to hush up his transgressions. Then he began . . ."

She paused for a moment, as if she were gathering her strength.

"My father raped me from age fourteen to age sixteen. He would climb into my bed and he would take me and afterward he would say, 'That's my little girl.' My mother knew this, of course. Her way of dealing with it was to commit suicide. My father insisted that Mother's death was the result of a traffic accident. Yet even as a child I knew you don't drive cold sober one hundred and twenty miles an hour into a bridge abutment on a sunny summer day by accident."

Cilla cursed under her breath. She moved her bishop carelessly.

"She was weak," Cilla muttered.

I moved a rook into position to counter the bishop.

Cilla shook her head to dislodge the black memories and sipped a generous portion of her drink before removing her bishop to its original position. I sent another pawn forward.

"I was not weak," she said, and moved a pawn to match mine. "Shortly after my mother's death, I went to my father's bed. I crawled in next to him—he seemed to like that—and I gently placed the blade of a ten-inch-long butcher knife I had spent fifteen minutes sharpening against his throat and assured him that if he did not leave me alone I would kill him. I spoke calmly, Mr. McKenzie. Softly, almost in a whisper. I think that's why he didn't believe me. He shouted at me, insulted me, told me to get out of his bed. I didn't move. But the knife blade did. It moved about an inch across his throat.

"The cut wasn't deep, but there was a great deal of blood. It spilled down his neck and onto the pillow and sheets. He clutched his throat to stem the bleeding. 'You're crazy,' he told me. 'You're insane.' But now he believed. I told him to leave me alone, to leave Robert alone. He said he would. He kept his promise. He never forced himself on me again. Nor did he ever again engage me in a conversation that lasted more than thirty seconds. He made it clear that I would need to fend for myself— myself and my brother. It was because of my brother that I stayed in the house even after I reached my majority. It's your move, Mr. McKenzie."

I was astonished. Not only at the story, but also at the matter-of-fact manner in which Cilla related it. She spoke about subjects that would send most people into an emotional frenzy, yet her voice held no anger or pain. Instead, it possessed a yearning, thoughtful quality, and when she spoke, she had a way of drawing out some words as if she wished she could think of better ones.

I moved my rook, and Cilla swept it off the board.

"Pay attention, McKenzie," she said.

"Tell me about Becker."

"In due time. First, allow me to tell you about my brother. Robert was an alcoholic, like our father, and like our father, he was abusive and totally amoral. Merodie wasn't the first young woman he corrupted by any means. If there was a difference between the two, it was that Father was also ambitious. He enjoyed money and power and wasn't above working long, hard hours to accumulate them. Robert did mind. He detested work, school, anything that required effort. Robert lived only to indulge himself.

"Make no mistake, my father adored Robert. At the same time, he was fearful of what Robert would do to the company he built from scratch. So he turned to me. I had a master's degree in chemistry. My father offered me a job in the company's R&D department and paid me nearly twice as much as everyone else with similar credentials and years of experience. A number of times I was invited to business functions and other gatherings. We rarely spoke at these events, yet he would introduce me to one and all as his 'favorite daughter.' That was as close as he ever came to saying, 'I'm sorry.' Later, after he died, my father left his entire estate—his business and the money to run it—to me. I was as surprised as anyone. For a time I amused myself with the delusion that he had a guilty conscience, but time taught me that he left everything to me because he did not trust Robert. I was all he had left.

"Now, this is important, Mr. McKenzie. When I first joined the firm, St. Ana Medical was attempting to develop a product that could compete with Ativan, Valium, and Xanax as a viable treatment for insomnia and anxiety. I was working on an analog of gamma-hydroxybutyrate—"

"GHB?"

"Yes."

"The date-rape drug?"

"Yes. GHB had been used productively in Europe as an anesthetic, as an aid to childbirth, and as a means to treat sleep disorders such as narcolepsy. We were hoping to develop a superior analog. And I succeeded.

"As a sleep aid—and this is GHB's primary disadvantage—as a sleep aid GHB has only a short-term influence. Even though sleep is deeper and more restful, people will wake up after only about three hours. This pattern is known as 'the dawn effect.' However, with my analog, people remained asleep for eight to nine hours. Something just as significant—while GHB can be detected in urine four to five hours after it is taken, my analog completely metabolized into carbon dioxide and water in less than two hours.

"Unfortunately, it was at about that time that GHB was banned in the United States by the FDA and later designated a Schedule I Controlled Substance because people, mostly men, used it to assist in sexual assault, mostly of women. As a result, my analog was shelved."

"Why is that important?" I asked.

"The analog allowed me to kill without detection."

"Kill who?"

"My father, to begin with."

I tried to speak. No words came out. It was as if I had suddenly lost the power of speech. Just as well. I didn't know what to say anyway.

"Your turn," Cilla said, indicating the chessboard.

I moved my remaining rook three spaces.

Cilla brought her queen out.

"You want me to tell you about it, don't you?" she said.

I reached for my iced gin-tea, hesitated.

Cilla chuckled.

"The drink is fine, Mr. McKenzie," she said. "Really it is."

I left the glass undisturbed just the same.

Cilla continued her story.

"My father came home after a night of carousing. He was visibly drunk. I knew he would be. I waited for him by the pool. I was dressed in the skimpiest bikini. I invited him to join me for a drink. Do you believe, Mr. McKenzie, that the sight of me in a bikini would make a man such as my father pause?"

"Yes," I said.

"I placed two grams of my analog into my father's drink. He fell unconscious in twenty minutes. I rolled him into the swimming pool, clothes and all. The shock of water awakened him, but by then he was suffering from acute loss of muscle control. He thrashed about ineffectually and drowned. I went to bed—after first tidying up, of course. His body was discovered by a maid the next morning. An autopsy was performed, and that worried me. I was concerned that Father had died before his system could absorb the drug. However, while multiple toxicology screens of blood and bile samples revealed that my father's blood alcohol level was enormously high, there was no trace of my analog. Perhaps, if the medical examiner had looked closer—but why would he? My father had a history of alcohol abuse; there had been many witnesses to his abuse the previous evening. His death was ruled an accident. I inherited everything."

"Do you realize what you're saying?" I asked.

"My father abused my mother, our maids, and God knows who else. He raped me for two years. Yet in the end, it was I who fucked him."

"That's murder."

"I prefer to think of it as irony."

The corners of Cilla's thin lips curled upward in a slight smile, yet her voice contained no trace of emotion.

"Should we continue our game?" she asked. "I think I'm winning."

I moved a bishop into a middle square, slamming it down on the board harder than I should have. Cilla's hand hovered above her knight. She wanted to move it but realized that I had pinned her. If she moved the piece now, I would attack her king.

"Very nice," she said, bringing a rook up to protect the knight.

I continued the assault, pressuring Cilla's queen with my own rook. Cilla surprised me by taking the rook with her other knight.

"What happened next?" she said. "Oh, yes. Robert. Several months passed, yet Robert did not change a bit. In many ways he became more and more like Father. I was somewhat disingenuous earlier when I suggested that I did not know about Merodie until after my brother's funeral. Of course I knew about her. My brother took particular delight in listing the sex acts he forced her to perform—acts that would make a hard-core porn star retch. He was proud of himself, proud that he could corrupt a child.

"Eventually, Merodie became pregnant," Cilla said. "She informed my brother, and my brother rejected her. He claimed he wasn't the father and called her a whore—he acted exactly the way you'd expect an egocentric child to act. In the past, Robert was able to run to Daddy, who would throw money at the girl and make the problem go away. Unfortunately—for him—Robert was forced to come to me for the money necessary to pay off Merodie. I refused to give it to him. He threatened to sue me for his share of our father's estate. I told him that was his prerogative.

"As was typical with my brother, instead of securing an attorney, he went that same evening to a bar and became drunk. Later, he called me from the bar and requested a ride home. It had begun to snow heavily. By the time I arrived, several inches had already fallen. It was the first stage of a massive blizzard. You might remember it. Seventeen inches of snow fell in about five and a half hours. While at the bar, I slipped a couple of grams of my analog into Robert's drink, then hustled him out to his car before the drug could take effect.

"I drove Robert's car. He sat next to me in the passenger seat. He called me vile, obscene names and demanded that I give him money for Merodie and his other projects until he fell into a nontoxic coma. My experience with my father taught me to be more circumspect. To be sure that my analog would not be discovered in his body, I was determined to kill Robert slowly in order to give his system time to metabolize the drug.

"I drove along East River Road until I found a likely spot near the park, and when I was sure there was no traffic about, I drove the car off the road. I realized later there was a certain amount of danger to me—I could have been injured—but I didn't consider it at the time. After we came to a stop, I pushed and pulled to get him behind the steering wheel. I locked the doors. After first making sure the exhaust pipe was buried, I climbed to the top of the ravine. The hardest part was trudging through the blizzard back to my own car. It was only a few miles, but the journey took nearly two hours in the storm. My feet and hands were wet and numb from cold—I was afraid I'd succumb to frostbite. Fortunately, I survived the ordeal, drove home, and climbed into a hot tub."

"What about Robert?" I asked.

"They discovered his car a couple of days later. Once again the autopsy found a great deal of alcohol, but not a trace of my analog. He was ruled dead of carbon monoxide poisoning, and his death was dismissed as an accident."

My head spun at the admission. I held it with both hands.

"You killed him!" I shouted.

"I most certainly did not," Cilla insisted. "I merely allowed him to die, just like Father. There's a difference."

"No, there isn't."

I was on my feet now. I stepped toward the unlit fireplace, then pivoted to face her. "Do you realize what you're telling me?"

"Yes," Cilla replied.

When I continued to stare at her, Cilla added, "Do you wish to hear the rest of the story?"

I didn't say if I did or didn't, but when Cilla motioned me back to the chair, I sat. She took another sip of her drink, stared at me for a moment, then slowly took one of my bishops off the board as if it were the easiest thing in the world.

"Check," she said.

I wasn't surprised by the move. I had seen it coming and simply slid a pawn forward two ranks to block the attack. Cilla pulled her queen back into the first rank next to her king. I slid my queen to the fifth rank of the H file, attacking Cilla's knight. She studied the move, shook her head, and slid her knight out of danger.

"Tell me about Brian Becker," I said.

Cilla's head jerked up. She held my gaze for a moment, then leaned back in her chair. She watched me over the chess pieces.

"Brian Becker abused Merodie, and I have no doubt whatsoever that in time he would have abused Silk. That, I could not allow."

"So you killed him."

"It was easy," Cilla said.

"Did Merodie know you were going to kill him?"

"Excuse me?"

"Did you conspire with Merodie to murder Becker? Did she trade custody of Silk for his death?"

"Mr. McKenzie. You've met Merodie. Do you honestly believe I would take the enormous risk of confiding in her?"

"I don't know what to believe."

A more amazing story I had never heard. Yet throughout it all Cilla's voice was at once warm and precise, as if she were confiding a minor personal secret to a lifelong friend instead of throwing open the closet door to a nosy stranger.

"Why are you telling me all this?" I asked.

"So you'll believe me when I tell you that I had nothing—absolutely nothing at all—to do with the death of Eli Jefferson."

Who said you did? my inner voice cried.

"Perhaps not," I said, "but aren't you even a tiny bit concerned that I'll run off to the county attorney and report that you confessed to three murders?"

"My father and Robert were both cremated, so there is no physical evidence to prove a crime was even committed, much less that I committed it. As for Brian Becker, you would need a court order to exhume his body, and I doubt you'd get one. After all, it's merely your word against mine. If somehow you did manage it, the embalming fluids used by the mortician to preserve his corpse would conceal any trace of the GHB—if there's any to be found."

I had nothing to say.

"Besides," said Cilla. "Why should you care?"

I didn't have an answer for that. At least not one that Cilla would understand. Yet I did care. I cared a great deal.

Cilla resumed her playing position. She brought her queen out again. I removed a pawn with my own queen. She moved her bishop one space, giving me a clear shot at her king.

"Ms. St. Ana, you've been unusually forthcoming. It makes me wonder why."

Cilla didn't reply. Instead, she watched me push a rook into position. I watched her watch me. *Two more moves and you have her,* my inner voice announced.

"The simple truth is, I have nothing to hide," she said. Cilla pressed her bishop against my king. "Checkmate."

10

For all practical purposes, Priscilla St. Ana had admitted to three counts of murder, and her candor made me squirm in the seat of my Jeep Cherokee. Why would she do such a thing? Cilla claimed she confessed her past crimes so I would believe her when she denied any involvement in Eli Jefferson's death. Well, I didn't trust that motive any more than I would an unsolicited stock tip. It wasn't that I thought Cilla was lying—I believed every word she spoke. It was more like Cilla was telling too much truth. The conversation reminded me of this time when I was still a rookie riding with a field training officer. A suspect had walked up to our squad and without so much as an "Excuse me, Officer" confessed to a burglary that my partner and I had known nothing about. Except here's the thing—the suspect was adamant that the crime took place at exactly 10:15 P.M. in Highland Park, which, according to the Ramsey County Medical Examiner, was the approximate time the suspect's wife and her lover were being slaughtered in a downtown hotel room.

The Anoka County Coroner's Office was located near Mercy Hospital in Coon Rapids. Except for a directory in the foyer that listed the names of the county coroner, five assistants, one chief deputy, seventeen deputies, and an investigative assistant, it didn't appear much different than your typical outpatient medical clinic. Although, when I told the receptionist that I wanted to see Dr. Timothy Ronning, I was shooed into his office almost immediately. That was different.

It was Dr. Ronning who had performed the autopsy on Eli Jefferson. I reminded him of that when he shook my hand and asked how he could help me.

"Eli Jefferson, yes." He shuddered as if he had just remembered a particularly shocking scene from a horror movie. "What about it?"

"I work for the attorney who's representing the woman accused of the crime."

"Then you know that I'm not at liberty to discuss my findings without a signed release of information form from the county attorney or next of kin."

"That's not why I'm here."

"Why are you here?"

"Dr. Ronning, I have evidence to suggest that before he died, Eli Jefferson had ingested GHB."

"I don't think so."

"He was probably given at least two grams if the killer's MO holds up."

"If there had been even a trace of GHB in Jefferson's system, it would have shown up in the urine drug screen."

"I've been led to believe that this particular drug is a highly specialized analog, that its metabolism is so efficient that can't be detected in urine two hours after it's taken."

"There is no such animal."

"It was developed by a chemist working for St. Ana Medical."

"Which doesn't exist anymore."

"Doctor, all I'm asking is that you take another look at Eli Jefferson. Confirm or refute my theory."

"One. I don't give a rat's ass about your theory. Two. I don't perform tests just because some guy walks in off the street and asks me to. If you have a problem, bring it to the county attorney or talk to a judge. Three—"

"Three," I said. "If you don't test for it, we're going to ask you why. In court. In front of a judge and jury."

Dr. Ronning barely concealed a yawn behind his hand. I don't think he was too impressed by my threat.

"If, however, you do test for it and find it, you'll be instrumental in helping to expose and capture one of the most clever, most heinous serial killers in the history of Minnesota."

"Oh, yeah?"

"Not to mention the publicity you'll receive. People will be lining up to shake your hand. You'll be asked to speak to every community group in the state. There might even be a movie or book deal in it—it's happened before."

Dr. Ronning looked me up and down as if I were suddenly interesting.

"You're not trying to appeal to my vanity, are you, Mr. . . . McKenzie, is it?"

"Yes, Doctor, I am."

"Well, you're doing a fine job of it."

"I'm not making this up, Doctor. If the GHB is there, it means that the woman who gave it to Jefferson killed at least three other men in the past sixteen years. Maybe more."

"If it's not there?"

"Then I'll go away. No harm, no foul."

Dr. Ronning stared at me some more.

"The standard urine drug screen is designed to detect certain classes of drugs—barbiturates, opiates, cocaine, heroin," he said. "I suppose it's possible that a light dosage of GHB might slip by. I could run a blood GHB-level test. Just to be sure."

"Just to be sure," I said.

"Oh, hell. How do I reach you?"

My cell phone rang as I was walking back to my Jeep Cherokee, and I thought, *That was fast.* It wasn't Dr. Ronning, though. It was G. K. Bonalay.

"We need to talk," she said.

"We most certainly do."

"My office, as soon as you can get here."

Thirty minutes later I was standing in the cubbyhole G. K.'s law firm deemed appropriate to her status as a newly minted associate and looking out the window. G. K. had a spectacular view of the office tower directly across the street.

"Do you think she's telling the truth?" G. K. asked.

She was sitting behind her cluttered desk, staring at her hands folded on a file directly in front of her. She was as surprised as I had been when I told her that Priscilla St. Ana had confessed to three murders, and like me, she was unsure what to make of it.

"It sounded like the truth when Cilla was telling it," I said. "Now I'm not so sure. If it is the truth, Jefferson's death would certainly fit her MO. She drugs him and then lets him die slowly—this time of blood loss instead of carbon monoxide poisoning. Anyway, we'll know for sure in a day or so. I asked the county coroner to test Jefferson's blood for GHB."

"You did what?"

"I asked the coroner—"

"McKenzie." G. K. shook her head violently. "You shouldn't have done that."

"Why not?"

"Because . . . because . . . because I'm in charge here."

"No one said you weren't."

"You have to ask me before you do things like that. What if—Listen, McKenzie. I think we should ignore her. Forget Priscilla St. Ana even exists."

"Why would we do that? She's a suspect. She's even more of a suspect than most suspects."

"It makes the case too complicated."

"Not if we find the GHB."

"No. Forget it. There's an easier way of getting Merodie off."

"Such as?"

G. K. unfolded her hands and picked up the folder. I took it from her outstretched fingers. The top page read:

Case #06-058939
Richard Scott Nye
Table of Contents
Gross Misdemeanor Domestic Assault

The file contained all the information gathered by the cops after Merodie had beaten on Nye with a Lady Thumper softball bat and he had broken her jaw—and more. Someone had done a judgment search on Nye, producing two sheets of computer paper filled with misdemeanors, gross misdemeanors, and felonies. According to the report Nye had a lifetime of arrests—yet few convictions—for arson, assault, possession, and disorderly conduct, plus two counts of sexual assault, both dismissed. God knows what he did as a juvenile, because the State of Minnesota wouldn't say. It was the last few lines of type that most interested me, however. They indicated that the Anoka County Criminal Investigation Division had arrested Nye for possession with intent to distribute nearly a pound of methamphetamine. He pled out and was sentenced to sixty months in prison, but the sentence was stayed on the recommendation of Anoka County Attorney David Tuseman. Instead, Nye was made to serve five days shy of a full year in the Aonka County Correctional Facility—jail, not prison—pay a five-thousand-dollar fine, undergo chemical dependency treatment, and remain law-abiding for a period of five years upon his release.

"He cut a deal," I said. Just what kind of deal the report didn't say.

Beneath the computer sheets I found still another case file, this one detailing Nye's meth bust. I paged through it quickly while G. K. waited until I came across a photocopy of the search warrant the sheriff's department used. The warrant had been issued based on information provided by an unnamed source that "has been proven to be true and correct"—or so a sheriff's deputy testified to the judge. However, they CIA'd the informant, giving him or her a "cooperative individual agreement"—the informant's name, sex, and age were not listed on the search warrant, nor were they revealed in court. There was no way for Nye to know with certainty who the informant was, but he could have guessed, couldn't he? After all, Vonnie Lou Lowman knew that Merodie had dimed him out. I was sure Nye could figure it out, too. Especially since—I compared the dates of the two reports against each other to be sure—the warrant was issued just two days after he put Merodie in the hospital.

"I tried to get this information earlier," I said. "I was told that Nye's files were in the custody of the county attorney. How did you get them?"

G. K. shrugged at me.

"Rollie Briggs?"

G. K. shrugged some more.

I tried to return the files, but G. K. refused to take them.

"What?" I asked her.

"Look again," she said.

I glanced through the folder a second time. "What am I looking for?"

"You tell me."

"C'mon, G. K. We haven't got time for this."

"There's an old saying. 'God is in the details.'"

"God is in a lot of things."

"Nye's physical description."

I found it under the heading

Defendant's Driver License Record

"He's blond," I said.

G. K. smiled triumphantly.

I said, "In Merodie's original statement to the deputies, she said a man with blond hair had broken into her home and fought with Jefferson. She said it could have been a former boyfriend."

"Now, was that so hard?" G. K. asked.

"But in her second statement Merodie said she couldn't identify the man. She said she wasn't even sure that he had blond hair."

"I don't care. We're looking for information that can be used to create reasonable doubt as to the guilt or innocence of our client. In this case, confusion is our friend."

"So now we can place two people at the scene of the crime," I said. "Nye and St. Ana."

"Forget St. Ana. Nye is more than enough."

That doesn't make sense, my inner voice said, but I didn't press the matter.

"I want you to meet me at the jail," G. K. said. "Make it about five. We'll hear what Merodie has to say. In the meantime, do you think you can find Nye? He was released to the Anoka County Department of Corrections a couple of months ago, but when I called, the flunkies refused to reveal his address to me. I think Tuseman is trying to keep him under wraps."

"Why?"

"I don't know."

"I'll find him," I said, and headed for the door. "Oh. You got my message earlier, right? You know that Merodie is in isolation?"

"Yes."

"Do you know why?"

"It seems that our girl has a bad temper."

While waiting for the elevator, I punched Bobby Dunston's code onto the keypad and my cell phone automatically dialed his office number. As usual, he was happy to hear from me.

"What do you want?" he asked.

"Geez, Bobby. Can't a guy just call up to chat? You know, find out how you are, how the family is?"

"Yes, a guy can do that."

"Well, then."

"I'm fine, the family is fine."

"Good."

"Now, what do you want?"

"I need a favor."

"I knew it."

I told him about Nye.

"You don't want to go through Corrections, you could probably find him through DMV," he said.

"I don't have the time."

"More likely you don't want to pay the nine fifty it would cost to do a search."

"There's that, too."

"A guy with your money—you are so cheap."

"A penny saved is a penny earned."

"I'll get back to you."

"Thanks, Bobby."

———

I stepped aboard the elevator car and, as convention demanded, turned to face the doors. They were polished to a high gloss, and I was able to study the female rent-a-cop as well as the other passengers in the reflection. The rent-a-cop wore a regulation blue uniform shirt. It was a man's shirt, and I remembered that when I was with the St. Paul Police Department some of the female officers would complain that they didn't make a woman's shirt in the same material and in a sleeve length that fit them comfortably. They also complained about the regulation men's pants that had to be tailored because the manufacturer didn't make them to fit the female body. Suddenly I could see his reflection in the elevator doors—Benjamin Simbi—and he was slowly raising his hands . . .

I wasn't aware that the elevator car had reached the ground floor and that my fellow passengers had departed until the doors closed again and I was heading up. I quickly punched the button that stopped the elevator on the skyway level. I stepped out of the car so quickly that you might have guessed there was a bomb on board. Sweat streaked my forehead and puddled under my arms, and my breath was coming much too fast.

"I can't go on like this," I said aloud. "This is nuts."

People moving past me on the skyway must have heard what I said but pretended not to. Which didn't surprise me. I tend to ignore crazy people as well.

You need help, my inner voice told me.

The skyway system was an elaborate network of streets in the sky—enclosed pedestrian bridges connecting the downtown Minneapolis office towers with each other. It stretched fourteen blocks north to south and another ten blocks east to west, and its purpose was to move pedestrians from one building to another without making anyone actually step outside. It has reached the point where you now often see people commuting from their attached garages in the suburbs to one of downtown's many enclosed parking ramps in nothing more than shirtsleeves and light jackets regardless of weather conditions. I didn't care for the skyway myself and seldom used it, yet followed it just the same, walking east, then south, until I reached One Financial Plaza.

Dr. Jillian DeMarais—called Jilly by those of us who have slept with her—had a two-room suite on the twenty-third floor. There were four paintings hanging on the walls of the outer room—Degas, Matisse, Chagall, and van Gogh. The few times I had been there, I had always been attracted to the Degas. This time I stared at the van Gogh. It was a print of one of Vincent's swirling color-and-light shows, and for a moment I felt I actually knew what he was going for.

How crazy is that?

"May I help you?"

The voice came from the inner room, Jillian's office, and the place where she actually did her headshrinking. A moment later she was standing in the doorway.

"Rushmore McKenzie," she said slowly.

"Hi, Jilly."

I smiled at her, but she didn't smile back.

"I don't know what to say, McKenzie. The last time I saw you, you were telling me what a nasty person I was."

"I'm very sorry about that," I said, and I meant it. Yet it was hardly my fault. Jill had hypnotized me to help me recall a license plate number. While I was under, she asked why I had broken up with her several months earlier. I told her the truth.

"I never meant to hurt you," I said. "I tried to avoid hurting you."

"You did anyway."

"I know. I'm sorry. Truly I am."

"Tell me. If I'm such an unlikable human being, why are you here?"

"Jill, the dream came back."

Her hard face softened. Not much—you had to look closely to see it, yet it was there.

"I told you it would," she said.

"I know."

"Come in."

Jillian led the way deep into her office. She maneuvered around her impressive desk and sat down. She told me to do the same with a gesture of her hand toward a wingback chair in front of the desk.

"Is the dream exactly the same as before?" she asked.

"It started that way, but now . . . I see it in slow motion. Other elements have been added, too. Things that occurred after the shooting."

"But all dealing with the shooting."

"Yes."

"When did the dream return?"

"The other night, when I was in jail."

"Jail?"

"It was a bogus charge. I was in and out in just a few hours."

"But that's when the dream returned?"

"Yes."

"What did you do to get thrown in jail?"

"It was nothing—a hassle with a young cop who was out of line."

"He was out of line?"

"Yes."

"Not you?"

"Well . . ."

"Well?"

"I could have handled it better."

"I understand."

"Do you? Because I don't."

Jill pressed her fingers against her temples and sighed. "I should never have allowed you to quit therapy," she said. "I should never have agreed to date you." She closed her eyes and shook her head at the memory of it. When she opened them again, she reached for a notepad. "I'll give you the names of a couple of therapists I know. They're good men."

She emphasized *men*.

"Can't you help me?"

"Not this time."

"Can't you— Jill, I dream the dream when I'm awake now. I dreamt it just a little while ago in the elevator."

"McKenzie, I can't be your therapist anymore."

"Why not? You know my history."

"It's unethical, and this time there's no pretending that it isn't."

"Jilly . . ."

"Ahh, Mac. Don't call me that. Those days are over."

"Jilly, I need your help."

"I can't be the one to help you."

"That's silly."

"Those are the rules."

"Rules are made to be broken."

"Are they, Mac?"

"Some are."

"Some?"

"Yes."

"Why did you shoot Benjamin Simbi?"

"What do you mean?"

"Why did you shoot him?"

"He had a gun."

"What else?"

"What else? He was going to shoot me. Maybe the others as well."

"Tell me about it."

"You already know what happened."

"Tell me again. Tell me what you see in your dreams."

"I see him coming out of the convenience store. He's carrying a gun. A Smith & Wesson .38. I tell him to drop the gun. He doesn't drop it. Instead, he raises his hands to shoot me. I shoot him first."

"Go on."

"What else is there?"

"What happened after you shot him?"

"I made sure he was disarmed."

"What else?"

"I called it in."

"What else?"

"What do you mean?"

"What else happened?"

"You mean the two people who witnessed the shooting? One of them called me a racist."

"Why?"

"Because he said I executed the suspect. He said Simbi was raising his hands to surrender when I shot him."

"Was he?"

"Jill, I did everything right. I did everything the way I was taught to do it, the way I was trained. I did everything according to the book."

"According to the rules."

"Yes."

"And you never break the rules."

"Not those rules."

"Why not?"

"Break those rules and people die."

"Someone did die."

"I know. Don't you think I know that?"

"Simbi had a gun."

"Yes."

"You told him to drop the gun. He didn't."

"That's right."

"Instead, he raised his hands."

"Yes."

"The gun was in his hand."

"Yes."

"You killed him."

"Yes."

"Was he trying to surrender?"

"Yes . . . I mean . . . I don't know."

Neither of us spoke for a long time. The silence was filled with the shouting in my head.

You didn't know. You didn't. He could have been raising his hands to surrender. Only you didn't wait to find out. Instead, you shot him. You shot him because that was what you were taught to do. You shot him because those are the rules. A man has a gun. You tell him to drop it. He raises the gun, you don't take that chance. You shoot him. Period. There's no room for argument here. No discussion. You shoot first and ask questions later, because if you stop to ask questions first, you could be killed. Others—civilians, the people you're paid to serve and protect—they could be killed, too. So you discharged your weapon. A righteous shoot. A textbook shoot. Everyone agreed. Everyone that mattered, anyway. But everyone wasn't there, were they? You were there. And you don't know. *He could have been giving up.* It only would have taken a second to find out for sure. Except you didn't have a second. A second's too long. A second is an eternity. It's the difference between life and death. That's how you were trained to think, and you were trained well. All sevens all the time. If only he had dropped the gun. You gave him a chance to drop the gun. No, not a chance. A choice. It's stupid to give them a chance. They could kill you if you gave them a chance. So you say, "Drop the gun. Or die." Simbi didn't drop the gun. He raised his hands. And that was that. Except, what if . . . You never thought about that, did you? The great what if. You never considered the possibility. Not in all these years. The possibility that you were wrong. You only pretended to deal with it. Even when you first went to Jilly you were more interested in her intelligent eyes and athletic body than you were in dealing with the truth of that long moment in the convenience store parking lot. The truth that you might have made a mistake. An error in judgment. And when the dream went away, well, out of sight, out of mind, right? Only it wasn't out of mind, was it? And now. . . .

"Fuck."

I noticed for the first time that Jillian was on her phone.

"I'll send his file right over . . . No . . . I appreciate this, Doctor. Thank you."

She hung up the phone and wrote on a notepad printed with her name and address. After a few flourishes of pen against paper, she tore the top sheet off of the pad and gave it to me. I stared at it dumbly while she spoke to me.

"This guy is the best. Dr. John Ridge. You have an appointment with him at 10:00 A.M. next Tuesday. I'll arrange to send your file over."

"Jill—"

"Promise me that you'll keep the appointment."

"Jill—"

"Promise me, McKenzie."

"I did the right thing when I shot Simbi, Jill. It was the right thing to do."

"Promise me."

"I promise."

A few minutes later, Jill was leading me to her door. My cell phone rang, and I paused to answer it.

"Got a pencil?" Bobby Dunston asked.

"Just a sec." I took a pen from my pocket. "Go 'head."

Bobby recited Richard Nye's current address. I wrote it down on the back of the sheet of paper that Jillian had given me.

"Thanks, Bobby," I said.

Jill was staring at me when I deactivated the cell.

"Don't forget," she said. "Tuesday morning."

"I've been such a prick to you, Jilly, yet twice now you've been there to help me. Why is that?"

"Don't worry about it, McKenzie. You'll be getting a bill."

11

I took a deep breath, let half out, and began marching down a long corridor on red carpet that looked like it hadn't been vacuumed since Bill was president. I halted at an apartment door, made sure it matched the address Bobby had given me, and took another deep breath, steeling myself, getting ready. I was nervous, but I was also happy—happy to be out and doing. I didn't want to think about my conversation with Jillian. I didn't want to linger over the experience at all.

A murmur of voices came through the door, but no words could be understood. I stopped listening and knocked. A shadow passed over the spy hole and the door was yanked open. At the same time, a TV studio audience erupted into frenzied applause.

I took him in all at once, tall and husky, with imposing muscles—prison gym muscles. My first thought was that they were so big they would get in the way if he should ever attempt to throw a solid punch. He was wearing a white tank-top undershirt and jeans, both noticeably snug. He was tanned, but it wasn't a healthy color. There seemed to be a tinge of green mixed with the gold. As advertised, his hair was blond and cut close to the scalp so that he resembled a Nazi officer in a World War II movie. Self-indulgence was written in his eyes.

"Well, hello," he said.

"Mr. Nye?"

"Come in, come in."

"Don't you want to know who I am first?" I asked.

"Why?" Nye smirked as he examined the bruises on the side of my face. "Do you think I should be afraid?"

I didn't say.

"I know who you are," Nye said. "You're McKenzie. I've been expecting you."

Expecting me?

I entered the apartment. The room smelled of stale beer, old food, unwashed sheets, and dirty socks and underwear. I could see the kitchen from where I stood in the hallway. The sink contained dozens of encrusted spoons, forks, knives, pots, and pans, but no cups, saucers, or plates. Instead, next to the refrigerator was a wastebasket overflowing with paper plates and plastic cups, as well as TV dinner trays, pizza wrappers, and empty beer cans.

"This way."

Nye led me deeper inside a living room that contained an ancient overstuffed chair and a TV set mounted on a stack of newspapers three feet in front of it. One of those daytime group-hug programs was being broadcast—I didn't know which one. Nye moved to the set and reduced the volume to a dull roar while I glanced around. There was no other furniture, only small piles of rubble, mostly beer cans and empty chip bags. Compared to this mess, I figured my house looked like the Taj Mahal.

I gazed out a pair of sliding glass doors that led to a small balcony. A courtyard lay beyond. A young woman reclined on a lounge chair on her balcony directly across from Nye's. The harsh sunlight made her bikini-clad body shimmer like gold.

"Nice view," I said.

"Bitch doesn't even close her drapes, you believe that?" he said.

That's when I noticed the binoculars resting on the top of the TV.

Nye had a jailhouse smile, insincere and off center. I had no doubt that he would shove a shiv in my back for the change you could squeeze out of a parking meter. Or a turn with the woman he had been peeping.

"You said you were expecting me," I told him.

"You're workin' for Merodie. Yeah, I figured you'd be around."

"How do you know I'm working for Merodie?"

"I have my sources."

Nye's eyes moved away and began slithering about the apartment, taking a nervous survey of windows and doors with the watchfulness of a paranoid. Then they came back to me.

"So, what do you want?" he asked.

"When did you last see Merodie?"

Nye stuck his thumbs in his belt and swayed side to side, but slowly. He nodded his head while I spoke, like a boxer taking instructions from his corner, all the while staring straight ahead at his opponent, giving me the mad-dog. Despite the air-conditioning, a light film of perspiration glazed his forehead.

"I haven't seen her in over a year, and it ain't been long enough, that's for sure."

"A year?"

"Yeah, that's right."

"You're sure?"

"Why? What did Merodie say?"

"What makes you think Merodie said anything?"

Nye was angry. He moved in close. You could have covered us both with a small umbrella.

"You want a piece of me?"

My hand drifted to the opening of my jacket. The butt of the Beretta was only inches away, and in my mind's eye I could see Nye on his knees begging my forgiveness, begging for his life. I was sorely tempted by the image, wanted to see it played out in real life, and would have pulled the nine, yes, I would have, if not for a second image that immediately replaced the first—the disappointed visage of Dr. Jillian DeMarais shaking her head and admonishing me: *See what comes of playing with guns?*

I let my empty hand hang loosely at my side and stepped back, putting space between us, giving myself plenty of room for hands and feet should the need arise.

Nye laughed it up. No doubt he thought that moving away from him meant I was frightened. My temper started to beat a high-tempo riff deep in my throat, but I swallowed it under control.

"You lived with Merodie for a long time," I reminded him.

"Too long," Nye said.

"You beat her up."

He gave me a smile that knew both humor and cruelty. He chuckled when he said, "I wouldn't want it to get around, but the truth is, she beat me up. She put me in the hospital."

"You were in the hospital for a day. Merodie was in for over a week."

"I wouldn't know. I was in jail by the time she got out."

"How did you like jail?"

"It's a nice place to visit, but I wouldn't want to live there."

Nye thought that was so funny he laughed for a good half minute. It annoyed him that I didn't join in.

He asked, "So, what you want, McKenzie?"

"You were busted for dealing meth."

"What of it?"

"Who do you think ratted you out?"

"Coulda been lots of folks."

"Could have been Merodie."

"Coulda been. If it was, I gotta tell ya, it was the best thing she ever did for me."

"Is that right?"

"Dealin' meth was a good living, I ain't gonna lie to ya. Before I got boxed, I moved a whole pound of methamphetamine every month. At a thousand to fifteen hundred per ounce, that's a lot of tax-free coupons, baby! And I wasn't just dealing to speed freaks, neither. My customers, I had yuppie businessmen, bored housewives, college kids on a rave— anyone who wanted a two-, three-hour ride. Basically the same customers who made cocaine such a big thing. One customer, a woman, bought a quarter gram of crank the last Friday of every month cuz that was when she cleaned her house, one of those big Victorian mothers with three floors and eighty rooms. She'd swallow the meth and then go into a Speedy Gonzales routine, cleaning that sucker from top to bottom in a single day.

"Only between the Mexicans and the fucking bikers, it wasn't exactly a healthy lifestyle, you know? Besides, crank is bad, man. Messes you up real good. Makes you paranoid, makes you think everyone's out to get you. 'Course, in my case, that turned out to be true, didn't it?" The laugh again. "'Cept I don't know who dropped a dime on me. Coulda been Merodie. Coulda been the Mexicans. All I know is all of a sudden the county cops were all over my ass, searching my car until they found my stash hidden behind the hubcap. Eleven months, three weeks in the Anoka County Correctional Facility, doin' nothing but pumping iron and watching cable.

"But I got clean. I got outta the game. And I ain't goin' back. That ain't no lie. You could say I learned the error of my ways. I didn't get religion, okay? I didn't turn into no pussy in eleven months. Only meth, man, that ain't no way to live. Don't need no building to fall on me to learn that, no sir. And if Merodie is responsible for that, well, thank you, Merodie."

"Is that why you went to her house after you got out of the joint?"

"Who said I went . . . ?"

"Were you looking to thank her?"

"Fuck you, McKenzie. You think I don't know why you're here? I know why you're here. Merodie killed her old man and you want to jam me up for it. Ain't gonna happen. No way. Merodie's goin' down. And listen to me. Ain't nothin' you can do about it. You don't believe me, just ask my friend the county attorney."

Nye placed a fist on his hip, posing for me.

"You and Tuseman are pals, are you?"

"Hell, yeah. Me and him, we're like this." He crossed his fingers and held them up for me to see. "Fact is, he wants me to testify against ol' Merodie."

"Does he?"

Nye liked the surprised expression on my face and was disappointed that it didn't last. "That's right," he said. "So back off."

"Does he know you were at Merodie's house the day Eli Jefferson was killed?"

Nye paused before answering.

"I was not at—"

"You were seen."

He grinned as if he knew a secret I was too dumb to grasp. "I was nowhere near Merodie's house the day Eli Jefferson was killed, and there ain't nobody around no more to say otherwise 'cept Merodie, and who's gonna believe her?"

Ain't nobody around no more to say otherwise—how can he be so sure? my inner voice wondered. While I was thinking it over, Nye leaned in close.

"Besides"—he was still grinning—"I got an alibi."

"What would that be?"

"Not a what. A who. I was with my girlfriend that whole day."

"How convenient."

"Ain't it, though?"

"What's her name?"

"Debbie Miller."

Nye pulled a torn slip of paper from his pocket and shoved it at me. On it he had neatly printed Miller's name, home address, business address, and telephone numbers. He smiled when I took it from him.

"She's waitin' for you, too," Nye said.

"Is she?"

"I told you, you was expected."

The radio switched off automatically when I shut down the Jeep Cherokee in the parking lot of the small shopping complex at County Road 10 and Round Lake Boulevard. I wasn't listening to it anyway. Instead, I had been thinking angry thoughts about Richard Nye. Maybe he was involved in Jefferson's death, maybe he wasn't. I sure would enjoy sending him back to jail for something.

I entered the branch bank where Debbie Miller worked. The woman who sat at the desk nearest the door greeted me and asked if she could be of assistance. After a moment's discussion, she motioned to Miller, who had been watching me from her cashier station. Obviously she had been waiting for me. Nye probably called her the moment I left his apartment.

Debbie Miller was one of those women that men fell in love with at a distance, aroused like Pavlov's dogs, not by a bell, but by her shapely figure and lustrous shoulder-length red hair. It was only when they were close enough to plainly see her blemished skin, thin lips, large nose, pointy chin, and eyes that didn't seem to go together that they had second thoughts. She wore a tight, high-collared dark blue dress that was trimmed from hem to throat with gold buttons that emphasized her generous breasts, thin waist, and narrow hips. Yet there was nothing she could do to flatter her face. It was not even remotely pretty and certainly not helped by the excessive amount of artwork she put in around the eyes and lips.

Debbie approached cautiously, as if she were afraid of stepping in something. She was smiling, but only out of professional habit. I introduced myself and said I hoped that she would answer a few questions if it wasn't too inconvenient.

"Certainly," she said.

Debbie glanced about the bank. She spied an empty desk with two chairs in the corner near the windows and pointed the way with her sharp chin. I followed.

We sat in the chairs, turning them so we faced each other. Debbie's front teeth were stained with peach gloss from chewing on her lower lip, and her eyes were red and flashing. The rest of her face was pasty white and displayed as much animation as the Pillsbury Dough Boy. She began defending Richard Nye before I even asked about him.

"He's a good man," she said. Her voice was tense and she spoke very low, possibly so her coworkers couldn't eavesdrop. Or maybe she was embarrassed. Not once did her gaze reach mine.

"He's been in trouble, I know," Debbie continued. "That's in the past. That's behind him now. He wants to start over. People should let him start over."

"Fine with me," I replied as pleasantly as I could. "I hope he lives long and prospers, or whatever it is that that guy in *Star Trek* says."

Debbie was surprised by my response. "Really?" she asked.

"Why not?" I opened my notebook and balanced it on my knee. "I'm not looking to cause him any trouble. I just want to dot some i's and cross some t's for the lawyer I work for, that's all."

"Oh. But he really is a good man."

"How did you meet?"

"It was— It was about a month and a half or so ago, I guess. He had come in to cash his first check from the printshop where he got a job after . . . after he got out of jail. You know about that?"

"Yes, I know about that."

Debbie seemed relieved that she didn't have to tell the story.

"Anyway, he made me turn the twenties into tens and the tens into fives and then the entire roll into twenties again while he flirted with me, asking me if I lived alone, asking all kinds of personal questions while he made the other customers wait in line. I wore my hair up and he said, 'I bet you look gorgeous with your hair down instead of in that silly bun.' I'm not gorgeous. Even with my hair down. I know that. But I liked it when he said I was. Richard was the first man to show interest in . . . in a long time. I have to admit— I have to admit I enjoyed the attention.

"And he never lied to me," she added quickly. "He invited me to dinner that night and I accepted, and during dinner he told me about . . . about his past, about going to jail. He told me that that was all behind him now and he was looking for a strong, honest woman he could love. A woman who would forgive him his trespasses and help him stay on the straight and narrow while he made something productive of his life. That's what he said."

"No reason it can't be true," I told her, although I could think of several.

"He's a good man," Debbie told me again. As she spoke, she pulled absently at the collar of her dress, and for a moment I could see bruises around her neck where someone had choked her.

"I'm sure," I said, and smiled my most sincere smile. "I just want to know a couple of things."

"Okay."

"If you can confirm Richard's alibi, that's jake with me."

I nearly started to giggle. *That's jake with me?* Where did that come from? The phrase seemed to turn the trick, though. Debbie smiled— although it didn't seem to do her face any good—and leaned back in her chair.

"Let's see," she said. "You want me to tell you . . ."

"Saturday, August first. Everything from the moment you saw him until the moment he left."

"Let's see." Debbie closed her eyes and spoke slowly. "Richard stayed over Friday night and didn't go home until early Sunday morning."

"What did you do during all that time?"

"On Friday night we stayed in— We just stayed in." Debbie was blushing now. "On Saturday we had breakfast at my apartment and then he built a bookcase for me and then—"

"Did he bring the materials with him?"

"Huh?" Debbie's eyes flashed open.

"When he came over Friday night, did he have the building materials for the bookcase, or did he get them Saturday?"

Debbie was seized by a moment of panic and indecision. I guessed that she and Nye hadn't covered that when Nye concocted the alibi.

"He brought the supplies with him," Debbie said.

"Okey-dokey," I replied, pretending that I was barely paying attention. "Then what did you do?"

"Umm, we went shopping for clothes. We went to the Northtown Mall because we wanted to buy some clothes. I wanted to buy some clothes. But we couldn't find anything I liked so we didn't buy anything."

"What happened next?"

"We decided to stay in again . . ."

"Sure."

"We rented a couple of movies. I don't remember what. Something with Bruce Willis."

"Where did you rent the movies?" I asked.

"Rent them?"

"Yes. Where did you rent the movies?"

"At the mall."

"Northtown?"

"Yes."

"Which store?"

"Store?"

"Which video store did you rent the movies from?"

"I don't remember."

"Well, that's easy enough to check."

"It is?"

"Sure. They keep records, the video stores."

Debbie's face grew even more pale, and she began to tremble slightly as if she were caught in a sudden draft. She pulled at her collar again, and I saw more bruising. I wondered if it was confined only to her throat or if Nye had damaged other parts of her body as well.

"What did you do after you rented the movies?" I asked.

Debbie bit her lower lip. "We stopped at Leeann Chin for takeout and went back to my apartment and stayed there together eating and watching movies and stuff until about three Sunday morning." Debbie spoke as if she were trying to get it all out in a single breath.

I made a production out of *not* writing down her answer. I closed the notebook instead and gazed idly out the window while pretending I wasn't watching Debbie intently in its reflection. I sighed dramatically.

"You really love this guy," I said.

Debbie was surprised by the question.

"You do, don't you?"

"Yes," Debbie answered weakly.

"Even though he hurts you?"

Debbie's hand leapt to her throat. "He doesn't," she said.

"Sure he does. He beats you. What else does he do? Does he embarrass you? Humiliate you? When you make love, is it fun? Fun for you, I mean. I bet it's fun for him."

Debbie turned her head away. The beginning of tears formed at the corners of her eyes. I was sure they were more from tension than sorrow.

"Yet you still love him?" I said.

Debbie nodded.

"Do you love him enough to go to prison for him?"

"Go to prison?"

"That's what's going to happen if you keep lying for him."

"I'm not lying," Debbie protested. There wasn't much energy in her words.

I turned in the chair so I could look the woman directly in the eyes. "Debbie," I said. "There is no Leeann Chin at Northtown."

Debbie's mouth fell open for a brief moment, and I half expected her to call me a liar. Truth was, I didn't know if the popular chain of Chinese restaurants had a store in the mall or not. Then, instead of calling my bluff, Debbie closed her mouth and shook her head.

"Tell me the truth," I told her.

Debbie shook her head again; with her lips pressed tightly together, she looked like like an errant child afraid to speak.

"Are you lying because you love Nye or because you're afraid of him? Because if you're afraid of him—" I rested my hand on top of hers. She tried to pull it away, but I held on tight. "If you're afraid of him, well, that's something I can take care of."

"You?"

"It would be my pleasure."

Debbie shook her head.

"You don't know him. He's . . . He doesn't feel."

He'd feel it if I put my hands around his throat and squeezed like he obviously did to you, my inner voice said, but I kept it to myself.

"I can protect you," I said. "You have my word." I removed a business card from my pocket and thrust it into Debbie's hand. "That has my home and cell number."

Debbie took the card but refused to look at me.

"Listen," I said. "Listen to me, please. Will you listen?"

Debbie didn't respond.

"You're making a big mistake helping Richard Nye. He's no good, and he's going to hurt you. Hurt you worse than he already has. It's just a matter of time. I think you know that. Here's the thing—you can get away from him. Free yourself. I can help. The lawyer I work for can help, too."

"It's not that easy."

"It would be a lot easier now with us than if you tried to do it alone later."

I thought I saw Debbie's head nod.

"Think about what I said," I told her. "Keep the card. If you need help or if you just need somebody to talk to, you can call me. You can call me anytime you want. Anytime. Okay? Will you do that? I want to help you."

Again, I thought I saw Debbie nod her head.

"Please, please, don't lie for him anymore," I said. "It's okay if you lie to me. It's okay if you lie to yourself. No one is going to do anything about it. But if you tell the same lie to the police or the county attorney, you're going to be in serious trouble. Do you understand?"

For the first time, Debbie looked me directly in the eye.

"Yes," she said.

Richard Scott Nye was leaning against my Jeep Cherokee, his arms folded across his chest, when I left the bank. He was smirking.

"How'd it go?" he asked.

"Get your ass off my ride."

I was angry and looking for any excuse at all to pop him one. Or two.

"Isn't this one of those soccer-mom cars?" Nye asked.

I grabbed a fistful of his shirt and yanked him into the neutral zone between my vehicle and a Ford Taurus. The smile stayed on his face.

"Touchy," he said.

I unlocked the door.

"Wait, don't go," Nye said. "I want to ask you something."

I turned toward him.

"What did Debbie say?" he asked.

"She said exactly what you told her to say."

"What's that supposed to mean?"

"You should know that when you make up an alibi, people automatically figure you have something to hide. It's better to have no alibi at all."

"I didn't do nothing. I ain't got nothing to hide."

I moved to the open door of the Cherokee. Nye stopped me. He spun me around and gave me the look—unblinking eyes burning with their coldness, a run-or-die expression on his face.

"Listen, bitch," he hissed.

I pushed him away and stretched my arms, giving myself room to maneuver.

Nye kept smiling while he took a few steps backward. His eyes found something behind my left shoulder. I knew what it was before I turned to face it: the gentleman from the Regis Center for Art.

"Meet my little friend," Nye said, trying hard to sound like Al Pacino in *Scarface*.

"What did I tell you, shithead?" the big Hispanic said. I could see it in his expression—he kicked my ass before and he was going to do it again. "Didn't I tell you?"

I remained still and waited. He approached rapidly, without caution, without fear, his head and shoulders leading the way, his fists clenched but hanging loosely at his hips. I tried to look scared. I didn't speak. I didn't move. I didn't so much as take a deep breath for fear that he might see it coming. As soon as he was in range, I raised my right leg and snapped a front kick to his groin, putting my heel where it would do the most damage. I kicked him as hard as I could. The force of the blow caused me to lose my balance and I had to reach for the Cherokee to keep from falling.

A lightning bolt of pain caused the bad guy to halt in his tracks. His legs locked. His hands moved to cover his groin. His mouth fell open, but instead of screaming he gargled like a seal. While he was immobilized, I stepped forward and raised my leg again. This time I brought my foot down hard against his kneecap. It snapped like dry kindling, and he collapsed against the dirty asphalt.

I glanced behind me. Nye hadn't moved an inch. He stood there with his mouth open, watching as if he couldn't believe what he was seeing.

I grabbed a handful of my attacker's dirty hair and pulled up. His eyes turned toward me and I hit him with a closed fist. I hit him in the face again and again, remembering with each punch how he had pummeled me. I hit him until my knuckles were rubbed raw and began to swell. His blood dripped from my hand.

"Look at me." I didn't mean to shout. I just couldn't help it. "Look at me."

His eyes turned toward my face.

"If I ever see you again, I'll kill you." I hit him again just to make sure he was paying attention. "If you ever go near the lawyer again, I'll kill you. Do you understand? Nod your head if you understand."

He nodded.

"Don't make me tell you again."

I released him and stepped toward Nye. Despite his prison muscles, he wanted nothing to do with me. He brought his hands up to fend off my blows and lowered his head. I hit him anyway, the heel of my fist catching him under the nose.

Blood spurted. Nye's hands wiped frantically at it. Like the Hispanic he refused to whimper or cry out. *Probably something you learn in stir,* I decided. I pushed him hard and he splashed against the asphalt.

"Yeah, you're tough," I said. I slid behind the steering wheel of my vehicle and started it up. I backed out of the stall. Nye saw it coming just in time to roll out from under the rear wheels. When he looked up, I gave him a wink.

"Bitch," he said, but not too loudly.

As it turned out, Leeann Chin really didn't have a restaurant in the Northtown Mall or anywhere close to it. Which was good news because it blew Richard Nye's alibi all to hell and bad news because it was already late afternoon and I hadn't eaten lunch. I had my stomach set on Peking chicken with fried rice and had to settle for a chili dog with fries on the side at the Hot Dogs 'R Us stand.

Afterward I did a tour of the local video stores. There were six within two miles of the mall. None of the clerks who worked at the stores were willing to reveal whether or not Richard Nye or Debbie Miller had an account with them until I claimed that Richard and Debbie were suspected of renting films, dubbing them, and selling the copies to other video stores. Suddenly each store was happy—and relieved—to report that neither of them was a member.

It pleased me to gain information that way. *Just like a semiprofessional private investigator,* I told myself. I couldn't wait to tell G. K.

There were police cars with decals plastered on the doors parked all over the place: County of Anoka, City of Anoka, Coon Rapids, Blaine, Fridley, Columbia Heights, Spring Lake Park, Ramsey, the Minnesota Bureau of Criminal Apprehension. Mixed among them were other vehicles, mostly vans, with decals that were even more garish: WCCO, KSTP, KMSP, FOX NEWS, KARE-11. Some of them were even parked legally.

It took me five minutes to find an empty meter along East Main Street and another five to walk back toward the courthouse complex. As I approached the impressive crowd gathered in front, I thought, *Either Tuseman is giving a press conference or the circus is early this year.*

Turned out it was Tuseman. He was standing in front of the entrance, his jacket off, his tie loosely knotted, his sleeves rolled up, the wind in his hair, and smiling like a man who just won the Powerball. Flanking him were uniformed representatives of the various law enforcement organizations, including Lieutenant John Weiner. They all seemed excessively pleased with themselves as well.

Arranged around them was a semicircle of TV cameras and klieg lights and the operators of both. Still photographers from the *Minneapolis Star Tribune, St. Paul Pioneer Press,* and Associated Press stood or knelt next to them. TV reporters and representatives from WCCO-AM and Minnesota Public Radio, each of them armed with a microphone, were scattered between the cameras, all of them vying for attention while trying not to block the camera lenses. Print reporters, their notebooks opened and pens poised, stood in back. Common folk, like me, watched from a distance.

I saw Genevieve Bonalay. She waved me to her side.

"What's going on?" I asked.

"Shhh," she hissed.

We listened to Tuseman. He was just getting warmed up, talking about the scourge of the drug methamphetamine; talking about its devastating long-term effects on the individual and its tremendous damage to the community. He spoke about how methamphetamine was spreading across the country, fueled by small rural labs and super labs in the Southwest and Mexico. He spoke about how he, personally, was dedicating the resources of his office to finding and punishing those that would "bring this poison into Anoka County, who would use it to poison our children." It took him a long time to get to the point, and the media people were becoming increasingly antsy—just think of all the editing they'd have to do.

Finally, he announced what the media had been enticed there to hear. All of the law enforcement organizations present, under his direction, of course, had just that day executed the largest, most sophisticated "sting" in the history of Anoka County—Tuseman seemed to like that word, because he used it a lot. The sting resulted in the arrest of "eighty-seven individuals involved in the manufacture and distribution of methamphetamine, also known as crystal meth.".The individual city, county, and state police organizations combined their resources in a co-ordinated assault—guess who did the coordinating—on suspected meth labs and stash pads throughout the county. The arrests were made with "lightning speed and precision" starting early in the morning and ending about noon.

Tuseman said the sting was the result of an intensive fourteen-month-long investigation by his office and the Anoka County Sheriff's Department. He said that the arrests were carried out without incident. Not a single shot had been fired; not a single officer was injured. What's more, Tuseman believed that these arrests would most certainly lead to even more arrests as suspects gave up fellow dealers and addicts in an ef-fort to gain lenient treatment.

He said it was a great day for Anoka County, and he issued a warn-ing to anyone who would bring crystal meth into *his* jurisdiction: "There is nowhere you can hide."

"Muehlenhaus isn't going to like this," I said.

A TV reporter asked a question. "Is it true that you relied heavily on the services of an informant during your investigation and the subse-quent arrests?"

Lieutenant Weiner leaned in and whispered in Tuseman's ear. Tuse-man nodded and said, "I cannot comment on that at this time. The in-vestigation is ongoing, and we expect to make more arrests during the coming days."

It sounded like "Yes" to me.

I couldn't believe the change in Merodie. After just a few days of sobri-ety, a balanced diet, and plenty of sleep, Merodie Davies looked ten years younger. 'Course, that meant she still looked a decade older than her chronological age, but what would you expect? She had been in jail only a week.

She greeted us when we entered Interview Room 109. "Good afternoon, Ms. Bonalay, Mr. McKenzie." Her smile was bright and warm.

"Good afternoon to you, Merodie," G. K. replied. "How are you holding up?"

"Oh, I'm getting along just fine. People have been very nice to me."

G. K. pulled a red plastic chair out from under the wooden table and sat across from Merodie. She set her briefcase in front of her. I found a spot on the wall and leaned against it.

"Don't get too comfortable," G. K. warned. "I intend to get you out of here as soon as possible."

Merodie smiled again. "I'd appreciate that," she said. "So, what's new?"

"You tell us," G. K. said. "What's all this about you being isolated from your fellow inmates?"

"Not all of them," Merodie said. "Just one."

"Which one?" I asked.

"Linda." She said the word as if it were a sexually transmitted disease. "What happened was, I'm having breakfast. They serve breakfast here at 7:00 A.M. whether you're hungry or not, and who eats at 7:00 A.M.? Usually, I eat breakfast at, I don't know, noon. But the screws, they don't care. Eat or don't eat, it doesn't matter to them. Only no raiding the refrigerator later. So I'm like sitting there, trying to choke down this, this—I don't know what it was—oatmeal, I guess, and this woman sits next to me that I've never seen before, and the first words out of her mouth are, 'Those bastards don't care about us,' which is what I'm saying, okay? So I start talking to her. Linda was her name. Turns out she was my new roommate, which kinda surprised me cuz it's not like the jail is overcrowded. There are twenty-two cells in the housing unit—that's what they call it, a housing unit—but four of the eighteen cells that have one bed, they're empty, and so are three of the four cells that have two beds. So why do I have a roommate, cellmate, whatever? Only Linda, she seemed all right. She was polite and considerate, a good listener, so I'm like, 'Okay.'"

"What did you tell her?" There was genuine alarm in G. K.'s voice.

"Nothing," said Merodie. "I said— Linda wanted to know about Eli, and I told her what a swell guy he was and that I loved him to death." G. K. and I both cringed at the word. "She wanted to know if we ever fought. She said she and her old man fought all the time. I'm like, 'That wasn't the story with me and Eli.' I said we would yell at each other sometimes, but we never hit and we never stayed mad for long. You just couldn't stay mad at Eli, no way. Only Linda, she wouldn't leave it alone. She kept saying, 'You never clobbered him?' She said she heard that I clobbered him. She said she heard that I clobbered him over the head with a bat. I'm like, 'That isn't true,' but she kept pushing me and pushing me and so finally I pushed her."

"Pushed her?" I said.

"We were in the common area. That's this place where we can sit at these tables and chairs that are anchored to the floor so you can't move them. And Linda just wouldn't stop talking about Eli, about how he must have been a jerk or something for me to hit him with a bat even though I kept saying I didn't hit him with a bat, so I pushed her over a chair—and a table—maybe I slapped her a couple times, too. And the guards, the detention deputies, they're leaning on this railing on the second floor above us. They see us, and all of a sudden they're hitting alarm buttons and spraying Mace at me. Next thing I know, they're dragging me off to segregation or isolation or whatever they call it."

"Merodie," said G. K.

"Yeah?"

"When they let you back into population . . ."

"Yeah?"

"Don't talk to Linda again. Don't even say hello to her."

"Why not?"

"She's either an undercover cop," I said, "or more likely a police informant who's trying to generate evidence to use against you."

Merodie looked like a child who had just discovered how hot dogs are made. "Can they do that?" she asked.

We assured her that they could and often did.

"That sucks," she said.

We agreed.

"Merodie," I said. "We've been speaking to Priscilla St. Ana—"

She was off her chair and across the room in an instant. Her fists were clenched, and I was sure that she was going to hit me.

"I told you to stay away from her," she said.

"Remember when I told you I was your friend?"

"Yeah, so what?"

"So shut up and sit down." I was pointing at the chair. "I mean it."

"McKenzie . . ." G. K. said.

I kept pointing at the chair. "I'm in a real bad mood," I said.

"Your cold is better," Merodie said. "Did you use the Vicks like I said?"

I nearly began to laugh. If they were going to strap her in the electric chair, Merodie would be warning her executioner not to stand too close.

When she was seated, I asked, "Why didn't your tell us about your daughter?"

"Look at me, McKenzie. What do you see? You don't have to say it, I'll say it. You see a pathetic drunk. If I didn't know it before, I know it now what with writing my history on a chalkboard all week. Silk, she shouldn't have to suffer cuz of that. That's why I gave her to Cilla, so she wouldn't have to suffer. She's got a good life with Cilla. My life has been just one thing after another, and some of it ain't my fault but most of it is, and my daughter, she ain't gonna suffer cuz of that. So you, you just shut up now about Silk. I'm the boss, I'm the client." She glanced from me to G. K. and back again. "You have to do what I say, and I say you don't talk about Silk and you don't talk about Cilla. I don't want no one pointing at them and saying things. I'd rather— I'd rather go away than let that happen."

"Go to prison," I said.

"Yes."

"Merodie," said G. K. "I think we have an opportunity to make sure that doesn't happen."

"Oh yeah?"

G. K. brought her hands together in a way that made it seem like she was appealing to the deity and said, "There's something I want to say, but I don't want you to interrupt until I'm finished. Okay?"

Merodie nodded.

"Now bear with me," G. K. added. "It gets a little complicated."

Merodie nodded again.

"It would be extremely valuable to us if we could furnish the county attorney with a *second* suspect in Eli's death. Now, we wouldn't need to prove this second suspect actually committed the crime—"

"The crime is hitting Jefferson on the head with the bat," Merodie said.

"Yes, exactly. But, please, don't—"

"I won't."

"Interrupt." G. K. said. "A second suspect would interject *reasonable doubt* into the case to the point where the county attorney might consider *dropping it* altogether."

"Do you really think—"

"Merodie, please," G. K. said, exasperated.

"Sorry."

"The question is, *who* would that second suspect be? Now, in your initial statement to the police, the one you gave when they first brought you to Mercy Hospital, you said, well, wait a moment . . ."

G. K. unsnapped the locks on her briefcase, opened it, and withdrew a copy of the Supplementary Investigation Report filed by the deputy who had taken Merodie to Mercy Hospital. I was looking at the door to the interview room, wishing I were on the other side of it. I always knew that defense attorneys would do almost anything to get their clients off, including coaching them into what might or might not be a lie, but watching it happen—it made me feel like a co-conspirator, and I didn't like the feeling.

Finally, G. K. found the passage she was seeking and quoted from it. "You said, 'Some guy with blond hair came into the residence and got into a fight with him,' meaning Jefferson."

Merodie nodded.

" 'I asked Davies'—that's the deputy speaking now—'I asked Davies who that might be and she told me that she felt it could have been a former boyfriend. I asked for the name of the boyfriend but Davies claimed she could not remember.' Now, here's the thing, Merodie. If you *could* remember who that former boyfriend was . . ."

"I'm not sure."

G. K. leaned forward in her chair.

"I was wondering if the former boyfriend might have been *Richard Scott Nye,* who has *blond* hair. Now, he had good reason to come to your house. He had just been released from jail on a drug conviction, and he believes *you* informed on him."

"I did inform on him," Merodie insisted.

"Yes. So Nye could have come to your house that day . . ."

"Yes."

"To get revenge . . ."

"Yes."

"And got into a fight with Jefferson."

"Yes."

"The question is: *Do you remember* Nye coming to your house and getting into a fight with Jefferson? In your statement you said that a man with blond hair who could have been *a former boyfriend* got into a fight with Jefferson. Do you *remember* now that the man was Richard Nye? Because if you do, *we might be able to get you out of here.*"

G. K. said that last part very slowly and very carefully, then sat back in her chair and waited while Merodie worked it over in her head.

It took Merodie forty-seven seconds by my watch before she said, "It wasn't Richard."

G. K.'s mouth hung open, but nothing came out. She closed it again, licked her lips, and said, "Let me explain this again." She did, too. Slowly. Carefully. Yet in the end, Merodie's answer was the same.

"It wasn't Richard."

"But it could have been him," G. K. blurted.

Merodie leaned across the table, her elbows supporting her weight. Her voice was like the first frost of autumn.

She said, "You wouldn't want me to testify to something that wasn't true, would you, Ms. Bonalay? Isn't that, whaddaya call it, suborning perjury?"

In that moment I searched Merodie's face and found something there that I hadn't noticed before—raw intelligence. Merodie Davies had a plan. I just didn't know what it was.

12

Dark and menacing storm clouds were gathering at the horizon by the time we left Merodie, but they were far too distant to worry about. We were walking toward our cars on East Main Street.

"I don't know what to do," G. K. said.

"Merodie isn't leaving us many options," I said.

"I could use a drink. McKenzie, would you have dinner with me?"

The question was so abrupt that I stopped walking.

"I'm sober, clear-headed, and feeling no pain," G. K. said. "At least not much."

"I don't think that would be a good idea."

A look of disappointment flashed across her face. I liked the look. A woman disappointed because I was turning her down for a date—you bet I liked the look. I wished for a moment that Nina Truhler had seen it.

"Is it because we're working together? Because I could fire you."

"It's not that. It's . . ."

It's Nina, dammit. Say it!

"Gen, the day we met, just hours before we met, I broke up with a woman—or I should say, she broke up with me. She was, she is— The thing is, I cared for this woman very much and I still do. The ego in me thought that the hole she left in my heart could easily be filled, but it just isn't true. You could drive a truck through the hole, it's that big. You're very smart and very tough and very considerate and very beautiful, but in the end— I'd love to spend time with you, it would be time well worth spending, but in the end . . ."

"In the end I'd be the rebound girl," G. K. said.

"Something like that."

"And if the other girl called, you'd go running to her."

"It's not very fair to you."

"At least you're being honest. Most guys wouldn't. Most guys would take advantage."

"Don't think I haven't considered it."

"I want to thank you anyway."

"For what?"

"For all those 'verys' you recited before. Especially the very smart and very tough. I don't always get credit for that."

"I'm sorry, Gen."

"Don't be. But you know, McKenzie, if that hole you're talking about ever shrinks to a manageable size—you know where I live."

"Yes, I do."

I didn't feel like returning to an empty house, so after I left G. K., I grabbed some fast food—which wasn't particularly fast and didn't taste much like food—and drove over to the Coffee Grounds coffeehouse in Falcon Heights and bought myself a double café mocha. Real Book Jazz was onstage, and Stacy, the pretty college girl who was fronting the group, gave me a little wave as I claimed a small table in the back. She did this partly, I'm sure, because I was a fine figure of a man—just ask G. K.—but mostly because I have been known to stuff a fifty into the tip jar. I waved back.

Real Book Jazz wasn't a group so much as it was an idea. Once a week a ragtag collection of amateur musicians would gather at the coffeehouse to play for tips and the love of music. Nearly anyone who had mastered the "real book," that near mythical compilation of standards that all jazz musicians are expected to know, was invited to sit in. As a result, the musicians changed from week to week and sometimes even from set to set. On this night a Lutheran pastor, a social worker, a part-time studio musician, a high school music teacher, and a bus driver had joined Stacy, a biochemistry major who was on summer break. They were riffing on "Scotch and Soda," the old Kingston Trio tune, and really had it going. The xylophone player in particular was outstanding, and I thought, *Nina should hear this guy.*

It was Nina who had discovered Coffee Grounds, who had first brought me to listen to Real Book, although I strongly suspect that she preferred the chocolate-covered coffee beans they sold to the music. Nina had a much more discerning ear than I had, and she prized consistency. Real Book Jazz, for all its virtues, was far from consistent. Yet sometimes they played the most extraordinary music—if only for a few moments—leaving behind a feeling of pure joy. In that regard the experience wasn't so much different from watching a journeyman ballplayer going yard in the late innings with the game on the line. It put a jump in your step and filled your heart with the sense that all things were possible.

That's why Nina valued out-of-the-way joints like this.

That's why I valued them as well.

God, I missed her.

Certainly, I had gone more than a few days without seeing or speaking to Nina in the past. Yet knowing she was out there and available had been reassuring to me; I always knew that I wasn't alone. Now that we were on the outs, suddenly I understood the anguish behind the Cole Porter song Stacy was singing from the stage—"Love for Sale."

It had been nearly two years since Nina and I met, and already I was having a difficult time remembering what my life had been like before she came along. There were things I had done prior to meeting her, events I had witnessed—Ella Fitzgerald at Northrup, Wynton Marsalis and Itzhak Perlman jamming on "Summertime" at Brilliant Corners, James Earl Jones playing Othello opposite Christopher Plummer's Iago at the State Theater, the Minnesota Wild skating to the brink of the Stanley Cup Finals, the Twins winning their second World Series. Only here's the thing—when I recalled these moments, and so many others, I nearly always saw Nina. She wasn't there; she couldn't possibly have been there. Most of these events occurred before I knew her, some when I was a still a kid. Yet somehow, in my memory, Nina is always at my side. Why was that?

I took a long pull of the mocha.

Real Book completely botched "Autumn Leaves"—that's what happens when you don't rehearse—did a decent job with "All of Me," and just soared on "The Girl from Ipanema." It was when Stacy let out that famous sigh that I decided I had had enough.

I dropped a twenty in the tip jar, bought a half-pound bag of chocolate-covered coffee beans, and went looking for Nina.

The storm the weathergeeks had been predicting all day had finally arrived, but it was coming in like a lamb, so I didn't bother with an umbrella as I crossed the parking lot and entered Rickie's. The sound of a jazz trio playing in the upstairs dining and performing area greeted me at the door, piano, bass, and percussion doing a splendid job covering the

Johnny Mandel tune "Suicide Is Painless." Half the tables in the downstairs lounge were occupied, and the customers seemed more animated than usual. I wondered briefly if the coming thunderstorm had anything to do with it. I found Nina Truhler behind the bar. Seeing her filled me with an almost adolescent glee that I instinctively worked to hide.

She and Jenness were both chatting with a customer, his back to me. For a moment I thought it was Daniel. I was relieved when I discovered it wasn't. As I approached, Nina moved casually down the bar, stopping in front of a few unoccupied stools. I greeted her there.

"McKenzie, nice to see you," she said. From the tone in her voice, she could have been welcoming any one of her regulars.

"Hi."

I presented her with the chocolate-covered coffee beans.

Nina took the bag from my outstretched hand, opened it and sniffed. "French vanilla, my favorite," she said without emotion, even as my own heart leapt. "You're spoiling me."

"That's the plan."

Jenness stayed with the customer but watched us. When she noticed me noticing her, she gave me a thumbs-up signal.

"What happened to your face?" Nina asked. "Did you get into a fight?"

"Yes."

"Are you okay?"

"You should see the other guy," I told her.

"That doesn't answer my question."

"Yes, I'm okay. It looks worse than it is."

"Good. That's good. So . . ."

"Yes?"

"Did you get my phone message?" she asked.

"I did. I tried to call back. You weren't answering."

"When did you call?"

"About eight this morning."

"McKenzie, you know the hours I keep. After I get Erica off to school I go back to bed."

"I didn't think. Why . . . ?"

"Yes?"

"Why did you call?"

"Oh, I don't know. Just to see how you were."

I nodded as if her answer actually told me something.

Nina set the coffee beans on the bar top. "What brings you out tonight?" she asked. "You know it's going to rain."

My plan on the drive over was to grovel. Grovel without shame, embarrassment, or pride. Only seeing her in front of me— The Nina I had come to know and love had no respect for groveling. I tried a different approach.

"I was thinking . . ."

"Yes?" she said.

"For the last couple of days all I've been thinking about is you, and us, and how much I messed up the other night, because . . ."

"Because?"

"Because I didn't tell you what I wanted to tell you, and I've been thinking about it ever since."

Nina leaned across the bar. "What did you want to tell me?" she said.

I bent toward her, slipped my hand behind her head, and held it there as I kissed her mouth. The kiss wasn't quick, but I broke it off before it could become something more.

"That's what I wanted to tell you."

I stepped back. I smiled at her. She smiled back, but it lacked the light-up-the-world brilliance that I had hoped for, that I was accustomed to. I had blown it.

"I'm sorry," I said. I took another step backward. "I should go."

"Hey," Nina said. Then, "Hey," again.

She rounded the bar and closed the distance between us. Her head listed forward, hesitated, then pushed forward again and kept going until her lips were pressed firmly against mine. She kissed me for a long time. The world changed with her kiss. Suddenly, I was an exhausted explorer discovering a new land. I liked it there. I wanted to live there.

When our lips parted, she smiled her usual confident smile and said, "I like men who know how to express their feelings."

I hugged her tight and muttered her name a few times.

"That's what I'm talking about," Jenness announced from behind the bar. We both turned toward her, and she immediately glanced up and down and around, looking anywhere but at us, pretending she wasn't eavesdropping. It was then that the storm finally broke over St. Paul. Rain fell, intermittently at first, then in torrents. Lightning flashed, thunder roared.

"Would you like to stay for the storm?" she asked.

I nodded and grinned, a child accepting a special treat.

She guided me to an empty table and we both sat.

"I want to thank you for not slugging Daniel the other night. I know you wanted to."

"Not in your place," I said. "Never in your place."

"I know you were angry."

"I wasn't angry at him. Well, yes, I was angry at him, but mostly I was angry at something else."

"You were angry because I was dating him."

"You have every right to date whomever you wish."

"No, I don't. After all the time we've been together—listen—the only reason I did it, the reason I had dinner with him the first time, was because he had asked when we were at the ball. The man dropped everything to help me out. How could I refuse?"

"What about the second time?"

"I did it to annoy you," Nina said. "I saw you parked outside my house, McKenzie. I recognized your car. You were spying on me. That was just plain psycho."

"I know, but . . ."

"But what?"

"Why did you invite what's-his-name into your house? Why didn't you shake hands and say thanks at the door?"

"I told you. I saw you parked outside and I wanted to give you something to think about. If you had waited another five minutes, you would have seen me push him out the door."

"Oh."

"Oh," she said, her tone mocking.

"Sorry," I said.

"Why did you do it?"

"I was concerned . . ."

"Concerned for my safety?"

"No, for *my* safety. There hasn't been a moment since we met when I wasn't aware that you could do better than me."

Nina waved a playful finger at my face and smiled. "That was a good line," she said. "I like it."

"It also has the virtue of being true."

"Ahh, McKenzie. It isn't true. If you'd been involved with as many men as I have, you would know that."

"How many men . . . ?"

"Never mind."

"I shouldn't have been jealous," I said.

"I shouldn't have given you reason to be jealous."

"I should have realized that you were *trying* to make me jealous."

"We need to work on our communication skills."

"Talk more."

"Yes. For example . . ." Nina gently stroked my cheek with her fingertips. "Tell me about your face."

"I had a run-in with a guy yesterday, no big deal."

"I think it's a big deal," she said.

So I told her about it; told her about yesterday and today, told her everything. Except I didn't tell her about my dream—maybe some other time. And I didn't tell her about Benny—maybe never.

"You take too many chances," Nina said. "This preoccupation with doing favors for others. Did you ever think of just working with a charity? The American Red Cross is always looking for volunteers."

"You don't think they take chances?"

"Not like you. Besides, they're actually concerned with helping people."

"I'm not?"

"I think you spend most of your life trying not to be bored."

"You think I'm an excitement junkie?"

"I think you need something to hold your interest."

"You hold my interest."

"You need more."

"All I need is love."

"Love?"

"I love you."

"Will you jump-start my car?" Nina said.

"What?"

"Will you mow my lawn, will you clean my gutters, will you give me sex?"

"What are you talking about?"

"I love you—the phrase. Sometimes it's a request. Sometimes it's an excuse. I love you, but I have to leave now. I love you, but I have to go to work, catch a plane, play golf. It asks questions. 'We're all right, aren't we?' 'You love me, too, don't you?' It means we'll go shopping, we'll go to the party, we'll visit your mother, we'll get a cat. It rarely means, 'I have an intense affectionate concern for you.'"

I grasped her hands. Holding them in mine was like mending a break in a power line—it allowed electricity to surge through me.

"I have an intense affectionate concern for you," I said.

"I have an intense affectionate concern for you, too," she said.

She leaned in close and we kissed.

"I suppose this is all my fault," she said when we finished. "I won't marry you because of my previous experience with the institution. You won't live with me because it's unfair to my daughter. So we date."

"Girlfriend and boyfriend."

"But since we have no formal commitment, theoretically we're allowed to see other people, and the freedom scares us. Isn't that why you were frightened about Daniel?"

"I wasn't frightened."

"No?"

"I was jealous."

"Big distinction."

"Hmmph."

"Hmmph, what?"

"I've been thinking lately that when it comes to relationships, we never actually leave high school."

"We're not kids anymore, McKenzie. We're mature adults."

"Sometimes I forget."

"In high school, it's impossible to hold our partners to their promises. There's just too much future in front of us and it's too uncertain. Adults—we're expected to keep our vows."

"What vows are those?"

"To have and to hold from this day forward, for better, for worse, for richer, for poorer, in sickness and in health, to love and to cherish, forsaking all others until *you* tell me otherwise. That vow."

"Or until *you* tell me otherwise," I said.

Nina extended her hand.

"Promise?" she said.

"I do."

We shook hands and held hands and spent several moments staring at each other.

"If we were in high school, I'd want to sit at your table," I said.

"I'd save you a place."

Jenness appeared. She set a Bailey's on the rocks in front of Nina and a Summit Ale in front of me.

"So," she said. "Are you guys good again?"

"Yes," said Nina.

That single word filled me with relief and joy that I simply don't have the words to express.

"Then I win," said Jenness.

"Win what?" I asked.

"The pool. We were all betting on how long it would take you guys to get back together."

"Really? How much?" I asked.

"Fifty-five dollars."

"A tidy sum."

"Don't you have work to do?" Nina asked.

"Ah, love," Jenness said, and returned to the bar.

"Fifty-five bucks," Nina said. "If I had known there was a pool . . ."

"This has all been so silly," I said.

"You're the one who was parked outside my house."

"You're the one who went out with some loser."

"You're the one who stood me up for an important date."

"I told you, I was in jail."

"I told you, it's always something."

"Arrrrgggggggg!"

My cell phone played the opening notes to Beethoven's "Ode to Joy." I untangled my fingers from Nina's—it took much longer than was necessary—and reached into my jacket pocket. I read the name on the caller ID and glanced up at Nina.

"I need to take this."

She nodded.

"This is McKenzie," I said into the mouthpiece.

Nina leaned forward to listen.

"Yes, Debbie. Are you all right? You sound . . . When . . . ? Did you call the police? Yes, yes, right now . . . You should . . . Okay . . . Okay, yes, I'm coming . . ."

The tone of my voice told Nina that it was trouble. She rested a reassuring hand on my wrist.

"Tell me where you are . . . Where is that?"

I pulled a pen from my pocket. Nina slid a napkin in front of me. I nodded my thanks to her and started writing.

"Tell me again . . . Yes, I have it. I'm coming, Debbie. I'm coming right now."

I deactivated the cell and turned my attention to Nina. "I need to go."

"McKenzie . . ." She let my name hang there. Then, "Another damsel in distress?"

" 'Fraid so."

"Is there anything I can do?"

"Forgive me."

"There's nothing to forgive."

I stood and moved toward the front door.

"McKenzie."

I looked back.

"Call me when you can. And for God's sake, be careful."

Nina couldn't have said anything more perfect.

I blew her a kiss and stepped out into the rain.

13

I took Selby Avenue to Dale Street to I-94 to Highway 280 to I-35W to Highway 10 to Anoka County Road 47, driving at speeds that invited disaster. A hard, slanting, remorseless rain, driven on by a steady wind, continued to fall from the northwest, and I drove straight into it. Water cascaded in sheets down the windshield, the wipers barely keeping up. Often I was forced to reduce my speed to as little as 20 mph. Light shimmered on my windows; the red taillights of the vehicles in front of me softened to pink smudges, and oncoming traffic seemed like a mirage. Gutters were clogged. Storm sewers backed up and overflowed, creating virtual ponds on the streets. All of it seemed designed to slow me down.

It took a long time before I could find Debbie Miller's apartment building in Coon Rapids—I passed it twice—and the delay tied painful knots in my stomach. Finally, I turned into the parking lot, splashing water that had pooled at a sewer grate. I found an empty spot at the end of a long line of cars and stopped. It was very dark beyond the ragged blur of light coming from the building's foyer. There were no people anywhere, no dogs—why would there be? I made a run for it, the heavy rain making noisy little thuds on my shoulders and bare head. I attempted to vault a puddle and failed. Water drowned my shoes and soaked the bottoms of my jeans. I reached the doorway and entered the foyer. There was no security system, no locked doors to get past. I checked the mailboxes for Debbie's apartment number, found it, and bounded up the stairs to the second floor. Debbie Miller's apartment was at the end of the corridor. The door was open.

I pulled my Beretta from its holster and thumbed off the safety.

Debbie was sitting in a chair, hunched forward, one hand clutching her stomach, the other supporting her head. She was swaying slightly from side to side, and her breath came in labored, sobbing gasps. The sight of her sent a shiver through me. Yet I didn't rush to her side. I had been too well trained for that. Instead, I quickly searched the apartment, the nine-millimeter leading the way, checking all rooms and closets. The place was surprisingly neat. Except for the tiny bloodstains that he had splattered on the arms and cushions of Debbie's chair, Nye had done his work without muss or fuss.

After I assured myself that we were alone, I went to Debbie and knelt next to the chair.

"I'm here," I said.

"I can't stop crying," Debbie managed to sputter.

I didn't blame her. Debbie's eyes were red and bruised. Her nose was broken, and her nostrils were caked with blood—she made sucking noises trying to breathe through it. There was a gaping hole in her mouth where two teeth had been. The right side of her jaw was swollen and discolored. The body I had admired only hours earlier now seemed frail and brittle. The way Debbie clutched her stomach, I knew some serious damage had been done there.

Debbie's voice was a hoarse whisper, and she spoke so low that I could barely hear her over the wind and rain that rattled the apartment windows.

"He hurt me," Debbie said. "He hurt me." Then, "He made me ashamed."

Her sobbing ceased, replaced with a quiet agony. I hugged her shoulder. I wanted to touch her in a way that would make all the pain and suffering disappear, but I didn't know how. Better not to try. *Vulnerability,* my inner voice told me, *is the curse of all those who care.*

"I'll call an ambulance," I said, although in this weather I wouldn't have wanted to make book on how long it would take to arrive. The plan was nixed anyway.

"Take me . . . hospital," Debbie begged.

"Yes."

As I helped Debbie to her feet, the phone rang. We both swung toward the sound, as startled as if it had been a gunshot.

"It's him, it's him," Debbie muttered through cracked and torn lips.

"Good," I told her. "That means he's not here."

I lifted her in my arms. The phone was still ringing when I carried Debbie across the threshold like a bride, hooking the apartment door closed behind us with my wet shoe.

Rain continued to fall, but not as relentlessly. Visibility had improved, and the streetlamps, imperceptible before, had turned each puddle into a silver pool. I struggled with Debbie's weight, staggering a few times as I carried her across the parking lot to the Jeep Cherokee. I leaned the nearly unconscious woman against the back door, holding her upright with my arm and shoulder while I fumbled for the front door latch.

The *crack* of a handgun—a sound as angry as thunder—caused me to drop to the wet asphalt, pulling Debbie down with me. She cried out so loudly that I thought at first she had been hit, but it was her injuries that caused the pain, not a bullet. I held her close, her face pressed against my wet shirt, and listened. Nothing. For a moment, I thought I had imagined the gunshot. Then I felt movement to my right. I spun toward it. There was no sound save the rumble of raindrops beating on the SUV.

"Get under the car," I told Debbie. She looked at me, but in the darkness I couldn't read her expression. "Get under the car," I repeated. She moaned and choked as I pushed her beneath the Cherokee. It was a tight fit, but there was just enough clearance.

I raised myself into a squatting position and leaned against the car door, gun in hand, and cautiously lifted my head above the hood. Raindrops caromed off the surface and splashed my eyes.

"Where are you?" I muttered.

As if in answer, the handgun exploded again and a bullet smacked the front quarter panel of the car directly behind me. I fired my gun in reply; fired at nothing, hit nothing. I fired it only for the sound it made. I wanted whoever was shooting at me to know I had a gun, too. I wanted him to know that I would use it.

I ducked and rolled across the asphalt to the rear of the Cherokee. The rain had flattened my hair and soaked my jacket, shirt, and jeans; the shirt and jeans were sticking to my skin. None of that registered at the time as I moved quickly behind the row of vehicles, keeping low, moving in the direction of the gunshot.

The rain mixed with cold perspiration. Muscles tightened in my neck and shoulders; my lungs compressed until I was taking only short sips of air; the pounding of my heart was loud in my ears; fear built. Yet my mind remained clear and pliant. The moment held no confusion for me. I understood what I must do and how to do it. For that I said a silent prayer of thanks to my skills instructors at the police academy and for what experience I had gained over the years.

I passed half a dozen cars and vans, poked my head up a second time. I saw nothing.

"Where are you?" I asked again, dragging breath into my lungs.

I moved several more car lengths.

Still nothing.

Then a scream, loud and painful.

Again I refused to panic. Instead of rushing to Debbie's side, I moved slowly and cautiously in a half-crouch back to the SUV. I halted at the rear bumper. A man was standing between my car and the one parked next to it, his gun pointed more or less at the pavement.

"Come outta there," Nye growled. His face was ominous, with thin lips curled over teeth made unearthly bright by the glow of the streetlamps.

I raised my nine and leveled it at his chest.

"Drop the gun, put your hands in the air," I shouted.

Nye looked at me. I had surprised him. Except not enough to drop the gun.

For a single instant that seemed much, much longer, the blood behind my eyes pulsated with a terrible sense of déjà vu.

Please, God, not again, my inner voice pleaded.

And then, "DROP THE FUCKING GUN!"

Nye was as startled by my voice as I was. I was moving toward him now, never lifting the front sight of the Beretta from the center of his chest.

"DROP THE FUCKING GUN. DROP THE FUCKING GUN. I'LL KILL YOUR MOTHERFUCKING ASS! I'LL KILL YOU, MOTHERFUCKER!"

Nye dropped his gun.

"ON YOUR KNEES. ON YOUR KNEES. HANDS BEHIND YOUR FUCKING HEAD. DO IT NOW."

I continued to scream at him until Nye knelt and laced his fingers behind his neck. I shoved him forward. He sprawled spread-eagle on the wet asphalt. I pressed my knee against his spine and jabbed the barrel of the nine against the base of his skull.

"Don't shoot me, please, don't shoot me," Nye said.

I thought how different my life might have been if only I had screamed obscenities at the first guy.

14

I was cold. I tried not to shiver in my rain-drenched clothes, my arms wrapped tightly across my chest, only there was nothing for it. No one had offered me a dry jacket to put on, or a blanket, or even a towel to wipe away the water that dripped from my hair and sloshed in my shoes. Certainly no one could be bothered to turn down the air-conditioning that added to my discomfort. Yet I refused to ask for those things. I didn't want these people to think I was a wimp. Instead, I chose to suffer in silence. Well, not in complete silence. My teeth chattered periodically, and try as I might I couldn't silence them.

Of the three people standing next to me in the small, unfurnished chamber, only one seemed to notice—an officer whose name I couldn't remember—and then only because he was afraid the video camera he was operating would pick up the noise. The other two, G. K. Bonalay and David Tuseman, were too busy watching the scene that unfolded on the other side of the one-way mirror to care.

The interrogation room of the Anoka County Sheriff's Department served also as a conference room. Fluorescent lights hidden behind marbled plastic ran the entire length of the ceiling. The opposite wall was a huge blackboard, and an audio-visual system mounted on a metal stand had been rolled into the corner. In the center of the room, surrounded by a dozen chairs, was a long table. Richard Nye sat silent and alone at the head of the table. He knew there were people behind the rectangular mirror—I bet he could feel our eyes upon him—only he refused to give us the satisfaction of looking our way, not even when he heard a loud sneeze from behind the glass.

"Bless you," G. K. said automatically, staring ahead.

"Yes, bless you," said Tuseman.

Like you guys care, my inner voice replied.

The door of the interrogation room opened and Assistant County Attorney Rollie Briggs stepped inside. He had been popping up throughout this case, yet this was the first time I had seen him. I wasn't impressed. He was middle-aged and flabby, about half a foot shorter and sixty pounds heavier than Nye.

Yeah, I can see how a clever beauty like G. K. could wrap him around her baby finger.

Briggs was carrying a yellow legal pad. The noise he made as he settled into a chair, dropped the yellow legal pad on the table, and swiveled to face Nye at the table's head sounded distant and tinny over the cheap speakers in the room behind the mirror.

"Where's Tuseman? Where's the county attorney?" Nye asked.

Tuseman stiffened. I knew he was having second thoughts about permitting us to witness the interrogation. I have no idea why he allowed it in the first place, except G. K. kept calling him David and "boss" and he kept calling her Genny and "kid." I had the impression that they had been close when she worked for him as an intern.

"If he's smart, he's in bed," Briggs answered.

"I want to talk to him," Nye said.

"But does he want to talk to you?"

"He's my attorney."

"Your attorney?"

"Yeah. Him and me had a deal."

"What deal was that?" Briggs asked casually.

"I was supposed to give up all the bikers and Mexicans I knew who dealt meth in the county," Nye said. "When I was in jail I was supposed to make as many contacts with the crankheads as I could. When I got out of jail I was supposed to lead you all to them. I did that. I did my part."

"And in return you drew less than a year in county jail instead of five in state prison," Briggs said. "What does that have to do with this?"

"We had a deal."

"Deal's done."

"Is it? He's gonna want me to testify, ain't he? Well, maybe I'll get a bad case of whatchacallit, amnesia."

"Maybe you'll go to prison for the rest of your life."

"Lookit," Nye shouted, stopped, lowered his voice, said, "Lookit, along with my testimony against the bad people, he said he was going to take care of me if I gave him some testimony against Merodie Davies."

"The county attorney said that?"

Behind the mirror, Tuseman said, "I never."

"He said he wanted me to testify that Merodie beat on my ass with a softball bat, which is true, so help me," Nye said. "He said he wanted me to say that Merodie had homicidal tendencies. He said he was gonna put her away, which was all right with me."

"Why did he want to put her away?"

"I don't know, man. Somethin' about teaching a lesson to some old guy thinks he's God. Lookit, I'm still willing to do that."

G. K. asked, "Are you getting all this?"

The camera operator nodded.

Tuseman made a noise that sounded like a growl. He formed a fist, but resisted putting it through the wall. Instead, he stared at his assistant.

"What does the sonuvabitch think he's doing?" he asked no one in particular.

Screwing you over, my inner voice replied. *He's been doing it all along.* I gave G. K. a sideways glance. *Was it for Muehlenhaus or for her?* I wondered. *I would like Briggs better if I knew he was doing it for her.*

Briggs said, "How was the county attorney going to take care of you?"

"He said he'd watch out for me, keep me out of trouble," Nye said.

"Tsk, tsk, tsk," G. K. clucked just loud enough for Tuseman to hear.

"Yeah?" said Briggs. "Well, that was Thursday, before you started beating up on women. Today is Friday. On Friday all the assholes belong to me."

"Fuck you," Nye said.

Briggs reached out with a flat, upturned hand. He made sure Nye got a good look at it as he slowly curled his fingers into a tight fist.

"I got your balls right here and I feel like squeezing," Briggs said.

Nye cut loose with a long string of obscenities, although he didn't put much effort into it.

"You want a lawyer?" Briggs asked. "We'll get you a lawyer."

"I don't need to pay some fancy-ass lawyer to cut a deal," Nye insisted. "I can make my own deals."

"You have the right to remain silent. Anything you say—"

"I know my fucking rights," Nye said. "I've been Mirandized a dozen times already."

"Just so you understand."

"Let's just get on with it, all right?"

"Let's."

Briggs removed a lacquered pen from his jacket pocket and slowly rotated the barrel to lower the tip into writing position. He turned the yellow pad on the table in front of him until it rested at a perfect angle before reviewing it. Nye beat an impatient rhythm on the tabletop with his fingers while he waited.

"First of all, you're already going to prison for five years," Briggs said. "That's prison. Not jail. You violated the terms of your parole the second you picked up the gun."

"Shit," Nye muttered.

"You have a criminal history score of three," Briggs added. "Do you know about the criminal history score? How it works?"

"Yeah."

"In Minnesota, the more crimes you're convicted of, the greater your score."

"Yeah."

"The greater your score, the more time you do for each conviction."

"I said I knew. Jesus Christ, get on with it."

"All right," Briggs said, not flustered at all and in no particular hurry. "We have you for first degree assault—"

"First degree?"

"Ms. Miller is in Mercy Hospital with a broken nose, fractured jaw, two broken teeth, three cracked ribs, and a ruptured spleen. Where I come from, that constitutes first degree."

"Shit," Nye said.

"With your score, that's one hundred and twenty-two months. We also have you for two counts of second degree assault for shooting at Ms. Miller and Mr. McKenzie. 'Course, if you had hit 'em, then it would be first—"

"Fuckin' McKenzie was shooting at me."

"Are you pleading self-defense?"

"I'm just saying."

"Well, let's say that charge holds up. We could go for attempted murder instead. You beat up Miller. Miller calls McKenzie. McKenzie comes running. You ambush him. Yeah, I think I can make a case for attempted murder. How 'bout you? Want me to try? It'll screw up the math, but I'm willing."

"Shit."

" 'Course, if we had been real lucky, McKenzie would have splattered your brains all over the parking lot—he's done it before."

I continued to shiver behind the glass.

Nye smiled the uncontrollable smile of a man who knew he was in deep trouble and it was just getting worse.

"Something funny, Nye?" Briggs asked.

Nye shook his head.

"I'll tell ya what I think is funny," Briggs said. "First degree assault, plus two counts of second degree assault at thirty-four months each, plus the five years for your parole violation . . . Why, Richard. You're going to prison for twenty-one years."

Nye studied Briggs's beaming face for a moment.

"Fourteen years if I get a third off for good time," he said.

"That's right."

"Fourteen years if the judge adheres strictly to the Minnesota Sentencing Guidelines."

"They usually do."

"Fourteen years if the sentences are served consecutively."

"Right again."

"The sentences, they all could be served concurrently with the parole violation."

"Could be," said Briggs.

"That would mean I would get out in"—Nye did the math quickly—"six and a half years."

"Six years, eight months to be precise," Briggs said.

"Or less."

"Could very well be less. Especially if you agree to testify in all the meth cases. Except . . ."

"Except what?"

"Do you see anyone around here willing to make a sentencing recommendation?"

Nye smiled and leaned across the conference room table. "What if I make it easy for you and cop a plea?"

"On what?"

"On everything."

"That would make me very happy," Briggs said. "Save the taxpayers a lot of money in court fees, too."

"How happy?"

Briggs rubbed his chin, pretending he was deep in thought, pretending he hadn't known exactly what he was going to offer Nye before he even entered the room.

Tuseman muttered something unintelligible, then added, "Get on with it."

"You go down for the nickel plus one," Briggs said at last. "Six years."

"Five," said Nye.

"Six," repeated Briggs. "And this time you do every fucking day."

"I can live with that."

"One more thing."

"Yeah?"

"I want you to tell me the truth about Eli Jefferson."

Behind the one-way mirror, G. K. Bonalay exhaled sharply.

David Tuseman stepped away from the glass and rested against the opposite wall.

I continued to shiver.

"I don't know nothing about Jefferson," Nye said.

Briggs rose abruptly from his chair, snatched the yellow pad off the table, and moved toward the door.

"Wait a minute, man," Nye called to him.

"Wait for what? You can do the fourteen."

"C'mon, man."

"Why did you force Debbie Miller to give you an alibi? Why did you beat her half to death when the alibi went sour?"

"Man, I'm telling you. I don't know nothing about Jefferson."

"Bullshit," Briggs shouted.

He crossed the room more quickly than I thought was possible for a man his size and shoved a finger in Nye's face, nearly poking him in the eye.

"I'll tell you what I think," he said. "I think you did it."

"No, man, no."

"If I can prove it, that's thirty years in prison," Briggs warned. "And I'll still nail you with the other shit just for the fun of it."

"Oh, man . . ."

"If you didn't do it, all you have to worry about is the six."

"I didn't."

"Convince me."

Nye rubbed his eyes wearily as Briggs backed off and resumed his seat at the center of the long conference table.

"I'm telling you the real thing, now," Nye promised.

"I'm listening."

"I went over to Merodie's house—"

"This was the Saturday Eli Jefferson was killed," Briggs said.

"Yeah. In the morning."

"Why did you go over there?"

"Do you want me to tell the story or what?"

Briggs spread his hands wide.

"I went over there to slap Merodie around, okay?" Nye continued. "I figured she was the one who put the finger on me on that meth bust. So I went over there to teach her a lesson. When I knocked on the door, this drunk dude answered. Jefferson. Man, I didn't even learn his name until the papers said he was dead."

"Go on," Briggs said.

"I swear I didn't say a word to this guy and he starts shoving me, you know, pushing me in the chest like he wanted to fight. I'm like, who is this jerk-off? He starts ranting about how I'm supposed to be Merodie's secret lover. I'm like, huh? So, he keeps shoving me. Pretty soon I start shoving back. Only there's nothing there. No strength in him at all, you know? It was like I was shoving a kid. I gave him one big push and he goes down. Then I notice, Christ, my hands are covered with blood. His blood, okay? This guy's bleeding like crazy. I look around—I'm standing in the living room—and I look around and there's blood everywhere. Just—fucking—everywhere. Then I see Merodie in the kitchen doorway. She's looking at me kinda strange-like, and I know it's because I'm standing over her old man with blood on my hands, and I'm thinking, I gotta get out of there. So I left."

"What happened next?" Briggs asked.

"You mean after I got rid of the blood?"

"Yes."

"I'm thinking that I'm going to get blamed for this somehow," Nye said. "I'm thinking that Merodie set me up on the meth bust, why not this, too? So I go to Debbie, and I work out an alibi."

"What did you tell Debbie?" Briggs wanted to know.

"I told her that some guys I knew before I went to jail were trying to force me back into dealing for them by blackmailing me with the cops."

"She believed that?"

Nye smiled knowingly. "Some women," he said, "who never had any real sex except maybe once in the backseat of some fool kid's car when they were in school, you start giving it to 'em real good, it's like their brains turn to jelly. They'll believe anything you tell 'em."

Nye went on to explain his theories on how to seduce lonely women, but G. K. and Tuseman weren't listening. G. K. turned her back to the mirror and faced the county attorney. She spoke just above a whisper.

"I like you David, I always have. You were very good to me when I worked here. You helped me a lot. Taught me a lot. I doubt I'd have my job today if it weren't for you. You must know that if I lived in the district, I'd be the first in line to vote for you come November."

Tuseman continued to lean against the wall, his arms crossed in front of him.

"I like you so much," said G. K., "I'm going to tell you my strategy for defending Merodie Davies. It's very simple, really. I'm going to put Debbie Miller on the stand to testify about Nye's phony alibi. Then I'm going to play the videotape of the interview we just saw for the jury, maybe, I don't know, a half dozen times. Especially the part about you cutting a deal for testimony. Do you believe it might create enough reasonable doubt to get Merodie acquitted? I think so. I also think there's a reasonable chance that you'll be brought before the bar on charges for witness tampering. 'Course, I could be wrong. What's your opinion?"

Tuseman spoke very slowly in a voice that could freeze ice cream. He said, "No charges will be filed against Merodie Davies in the death of Eli Jefferson."

"What about the case?"

"The case will be closed. Jefferson's death will be ruled an accident." Tuseman smiled. "It would have been a difficult case to win anyway."

G. K. glanced my way.

"I told you he was a reasonable man."

"Salt of the earth," I said.

"One more thing, David." G. K. moved close enough to Tuseman that they could have kissed. "I want Merodie released."

"After she serves her thirty days."

"Today, David. I want Merodie out today. If she's not free by 3:00 P.M., I'll conduct a press conference outside your office at 3:30 P.M. That should give the TV people plenty of time to prepare for the six o'clock news."

"Are you threatening me, Genny?" Tuseman wanted to know.

"You betcha."

The sun came up like a flamethrower, scorching everything in sight, setting even the shadows on fire. I felt the heat on my wet clothes as G. K. and I left the court building. Water vapor condensed and rose as fog from my shoulders. My clothes were streaked with dirt, and the knees of my jeans looked like I had knelt in a mud puddle, which, of course, I had. I slipped off my now shapeless sports jacket and pulled my shirt away from my skin. I felt like I was breathing through a damp washcloth.

"Where are you parked?" G. K. asked.

I pointed east on Main Street.

"Me, too," she said.

"I didn't want to say anything in front of the county attorney," I said as we followed the sidewalk, walking directly into the rising sun.

"Always a wise decision," G. K. said.

"I think Nye was telling the truth."

"About what?"

"About Eli Jefferson. We have a witness. Priscilla St. Ana. She was on the scene after Nye had his alleged shoving match with Jefferson."

"I like that word—alleged," G. K. said.

"St. Ana said there was no body on the floor when she arrived."

"Forget about St. Ana."

"Forget her?"

"Forget everything. Look, McKenzie. I'm not Perry Mason. I'm not here to solve a crime. I don't even care who committed the crime. My job—and your job—is to show that our client is not guilty of the crime, and yes, we both know that's not the same thing as being innocent."

"But what if . . . ?"

"There are no 'But what ifs.'"

G. K. placed a hand on my arm, stopping me. She looked up into my eyes. There was nothing sexual about it. She merely wanted my undivided attention.

"When I was young and just starting out, I believed that justice was more important than life." She spoke as if she had made the same speech before—maybe to herself. "That's why I wanted to do the work I did, to serve justice. It was only after I became older and wiser that I realized justice belongs to God alone. The best the rest of us can do is serve the law. Well, McKenzie, the law says if there's reasonable doubt, the defendant goes free. Merodie Davies will go free today because after Richard Nye's behavior and the remarkable statement he just made there's plenty of reasonable doubt. Understand?"

I understood. That didn't make me any happier.

"You said that justice belongs to God alone," I said.

"Yes."

"Then where does Mr. Muehlenhaus come in?"

G. K. refused to answer. She continued down the sidewalk. She didn't take half a dozen steps before her cell phone rang.

"Speak of the devil," I said.

She answered the phone without breaking stride, listened for a moment. "Thank you, sir," she said, and glanced away from me, refusing to meet my eyes.

"What did I tell you?" I said.

"Yes, sir . . . That's very kind of you . . . No, sir . . . I appreciate it very much . . . He's standing right here . . . Not at all . . . Just a moment."

G. K. thrust her phone at me. "He wants to speak with you."

She didn't identify who "he" was. There was no need.

"Good morning, Mr. Muehlenhaus," I said.

"Good morning, Mr. McKenzie. How are you? No worse for wear, I hope."

"Fit as a fiddle and ready for love."

"That's my boy."

I didn't like that he called me "his boy," but I let it slide.

"My sources tell me that Ms. Davies will soon be released," Muehlenhaus said. "It seems that once again I am in your debt."

"What's the going rate for such things?" I asked. "The hand of your eldest daughter and half your kingdom?"

"Alas, my daughters are all spoken for. I do, however, have a rather attractive granddaughter, if I do say so myself, who I am sure will find you just as fascinating as I do."

"Is she as duplicitous as her grandfather?"

"Mr. McKenzie, there is no need—"

"Stop it," I said. "According to my birth certificate I was born at night, Mr. Muehlenhaus, but I wasn't born *last* night. You weren't the slightest bit interested in getting Merodie off the hook. Nor were you concerned that Tuseman would use her murder trial to get publicity for his campaign. He'll get plenty from the meth busts—and don't tell me you didn't know about them ahead of time. No, you wanted the case kicked to protect someone else, and we both know who. Do I need to say her name?"

"No."

"My question is why. Why would you protect her?"

"For the same reason you protect your friends. Because they are friends."

"Still, why go to all this trouble? Why didn't you just pick up the phone and call Tuseman?"

"I did."

"And?"

"The price was too high."

"He wanted your support in the election."

"I had already promised my support to another, and I never break my promises, Mr. McKenzie. That's another quality in which you and I are much alike." I wished he'd stop saying that. "Unfortunately, it would seem that Mr. Tuseman will prevail, in any case."

"Don't worry about Tuseman," I said. "I'll stick a fork in that sonuvabitch."

"Indeed, Mr. McKenzie."

"Only I'm not going to stop there. Unlike Ms. Bonalay"—I looked directly in her eyes when I spoke—"I believe in justice on earth, and I'm not above manufacturing some when the need arises."

Muehlenhaus started to laugh, but only to prove that he could.

"Yes, I am sure my granddaughter would find you quite fascinating."

I deactivated the cell phone without saying good-bye and handed it back to G. K.

"What are you going to do?" G. K. asked.

"Whatever I can."

"McKenzie, you did good today. You probably saved one woman's life, and you helped get an innocent woman out of jail. Can't you be happy with that?"

"Genevieve," I said, drawing out the name. "That little speech you gave me before about serving the law—all I can say is, thank God, I'm not an attorney."

I was in my Jeep Cherokee heading east on Highway 10 toward New Brighton. It was slow going. Over one and a half million people were driving to work, and the Cities' overburdened freeway system was clogged with traffic, most of it heading in the general direction of downtown Minneapolis and St. Paul. It was becoming increasingly hot inside my car, but I had the air-conditioning off and windows open—I was trying to dry off.

My cell phone sang "Ode to Joy." Normally, I don't answer it when I'm driving for fear it might lead to an accident, but considering the speed at which I was traveling, I decided to take that chance.

"McKenzie, this is Dr. Ronning with the county coroner's office."

"Yes, Dr. Ronning."

I was so surprised to hear from him that I nearly rear-ended the van in front of me.

"I ran a blood test on Eli Jefferson as you requested, this time specifically looking for GHB. I ran it twice."

"And?"

"Negative."

"Negative?"

"There was nothing there. Not a trace. I looked very hard."

"Are you sure?'

"McKenzie, it's what I do."

"I don't know what to say."

"How about, 'Sorry for wasting your precious time and resources,
Doctor'—that'll do. Oh, never mind."

Dr. Ronning hung up.

Suddenly, I felt like the tiredest man on the face of the earth.

I had asked Muehlenhaus why he was protecting Priscilla St. Ana.
What I should have asked him was why Priscilla St. Ana needed protec-
tion. The answer had seemed obvious to me. She had killed Jefferson.
She had all but confessed to it, along with the murders of her father, her
brother, and Brian Becker. I thought I knew why. It was the reason I
was driving to New Brighton. Now I wasn't so sure.

Vonnie Lou Lowman was making a beeline from her front door to her
car in the driveway, a Plymouth Reliant that couldn't have been much
younger than she was. I pulled in behind it.

My brain was all a-jumble with thoughts of signatures and motives
and opportunities and the means of murder. Cilla claimed she had put
Robert St. Ana and Brian Becker to sleep with her GHB analog and
then allowed them to die of carbon monoxide poisoning. Eli Jefferson
had also been asleep when he bled to death. The coroner now says there
was no trace of GHB in his blood. If Cilla hadn't killed Jefferson, why
was she so anxious that I believe she had? Or maybe she did kill him,

but instead of using GHB, she used the softball bat to make him unconscious.

Put that aside for now, I told myself. *Instead, concentrate on motive. Concentrate on the why.* Cilla killed her father for herself. She killed her brother for Merodie. She killed Becker for Silk. Why did she kill Jefferson?

"What is it?" Vonnie Lou wanted to know as I approached her car. She was dressed the way lots of women dress for work in the office nowadays, in a matching blue blazer and skirt and a white blouse with notched lapels. The outfit reminded me of a private school uniform.

"I need you to look at a photograph," I said.

"I don't have time," Vonnie Lou insisted. "I just got a call for a receptionist gig that could last three weeks, maybe longer. I can't afford to be late."

"It'll only take a sec."

I showed her the computer printout of a photo of Priscilla St. Ana, the one that appeared in *Women's Business Minnesota*.

"Is this the woman you found with Eli in your bedroom that day?" I asked.

Vonnie Lou was definite. "No," she said. "I told you, the bimbo was younger. A college girl."

"Are you sure? She looks young for her age."

"Not that young. Besides, the bimbo had auburn hair. This one is blond."

"It's a dye job. Imagine her with auburn hair."

"It's not her."

I was disappointed. I thought I was on to something.

"You don't look so hot," she told me.

"I haven't been to bed yet."

That's why you're punchy, my inner voice told me. *That's why you're not thinking straight.*

"Can you move your car now, McKenzie? I'm really late."

I returned to the Cherokee. I was about to back out of the driveway when I had another brainstorm. A moment later I was standing in front of Vonnie Lou's driver's side window. Vonnie Lou rolled it down.

"Now what?" She was losing patience with me.

I shoved another printout at her. "One more photo. Look carefully. Is this the woman you found in your bed?"

Vonnie Lou studied it for a moment.

"Yep," she said. "That's her."

"Are you sure?"

"I am absolutely sure. Now can I go?"

I was the first one in line when they opened the doors to the Minnesota Driver and Vehicle Services office in the Town Square Building in downtown St. Paul. The woman behind the desk was happy to furnish me with both a Records Request form as well as an Intended Use of Driver License and Motor Vehicle Information form. I filled both out carefully, then returned them to the clerk, along with the nine fifty search fee.

It was only a few minutes before I was rewarded with the information I sought—Priscilla St. Ana's complete motor vehicle information and driving record. According to the printout, Priscilla St. Ana owned two cars. The first was the Saab she had told me about. The second was a Mazda Miata MX-5.

"Would you call that a sports car?" I said.

"One-forty-two horsepower, four-cylinder, five-speed transmission, two-seat convertible—yeah, I'd call it a sports car."

I glanced up at the clerk. She gave me a toothy grin and said, "I like cars."

I went back to the printout. Under color, it read "black cherry."

May I take the Mazda? Silk had said.

You always do, Cilla told her.

That's because I look so good in it.

"Nuts," I said.

15

By midmorning the hot sun was shimmering off the gray tiles on the roof of Priscilla St. Ana's estate in Woodbury—and off the tiny black-cherry sports car parked in the long driveway. I spent a good deal of time staring at the car. It reminded me of something G. K. Bonalay had said—was it just yesterday?

God is in the details.

My inner voice scolded me. *So much misery could have been avoided if only you had looked in the garage,* it said.

Yeah, but there are no windows in the garage.

Excuses, excuses.

The way I looked, I didn't think I had much chance getting past the maid, Caroline. Besides, I didn't want to speak with Cilla. So I ignored the front door and made my way around the sprawling house to the backyard patio. I heard the rumbling sound of the diving board and saw Silk slicing into the water as I turned the corner. I watched her pull her-

self from the pool as I approached. She was wearing a pale gray swimsuit with some pale blue splattered here and there. The sun touched
droplets on her face and shoulders and the top of her breasts, turning
them to silver. Silk smiled as she took a big white beach towel from the
back of a chair and brushed away the droplets.

"Mr. McKenzie," she said as if it were the answer to a question.

"Ms. St. Ana," I said.

She seemed amused by my appearance—bruised, unshaven face;
flat, disheveled hair; dirty jeans and shirt; damp, shapeless sports jacket.

"You look like you fell into something," she said.

"I suppose you could say that."

I sat in an iron chair next to the glass table without asking permission, stretching my legs out in front of me. I hid a yawn behind my hand.

"Sorry," I said. "I've been up all evening."

"Must have been an interesting night."

"It had its moments."

"Are you here to see Aunt Cil?" she asked.

"No. I'm here to see you."

"Me?"

Suddenly, Silk seemed bashful. She took a tentative step backward
and brought the huge white towel in front of her, concealing her body.

I set a heel on the seat of a chair and launched it forward. It slid
across the tile and came to a rest next to Silk.

"Take a seat," I said.

Silk did what I told her, an obedient child listening to the voice of
authority, holding the towel in front of her as if it were a life preserver.

"What do you want?" she said. Her voice made me believe she was
willing to do whatever I requested. *Where was her confidence?* I wondered. *Where was her audacity?*

I said, "The clock is striking midnight, Cinderella. It's pumpkin
time."

Priscilla came through her French doors in a hurry.

"McKenzie," she called. "McKenzie, stop. McKenzie . . ." She reached the table. "What are you doing here?"

Cilla was also wearing a swimsuit, dark blue with gold trim. It was dry, so I figured I was either delaying her swim or interrupting a bit of sunbathing. Without the camouflage of her tailored clothes, I could detect a heaviness in Cilla's hips and thighs, a bulge at the belly, and a softness in her upper arms and shoulders. It was the body of a forty-plus woman, although I knew a great many twenty-year-olds who wished they looked as fit.

"You look awful," Cilla said.

"People keep telling me that, so I guess it must be true."

"What are you doing here?"

"Merodie Davies will be released from jail today," I said.

"That's wonderful," said Silk.

"You came here to tell me that? I'm grateful, of course."

"Sure you are."

"Is— Is the Anoka County Attorney going to arrest someone else?"

"The case is closed and will soon be buried along with Eli Jefferson."

Cilla sighed as if a great weight had been lifted from her shoulders and settled into a chair across the glass table from me.

"I'm surprised Mr. Muehlenhaus hadn't told you already," I said.

"Who?"

"Stop it, Cilla. I'm not in the mood."

"What do you want? Why did you come?"

"You had me, Cilla," I said. "You really had me with the story about your father and brother and Brian Becker. Tell me, was any of it true?"

Cilla gave me a slight smile and an even less perceptible shrug. I might as well have asked a professional gambler if he had the cards after he bluffed me out of a pot. I didn't pay to see her cards, so she wasn't going to show them.

"True or not, it worked," I said. "You talked me into believing that you killed Eli Jefferson. You didn't, though, did you?"

I turned my gaze on Silk. She began to squirm.

"I want you to leave now, Mr. McKenzie," Cilla said. "Right now."

"In a minute."

"Leave now, or I'll call the police."

"Here." I slipped my cell from my pocket and pushed it across the table at her. "Use my phone."

"McKenzie."

I kept staring at Silk.

"Cilla, you said you put the envelope containing Merodie's check on the coffee table in the living room," I said. "But I saw the crime scene photos, read the reports—there was no coffee table in the living room. You said that there was nothing amiss in the house. But the living room was practically awash in blood, Jefferson's blood, by the time you said you arrived. You couldn't possibly have missed it—if you had actually been there. You weren't. It was Silk who delivered the check."

"No," Cilla said.

"You lied when you told me you hadn't seen your mother for eons, didn't you, Silk?"

She nodded her head.

"You were there the day Eli Jefferson was killed," I said. "Your little black-cherry sports car, the one that makes you look so good when you're driving—it was seen parked in Merodie's driveway."

"No," Cilla shouted again.

"How about it, Silk?" I asked.

"Eli wanted sex and I refused to give it to him," she said. Her voice was just above a whisper, and I had to lean forward to hear her.

"Silk, don't say anything," Cilla said.

"It's okay, Aunt Cil. I was going to come forward anyway if my mother had been charged with Eli's murder."

"But she's not being charged. She's free."

"Is that true?" Silk asked me.

"Free as a bird by three this afternoon."

"Thank God," Silk whispered.

"Silk, don't say anything more," Cilla said.

"The case is going to be dropped," I said. "Eli's death will be ruled an accident—so you're off the hook, too."

"Thank God," Silk whispered again.

Cilla was on her feet. She moved next to her niece and clutched her shoulder.

"You're not to say another word until we hire a lawyer," she said. "Do you understand me, young lady?"

Silk took her aunt's hand between hers. She brought it to her lips and kissed it lightly. "You can't protect me forever," she said.

"The hell I can't. See if I can't." Cilla turned on me. "Get out," she shouted.

"Shut up," I said.

"You can't speak to me that way."

I pointed at my cell phone, still on the glass table. "Call Muehlenhaus," I said. "I bet he tells you I can speak however I damn well please."

That quieted her right down.

"Silk—" I said.

"Who's Mr. Muehlenhaus?" she asked.

"Your fairy godmother. Silk, tell me what happened."

"Is it important?"

"Yes, to me it is."

Silk sighed heavily and gripped her towel with both hands.

"I met Eli in July when I delivered Mother's check," she said. "He came on to me. I let him."

"Silk." The cry came from deep inside Cilla's throat.

"Eli made me feel . . . he made me feel things I hadn't felt before with a man. Not like the other men I knew, the boys I knew. He— I suppose he seduced me. I can't explain it any better than that. I don't have the vocabulary. He asked me to meet him at his sister's house. I did. He offered me alcohol. I took it. He asked me to go to bed with him. I said yes."

"Silk, oh, Silk," Cilla cried again.

"Nothing happened, Aunt Cil. Eli's sister came home before . . . before anything happened. I didn't . . . I didn't . . ." Silk hung her head. "It wasn't until later that I realized just how fortunate I had been."

Cilla wrapped her arms around Silk's shoulders and hugged her from behind. There were tears in Cilla's eyes.

Suddenly, I felt like an intruder, but I couldn't bring myself to leave without hearing the entire story.

"What happened next?" I asked.

Silk answered even as Cilla held on to her. "Eli called a few times asking for a rematch—that's the word he used, rematch. I turned him down. Over and over again."

"You should have told me," Cilla said.

"I was too embarrassed," Silk said. "Anyway, when I went to deliver Mother's check, he was there. It's hard for me to tell you exactly what happened next. It's all kind of blurry. He was drunk. At least he seemed drunk. He kept pawing at me. He kept telling me to take off my shirt. I called for my mother, but she didn't answer. When I pushed him away"—Silk held up her hands—"my hands were bloody. He was bleeding very badly. I don't know why. I couldn't see a wound. I called for my mother again, only she never came. I tried to escape. Eli stopped me. I grabbed a softball bat—it was leaning against the wall and I just grabbed it. I didn't even think about it, I just . . . I told Eli to leave me alone. He came at me anyway. He said he knew just what I needed. I swung the bat. I hit him. I hit him in the back of the head. He said, 'Strike one.' I hit him again. Harder. He fell. I dropped the bat and ran out of there just as fast as I could."

"Okay," I said.

Silk's hands were folded on the towel in her lap. She was looking down at them as if she had never seen them before. They were dotted with tears.

"I believed you when you said you would have given yourself up to protect your mother," I told her.

Silk nodded.

"So now what?" Cilla wanted to know. "So now you're going to ruin her life? For what? For Jefferson? For that piece of filth? Silk has an incredible life in front of her. She's going to the Olympics. Are you going to take that away from her? Silk was acting in self-defense. She was only protecting herself. Are you going to ruin her life over that? Answer me! What are you going to do?"

Nothing, my inner voice replied. I didn't believe that Silk was responsible for Jefferson's death. The best a prosecutor could argue was that conking him on the head was a contributing factor. Clearly not murder, and probably self-defense. No, Silk didn't kill Jefferson. It was the booze that done him in. That's what a good defense attorney would argue, and Cilla would hire the best that money could buy. So why bother? Why ruin Silk's life? The law might be satisfied, but would justice be served? G. K. said it earlier. *Justice belongs to God alone.* Besides, Merodie would hate me forever, and I just didn't want that.

I stood up and retrieved my cell phone from the table.

"I'm going home to get some sleep," I said.

I began to walk away.

"Have a good life, Silk," I called over my shoulder.

"Wait a minute," Cilla said. She jogged to my side. She wasn't pretty now—not for any age.

"Do you think you're going to come back later and ask for money?" she wanted to know. "Do you think you're going to blackmail me over this?"

She grabbed my arm with both hands and pulled it until I spun toward her. She had a strong grip, and she didn't let go.

"I know your kind," she said. "I've dealt with your kind all my life. Men like you. Selfish and cruel and greedy beyond belief. All you care about is what you can get for yourself—what you can take from me for yourself! Just like my father. And my brother. And all the rest. Well, you're not taking anything from me, do you hear? Not a dime. Nothing. If you come back here, I'll kill you."

I regarded Cilla closely. There was much to admire. There was much more that made me want to bash her brains in. The story she had told about her father, her brother, and Brian Becker—it was true. Looking into her hate-filled eyes, I knew it was true. I could forgive her all the rest. Trying to protect her niece, going to Muehlenhaus, certainly, I could forgive her for that. But cold-blooded murder? The men who died around her might have been bastards, but one of the first things I was taught as a cop was you can't choose the vic, and I was still too much of a cop to let it slide. Yet what could I do about it? If I took it to the cops, I'd have to give them all the rest, too, and I couldn't do that. Not to Silk. Not to Merodie. Besides, where was the evidence? It was my word against hers, and my word consisted solely of repeating an admittedly outrageous story she told me that might or might not be true. Except it was true.

I gripped Cilla's elbow in a way that made her cry out in pain and release my arm. She stepped backward, rubbing her elbow. There was no pain in her eyes, though. Only anger and hatred.

"You're a dangerous woman, Cilla," I said. "Someone ought to do something about you."

They call Minneapolis City Hall the "Pink Palace" because of its Camelot-style Gothic architecture and the color of its granite facade. Room 108 in the Pink Palace was reserved for the Minneapolis Police Department's homicide unit. No outsider was allowed entry without an escort, so I had called ahead to warn Lieutenant Clayton Rask that I was coming and to request that he fetch Lieutenant John Weiner from Anoka for a brief meeting. I was quickly ushered to Rask's desk. It was made of rich mahogany. Basic gray metal government desks served all the other officers in the department. *Rank does have its privileges,* I decided.

Neither officer rose to his feet or offered me a hand in greeting.

Rask said, "Look at you. What rock did you crawl out from under?"

I was hoping he was referring solely to my appearance.

"You have a homicide," I said.

"I have several homicides," Rask said.

"Mollie Pratt."

"Have you come to confess?" Weiner asked.

I guess that was his idea of humor.

"We both know who did it," I said.

He rose quickly from the chair next to Rask's desk.

"Don't push it," Weiner warned.

"I don't know who did it," Rask said. "Tell me."

"Richard Scott Nye," I said. "He lived next door to Mollie Pratt before he was busted for dealing meth—that's how they met. You shouldn't have any trouble finding him, either. Weiner here has him in custody at the Anoka County Correctional Facility. He and the county attorney are protecting him. He's their chief witness in the meth busts they made yesterday. You might have heard about them. It was in all the papers."

"I have no idea what you're talking about," Weiner said.

"Then I apologize in advance for accusing you of shitting on your badge."

"I bet this is going to be an interesting story," Rask said.

I told it as concisely as I could, filling in the blanks with assumptions that I had made. Mollie knew Nye was dealing; she was one of his customers. Mollie told Nye that she had seen him at Merodie's house the day Eli Jefferson was killed either as a favor or to blackmail him into giving her dope. Nye raped and killed her; that was why he had been so confident that no one could testify against him when I confronted him at his apartment. *Ain't nobody around no more to say otherwise.*

"Weiner knew about Nye," I added. "That's why he hustled me out of his office the other day when Nye's name first came up."

Rask didn't speak, but I had seen the expression on his face before. Lordy, but I was glad he wasn't angry at me.

"This is nonsense," Weiner said.

"It is a tad thin, McKenzie," Rask said.

"It should be easy enough to check out," I said. "You have the DNA the killer left on Mollie's body. Match it against Nye's. You won't even have to get a warrant. Nye was busted twice for sexual assault in the past. His DNA is on file."

"What do you think, Lieutenant?" Rask asked.

"It's your case," Weiner said.

"So it is."

"Something else," I said.

"What's that?" Rask asked.

I was going to tell him about Priscilla St. Ana, I really was, but at the last moment my mind's eye focused on Silk's face—and Merodie's. I couldn't see past them.

"Never mind," I said.

My sticky eyes jerked open and landed on the digital display of my bed-side clock radio. It was 5:05 and the sun was shining brightly. For a moment I pondered how that could be, but there was a heavy pounding on my front door—that's what had awakened me—and I gave it up. I was a third of the way down the stairs when I realized that I was wearing only blue boxers. I went back upstairs, took a robe from my closet, and wrapped it around me. The pounding continued.

"I'm coming," I shouted.

A moment later I pulled open the door.

Genevieve Bonalay smiled at me.

"Good evening," she said.

Evening?

"I figured I was pounding loud enough to wake the dead," she added. "Apparently I succeeded."

"I didn't get home until late this morning," I said.

"You clean up good, though," she told me. "Nice outfit."

"Come in," I said. I pulled the robe tighter around me and stepped back so G. K. could enter. She was carrying a bottle of Krug champagne. It had been opened. She waved it at the empty living room.

"Love what you've done with the place," she said.

Oh yeah, she's been drinking, my inner voice warned me.

I led her to the kitchen.

"Would you like some coffee?" I asked.

"No, this is fine." She held up the Krug. "Care to join me? The least I can do is buy you a drink since you're not getting paid for this fiasco."

"Satisfaction is my reward."

I took two crystal champagne glasses from the cupboard. G. K. quickly filled them both. She held up her glass by the long, narrow stem.

"What should we drink to? I know. To justice."

"To justice," I said, and drained half the champagne.

G. K. drank all of hers and refilled the glass.

"I thought you didn't believe in justice," I said.

"Oh, I do today. That's why I'm celebrating. Today I've seen justice firsthand. Poetic, ironic—McKenzie, will you go to bed with me? Will you go to bed with me right now? I could use some TLC."

"I don't think so."

"That's right. You don't go to bed with women who have been drinking. No problem. I know plenty of men who don't have your scruples, who don't have any scruples at all." She curled her nose and furrowed her brow. "Come to think of it, most of them are lawyers. Oh, well."

She drank more Krug.

"Talk to me, Gen."

"I like that you call me Gen. I wish you would call me Gen more often."

"Tell me what happened."

"I don't understand the things people do anymore. I really don't. Once I thought I did. No more. I can't, what's the word? Empathize? I can't empathize with them. I can't put myself in their place. People have become such strangers to me."

"You'll find as you go along that they get stranger," I predicted.

"Will they? God."

Gen was starting to take another long drink. I seized her hand, gently removed the glass, and set it on the counter. G. K. made a small sniffling noise and bowed her head. She brushed away tears with the back of her knuckle.

"There's no crying in baseball," I said.

"I'm not usually this emotional. I can't remember the last time I cried before today. But today . . ."

"Something happened to Merodie, didn't it?"

"In a manner of speaking."

"What happened to Merodie? She should be out by now."

G. K.'s head came up abruptly. "Out and then back in again," she said.

"Tell me."

"It was a fluke. Merodie was being processed out. I was with her. They were taking her—us—down in the elevator. Richard Nye was being processed in. He was waiting for the elevator to take him up to booking. The elevator doors opened. Merodie saw Nye standing there and she jumped him. Bam. Just like that. Nye's hands were cuffed, but Merodie's weren't, and she knocked him down and started beating him and scratching him and trying to strangle him until the deputies dragged her off. All the time, Merodie was screaming that Nye had killed Eli Jefferson and she was going to make him pay for it."

"That's why she refused to roll on him," I said. "Merodie really did believe that Nye had killed Jefferson. She wanted him out of jail so she could get her revenge. See what I mean about people doing strange things."

"Hell hath no fury . . ." G. K. began to quote, but changed her mind and took a swallow of champagne.

"Did she hurt Nye badly?" I asked.

"Yes."

"How badly?"

"She scratched out one of his eyes."

Just So You Know

Things went very, very badly very, very quickly for David Tuseman. After word of what Merodie had done leaked out, he was thoroughly chastised in the media for not being able to protect his prisoners. Next, a district court judge rejected his claim on Richard Scott Nye and ordered that he be transferred to the custody of the Hennepin County attorney. It was more or less a technicality anyway, since Nye was in Mercy Hospital at the time having a glass eye inserted into his socket. The prosecutor immediately charged him with second degree murder and first degree criminal sexual conduct, which pretty much removed any remaining incentive Nye might have had to testify in Tuseman's meth trials. As a result, Tuseman was forced to drop the charges against half the suspects, and of the nine he actually brought to trial, five were acquitted. The TV and newspapers—along with his political opponents—crucified him for his incompetence. True, he wasn't entirely to blame, but hey, he who lives by the mass media dies by the mass media. Eventually, he was forced to resign as county attorney, and Rollie Briggs took over.

As for the State Senate, Tuseman was defeated in the primary by a three-to-one margin. The next day, Mr. Muehlenhaus sent me a case of Aberlour ten-year-old single malt, sherry-cask scotch. I would have sent it back except, well, it was Aberlour ten-year-old single malt, sherry-cask scotch.

Meanwhile, Richard Scott Nye was sentenced to 366 months in Stillwater State Prison. He might have been hammered for 488 months, but he cut a deal: In exchange for guilty pleas, he was ordered to serve his sentences for murder and rape concurrently. He was never tried for beating Debbie Miller or attempting to shoot me. Such is life.

I went to see the therapist Jillian DeMarais had set me up with. He was a nice enough guy, but after three sessions I didn't think we were making much progress, so I stopped going. Besides, the dreams went away after a couple of weeks, just as I had predicted they would.

Silk St. Ana finished eighth in the ten-meter platform diving competition at the Summer Olympic Games, but you'd think she won the gold by the way the TV cameras followed her around and network announcers gushed over her bright future and stunning good looks. Twice during the competition she waved at the cameras and mouthed, "Hi, Mom."

Merodie Davies probably didn't notice. At the time, she was doing thirty-four months and a day for second degree assault at the Minnesota Correctional Facility for Women in Shakopee. Cilla did notice, though, sitting in the stands, yet also following the action on a miniature TV. Cameras caught her watching Silk wave her greeting. She cried both times.

As for me, I was left with a couple of questions. Did Priscilla St. Ana kill her father, her brother, and Brian Becker? Did I help let a stone killer go free? Not knowing the answers bothered me for a long, long time.